9/09

TROUBADOUR

ALSO BY MARY HOFFMAN

The Falconer's Knot

The Stravaganza series:
City of Masks
City of Stars
City of Flowers
City of Secrets

TROUBADOUR

Mary Hoffman

BLOOMSBURY

NEW YORK BERLIN LONDON

Raymond Lévesque, *Quand les hommes vivront d'amour* . . . , used by permission
of Éditions Typo, 1989 © 1989 Éditions Typo and Raymond Lévesque

First published in Great Britain by Bloomsbury Publishing Plc
Published in the United States by Bloomsbury U.S.A. Children's Books
175 Fifth Avenue, New York, New York 10010

Library of Congress Cataloging-in-Publication Data
Hoffman, Mary.
Troubadour / by Mary Hoffman. — 1st U.S. ed.
p.   cm.
Summary: In the winter of 1208 while the dispute between the Pope and the Cathars intensifies,
thirteen-year-old Lady Elinor, secretly in love with the troubadour Bertran de Miramont and
determined to avoid her imminent marriage to an older man, runs away from her family's castle
disguised as an apprentice troubadour, unaware of the dangers ahead as the Albigensian Crusade
begins its onslaught on her native Languedoc.
ISBN-13: 978-1-59990-367-5 • ISBN-10: 1-59990-367-9
[1. Troubadours—Fiction. 2. Sex role—Fiction. 3. Albigenses—Fiction. 4. Crusades—Fiction.
5. Languedoc (France)—History—13th century—Fiction. 6. France—History—Philip II
Augustus, 1180–1223—Fiction. 7. Middle Ages—Fiction.] I. Title.
PZ7.H67562Tr 2009   [Fic]—dc22   2008046440

First U.S. Edition 2009
Typeset by Dorchester Typesetting Group Ltd
Printed in the U.S.A. by Quebecor World Fairfield
2 4 6 8 10 9 7 5 3 1

All papers used by Bloomsbury U.S.A. are natural, recyclable products
made from wood grown in well-managed forests. The manufacturing processes
conform to the environmental regulations of the country of origin.

For Rebecca Lisle and Linda Strachan,
the other two sides of the Trieste Triangle

Quand les hommes vivront d'amour
Ce sera la paix sur la terre,
Les soldats seront troubadours
Mais nous nous serons morts, mon frère.

(When men live in brotherly love
There will be peace on earth
Soldiers will be troubadours
But as for us, we shall be long gone, my brother.)

Raymond Lévesque
(Author's translation)

Note: The following are imaginary places: Sévignan, Selva and Castelnuovo.

The region of
Occitania
in the
Early Thirteenth Century

Contents

A Fatal Blow

15 January 1208

A small group of monks was making its way down to the river crossing. They wore the distinctive white robes of the Cistercians, although the colour was actually more of a dirty grey. Their leader, Pierre of Castelnau, rode a mule but he was not a humble man.

When the monks reached the shore of the Rhône, they could see that the ferry-boat was on its way back to their side of the river. The group settled down to wait. The leader dismounted from the mule and rubbed his hands over his face. He was as angry as he was tired. It was still early in the morning and he had celebrated Mass fasting, but with little charity and compassion in his heart.

Pierre and his companions had come from Saint-Gilles. He had been sent by the Pope as his Legate to reason with its mighty ruler, the Count of Toulouse, but the Count had proved unreasonable. He would not agree to the Pope's order to rout out the heretics from his lands, even though he had already been excommunicated for failing to obey his Pope. Pierre's mission had failed.

What can you do with a man who does not fear separation from the Head of the Church? thought Pierre. *Such a man is practically a heretic himself.* The Count's last words to him yesterday, shouted as the Papal Legate left the court at Saint-

Gilles, had been 'Wherever you go and whatever you do, Pierre of Castelnau, take care! I shall be watching you.'

Empty threats, thought Pierre, who had spent the night at an inn with his companions before heading down to the river. From the other side, at Arles, he would make the long journey to Rome and tell the Pope that the Count would not obey his master on earth or his Master in Heaven. The Count himself was a stubborn bully but Pierre was not afraid of him.

The ferry-boat drew nearer to the shore. It had only one passenger, a handsome man a little over thirty, with aristocratic features but clothes no longer in the best condition. Bertran de Miramont looked at the group on the bank with little interest. Monks were everywhere these days, as involved in politics as in religion. Bertran tried not to concern himself in their affairs. But, along with many in the region, he had his reasons for not wanting to associate with these monks.

So he turned his head to one side to avoid making eye contact with the group. He would give a formal bow as he led his horse from the boat and quickly take his leave but he did not want any conversation with the Cistercians, particularly their ascetic-looking leader.

And so it was Bertran who first saw the man riding out of the woods full pelt towards the monks. He thought it must be a courier with an urgent message until he saw the lance. The rider didn't hesitate but spurred straight towards the man standing by the mule.

Bertran cried out a warning and the Cistercian looked up towards him, fixing him with his gaze, as the horseman's lance ran through his back, throwing him to his knees.

'Faster, faster!' Bertran shouted at the shocked ferryman

and leapt from the boat as soon as it reached the shallows. He ran splashing through the water and reached the bank in time to see the murderer wrench his lance out of the body and turn his horse's head back to the woods.

The dying monk, his robe startlingly colourful now, twisted his body to see where his attacker had gone. Supported by his companions, he called out after the retreating horseman with the last breath left in his lungs, 'May God forgive you, as I forgive you!'

Bertran, whose very business was words, had time for the fleeting thought that the monk's language was cleverly ambiguous, before the stricken man's eyes filmed over and his spirit left his body.

All was chaos in the little scene: monks not knowing whether to pray, howl or pursue the attacker; Bertran, dripping wet, offered his services and the ferryman disembarked his horse for him.

'Please, sire,' said one of the older men; Bertran saw he wore a bishop's ring. 'Follow the villain. For he has killed the Pope's representative. Lying here on the ground is Pierre of Castelnau, sent by His Holiness Pope Innocent to the Count of Toulouse.'

'And it was the Count's hand behind that lance, even if another wielded it,' said a younger monk bitterly. Another was vomiting discreetly into the river.

Bertran was stunned. He was a troubadour, a master of words and music, not a politician or a knight. He had offered to help bring a murderer to justice and he would do his best to track the man down. But the victim was his bitter enemy, the enemy of all who, like Bertran, shared a dangerous secret, a secret that was getting more dangerous by the day.

And, even as he heaved himself all sodden into the saddle and spurred his horse towards the woods, Bertran knew that whether he succeeded or failed, what he had just witnessed was only the beginning.

For he was a heretic and Pope Innocent was pledged to eliminate all heretics. Pierre's murder was just the first blood in a war to the death.

Part One

Donzela

The Troubadours liked best to lead the wandering life of
the Pure, who set off along the road in pairs.

From *Passion and Society* by Denis de Rougemont,
tr. Montgomery Belgion (1956)

CHAPTER ONE

Love Song

The hill town of Sévignan was not at the heart of a great estate. Lanval de Sévignan was only a minor landowner but within the walls of his town, he was the absolute lord. And within his castle, his word was law.

Except, he sometimes felt, when it came to his older daughter. His lady, Clara, was an exemplary wife; she had borne him first a son, Aimeric, and then two daughters, Elinor and Alys. And though Lord Lanval might have preferred one more son, to be certain that his name would be carried on, no further pregnancies had been successful and he was content with his lot. Aimeric was a healthy, strong sixteen-year-old, skilled at arms and ready to defend his home or that of any local noble who called on him.

Alys at eleven was really the only one still a child. But even Elinor at thirteen was far from grown up or ready to be married, either in temperament or suitability. She was headstrong, opinionated and always at war with her mother. There were times when both her parents felt that she should have been a boy. And she was passionate. Lanval was sure that she had cast immodest looks at several of his knights, including three youngsters he was fostering for another local landowner, who was richer in sons than the Lord of Sévignan.

Perhaps Elinor *should* be married, thought her father, but at present he had more serious matters to worry about. He already had a troupe of *joglars* and their troubadour wintering with him, but a few days ago Bertran de Miramont had arrived unexpectedly. It was unusual for him to change courts in January. As soon as Bertran rode into the bailey, Lanval had known it meant bad news.

But it was worse than he had feared: the Papal Legate murdered and the Count of Toulouse suspected! Bertran had ridden hard on the heels of the attacker but lost him in Beaucaire.

'You didn't tell the monks your name, did you?' had been Lanval's first question.

'They didn't ask, sire.'

'What about the ferryman?'

'He knows me well enough. I travel often to Saint-Gilles when I am based at Count Alfonso's court in Arles.'

'And how long before news of the murder reaches Rome?' asked Lanval.

'Not long,' said Bertran. 'And then we must all be on our guard.'

⚜

Elinor was trying to learn to dance the *estampida* but her feet kept getting tangled up in the hem of her dress. What was even more galling was that Alys was doing it perfectly. Today was a saint's day – the Feast of Saint Bertran of Saint-Quentin – and there would be dancing and music and a fine dinner in their father's great hall. Elinor would make her first appearance there as a young woman. Alys was too young to

8

attend and join in the dancing but, since she was not only neater-footed but also taller than her older sister, Elinor wished with all her heart she could absent herself and send Alys in her place.

Not that Elinor would – or could – really stay away. She would have just preferred to watch from the dark alcove where she had always been a keen observer of the court's entertainments, where she and her sister had eavesdropped on music and poetry from an early age: the hiding-place from which she had first seen Bertran de Miramont.

Elinor still could not believe that Bertran was here, in the castle, on his own name day. She had been expecting a wait of months, till he returned in the spring. But a day or two earlier, some heightened instinct had taken her up on to the walls that enclosed the castle keep.

She was often restless these days, feeling that her childhood was disappearing fast and fearful for the future she must face as a woman, and a noblewoman at that. The evening was cold and she clutched her long fur-lined cloak close around her. She must expect to be married by fourteen at the latest, even though her parents had said nothing to her about it yet. The presentation of her in the great hall as *donzela* of the castle was just the beginning.

Elinor spent no time, like Alys, wondering who her husband might be. She knew that once her father made up his mind, she would have no choice. Or, more likely once her mother's mind settled on a suitable man. He would be older, much older, that was certain. Men of the Languedoc did not marry till they were in their thirties and their brides were commonly half their age. And it was usually only the oldest sons who married. Her brother, Aimeric, might have all his years so far over again before he stood in the great cathedral at Béziers with a young woman at his side.

Elinor sighed. Not for the first time, she wished she had been born a boy. Then she could have been a knight and as second son wouldn't have had to marry. She could have joined another lord's household and lounged about flirting with the prettiest serving-maids and eating copious amounts of mutton.

But it was no good repining over what couldn't be changed. She had more or less two choices: marry or go into a convent. She had to smile at the thought of being a nun. Her mother would scorn the very idea. But not as much as she would mock at the name of Bertran of Miramont. Troubadours were all very well in their way and were often noblemen, even if only younger sons. Bertran was a great favourite with Lady Clara and the other women of Lanval's household but also had the knack of making himself pleasing to the house knights and lordlings. Lady Clara enjoyed his compositions more than those of any other poet. As the Lord's wife, she was his *domna*, his inspiration for love poems and the mistress of his heart – at least on paper. And he was her indulged favourite.

But marry her daughter to him? Out of the question. That was one of Lady Clara's favourite phrases where her older daughter was concerned and Elinor could hear her mother's voice in her head as she paced the battlements. 'Marry a troubadour? Out of the question!'

And that was when she had seen him, riding full pelt towards the castle. She would have known Bertran's horse and colours anywhere. Elinor had hurried down from the walls but there was no further sight of him that night. She had caught glimpses of his familiar moss green velvet jerkin once or twice since but it was tonight at the feast that she was bound to see him.

And perhaps dance opposite him. The very thought tripped her disobedient feet again and it was the dancing master's turn to sigh.

Perrin was a *joglar*, one of the troupe of minstrels wintering at Sévignan. He was used to singing Bertran's new compositions but like everyone else was surprised to see him turning up so early in the year. It was only a short time before the poet sought him out and took him into the stables where they could talk without being overheard.

'Murdered?' said Perrin, horrified at the news. He was a young man, little more than a boy, but quick to realise what this meant for heretics like themselves. 'Vengeance will be swift!'

'And bloody,' agreed Bertran. 'I must not stay but will leave as soon as the saint's day is over. Someone must take the news to more of our brothers and sisters.'

'But what can they do?' asked Perrin.

'They can warn the Believers,' said Bertran, lowering his voice even further. He looked watchfully round the stable, unsure whether the slight clink of harness he heard had been caused by the January wind. 'And all sympathisers,' he added. 'We must learn to dissemble.'

'What reason are you giving for coming back to court now?' asked the *joglar*. 'I mean the official reason.'

'Why,' said Bertran, smiling and talking in a normal voice.

'I have written a song for my *domna* that could not wait. And you must learn it by tonight.' Then he added in a whisper. 'I shall take the same song to courts all over the south and many a *joglar* will have to learn it just as quickly.'

As soon as the dancing lesson was over, Elinor sneaked down to the kitchens to find out what was to be served at the great saint's day feast. Hugo the cook was sweating over the pans, roaring orders to the kitchen boys to fetch more firewood, stir the frumenty and turn the spits. Elinor turned her eyes away from the rotating corpses of sheep and deer; she hated to look at them but the savoury smell coming from the roasting flesh made her mouth fill with water and her stomach grumble.

Above the shouting and the clanging and the general kitchen chaos, she could hear the sad notes of the rebec. In a dark corner was the familiar figure of Huguet the *joglar*. 'Little Hugo' his name meant, to distinguish him from the cook. The *joglar* spent so much of his time in the kitchen, especially in the winter, because he felt the cold badly, that Hugo and all the other servants took him for granted. He was as much a fixture as the powderer, who spent his days pounding lumps of salt into fine crystals.

And he and Elinor had been friends for years; the *joglar* was only a few months older than her.

Elinor picked her way across to Huguet, automatically lifting her skirts out of the grease and blood on the floor. As soon as he caught her eye he stood and made a formal bow.

'Oh, don't stop playing, Huguet,' she said. 'Pretend I'm not here.'

That was impossible for servants, Elinor knew well. Her very presence in the kitchen made them tense, carrying out their duties more meticulously. Hugo wiped the sweat from his brow before rolling out the pastry for his capon pies. The spit boys stood up straight and turned more regularly, as if afraid she would inspect their work.

Huguet began to play again, softly.

'What is that tune?' asked Elinor, wondering how to broach the subject of Bertran.

'It is to accompany the new *canso*,' said Huguet. 'An old tune tricked out new, as a maid might put a fresh ribbon on an old dress. There is no time for Perrin or me to write a new one. De Miramont wants it for his new song tonight.'

'Oh,' said Elinor casually. 'Is he here then? It's early in the year for him to change court.'

Huguet grinned. He and every other musician, singer, dancer and acrobat in the castle knew perfectly well that the Lady Elinor had eyes for no one but the handsome troubadour. But she was young and de Miramont was an appealing prospect. Few people knew that his secret meant he was unlikely ever to marry, even though his songs were all of undying love. It was a secret that Huguet and Perrin shared, being Believers themselves.

'Indeed, my lady, Bertran is here. He told Perrin he could not wait to sing your mother, the Lady Clara, his latest song.'

'So is he staying long? Has he forsaken the court in Arles?'

Huguet's eyes turned vague, as if he were concentrating on a difficult key change. 'I think not. He spoke of other courts he must visit.'

'Must?' asked Elinor sharply. 'Is he so in love with the lady of every one that he must take his new song to them?'

Huguet cursed silently. He always forgot that, young as she was, Elinor was as sharp as a pin, particularly where Bertran de Miramont was concerned. He resolved to be more discreet in future.

He need not have worried. Elinor was entirely focused on the unfairness of being the daughter of the Lord, the *donzela* of the castle, who would never have a love song addressed to her. All the troubadours wrote songs of everlasting devotion to her mother, the *domna* of the castle; it simply wasn't the custom to serenade young unmarried women.

Everyone knew that neither Bertran nor any other troubadour was really in love with Lady Clara. Why, she was an old woman – over thirty years of age! But they had to pretend that they were and Lord Lanval understood this and didn't mind at all. He would have felt his hospitality insulted if a poet fed at his table had not sung the praises of his wife.

Bertran would not sing the song himself, of course; he was a nobleman in his own right, even if a poor one. It would be up to Perrin to sing it, accompanied by Huguet on the rebec. But Bertran would stand beside him, casting longing looks at Lady Clara and perhaps even sighing. And Elinor wanted him to sigh for her.

Bertran was over thirty too, but it was of no consequence in a man. He had no childbirths to slacken his figure or other womanly ailments to take the colour from his cheek or the vigour from his voice and sparkle from his eye. He was simply the handsomest man that Elinor had ever seen and she was so entranced by him that she wanted to *be* him almost as much as she wanted him to notice her and compose a poem to her beauty.

She smiled at the very thought and Huguet saw that the moment of danger had passed. The daughter of the castle was far too caught up in her own fancies to have noticed his slip about Bertran's movements.

'Out of the question,' said Lady Clara, when Elinor asked if she might be excused the dancing and yield her place to Alys.

She looked at her older daughter hard and what she saw pleased her no more than usual. It was difficult for a once beautiful woman to feel that she must soon yield her place to her daughters. Clara often wondered if it would be easier if Elinor were like her in any way but it was her younger daughter, Alys, who favoured her. Alys was naturally demure and never forgot to cast down her eyes when a male courtier or a knight passed her in the castle. She was fair-haired and grey-eyed like her mother, while Elinor was a sort of nut brown all over – hair, eyes and skin. It was in vain that her mother exhorted her to keep out of the sun; Elinor was outdoors on the castle walls in all weathers. But the rays that darkened her skin did nothing to lighten her hair.

She should have been a boy, thought Lady Clara, like Aimeric, who shared his sister's dark colouring. They were both like their father but it didn't matter in a son. Clara was happy to see Aimeric's complexion as a sign of manly hardiness. But girls should be fair and quiet and Elinor was not only dark but unruly and unladylike. If only she had been the younger daughter!

'You must dance, Elinor,' said her mother. 'Why else does your father feed and clothe a dancing instructor? And tonight is your first opportunity to show how the *donzela* of the castle dances.'

'But, Maire,' said Elinor desperately, 'I am so very bad at it!'

'Then you must just practise until you are better,' said Lady Clara. 'Look – it's not difficult.'

She started to hum a vigorous tune and slid her feet sideways, before giving a neat little hop and skip.

'You see?' she said. 'Easy.'

'For you, Maire,' said Elinor, looking at her own feet. 'But the music goes so fast!'

'You must not look down, Elinor,' said Lady Clara. 'Just listen to the music, feel the beat of the tambour and let yourself be led. Close your eyes if it will help.'

It sounded pleasurable, even blissful, the way her mother described it, with her head thrown back and her eyes half-closed and her face all dreamy. But Elinor couldn't imagine doing it.

Still, she could see she wasn't going to get anywhere with her protests.

Lady Clara opened her eyes and looked into her daughter's wayward expression. Her own face softened.

'You have to try, Elinor,' she said, more kindly than usual. 'Dancing, singing, fine needlework, they all seem so hard to you, but what else can you do? You must have the accomplishments of a noblewoman if we are ever to find a husband for you. You will not get one on your looks alone.'

Elinor was glad of that 'alone'.

'I can read and write,' she said. 'And perhaps I do not have to marry?' (*If I cannot marry Bertran, the troubadour,* she added in her mind.)

16

'Out of the question,' said Lady Clara, her mood harden-ing again. 'You must marry. You cannot turn your skills with parchment and quills into land and rents, can you? You will have a husband, willing to pay a good bride price, if it's the last thing I do.'

Only you won't be the one that has to do it, thought Elinor bitterly.

The great hall was full of long wooden trestles and behind the one set at the head of the room green branches of fir, holly and hemlock hung from the beams. Perrin and Huguet and the other *joglars* were already in place with their instruments, ready to play during dinner and for the dancing afterwards. They would not eat till all the guests had gone but there was already a flagon of wine at their feet, which would be refilled often during the evening.

Bertran would sit near the Lord's table, among Lanval's knights and foster-sons. They were beginning to drift into the great hall now. It wasn't until the musicians played a little fanfare that everyone took their place and stood for the entrance of the Lord and his family.

Lord Lanval, Lady Clara and their son Aimeric walked into the hall like the landed nobles they were, accustomed to deference from all the rest of the '*familha*' – the family – that made up the population of the castle. They were followed, for the first time at a saint's day feast, by the *donzela* of the castle, looking unusually demure, because her eyes were cast down towards her feet, something she did not usually manage.

But Elinor was terrified of all the gazes directed at her. As the family arrived at their places, she risked a swift upwards glance and saw Bertran smiling back at her encouragingly. She remembered just in time not to grin back at him – which would have counted as unladylike – but inclined her head so slowly that it could have counted as gracefully.

Then Perrin broke into a lively *virelai* on his lute and the moment passed. All during the meal Elinor felt her eyes darting back to where Bertran sat but he hardly ever looked at her again. If she was very careful, she could just sneak a glance now and again without her mother's notice. As well as the family there were some senior knights at their table, together with some lords and ladies from neighbouring towns, and a visitor Elinor had never seen before, who was engaged in courtly wordplay with her mother.

Elinor's feast partner was Aimeric, so after a while she relaxed. It would have been too awful to share dishes with a stranger. But her brother was not too daunting, at least when he wasn't teasing her.

'You look nice tonight, sister,' he said. 'That dress suits you.'

She was relieved; she had feared the rose velvet would make her look like something Hugo had concocted from berries and cream. And Aimeric had understood that she couldn't take any teasing tonight of all nights, on her first public appearance as *donzela*. But Elinor didn't want him to see her watching the troubadour.

Bertran was a fastidious eater, taking food from the shared dishes with his knife or a spoon and not using his fingers. He didn't wipe his hands on his bread trencher either, and when the savoury courses had been cleared away, he tore the gravy-smeared bread into small pieces for the dogs, like a true nobleman and didn't wolf it down himself like a peasant.

All in all, the meal went better than Elinor had feared, though she was too nervous to do justice to Hugo's capon pasties or his roast venison and frumenty. But when all the many dishes had been cleared away, she was able to nibble at some gingerbread and almonds. And she drank gratefully of the spiced wine, which her father always served at the end of a feast.

And then Lanval and Clara were getting up and servants were coming in to move the tables away. That meant the dancing was about to begin and Elinor hastily gulped the last of her wine, her panic returning.

Before the dreaded *estampida*, there were jugglers and acrobats and even someone with a monkey that danced on its hind legs. But the moment couldn't be postponed for ever and at last Elinor heard the familiar rhythm being beaten out on the tambour. The *joglaresas* – the female entertainers – were beginning to swish their skirts.

Noblemen and women assembled on what had been quickly transformed into a dance floor and Elinor soon found herself separated from Aimeric, who she had hoped would be her partner. Instead she was opposite Gui, one of her father's foster-sons, a *noiretz*. He was a good dancer, Elinor knew from her spying in the alcove, but not someone she wanted to see her awkward steps.

But the wine seemed to have done something strange to her feet as Perrin began to sing the opening verse of 'Kalenda Maia' – the May Day song. It was not at all appropriate for the middle of winter but ever since Perrin had been taught it by an Italian troubadour it had been all the rage in Lanval's

19

court. It was a song written by a troubadour called Raimbaut to his lady love, Beatrice, the sister of his lord.

Everyone in the hall knew it and several joined in with the words.

'*Ma bell'amia*,' mouthed Gui. 'My beautiful friend.'

Elinor blushed; he nearly put her off her steps. But she made it to the end of the last verse: '*Bastida, Finida, N'Engles, ai l'estampida!*' which meant 'Enough, I've finished my composition, *Senhor* Engles, my *estampida*.'

Elinor wondered about *Senhor* Engles; perhaps he was a noble in Italy, at Monferrato, where Raimbaut had composed his song. She caught her breath, glad not to have made a fool of herself with Gui.

But the rest of the dancers were still moving and Huguet had launched into a lively *saltarello* on his fiddle. Elinor was appalled even though she had learned that it could follow straight on from the *estampida*. Her feet faltered because the music was much faster now and Gui's face was beginning to blur before her eyes in the spin and whirl of the dance. She was going to fall, on her first appearance as a grown-up woman in her father's court. And the young knights and *noiretz*s would laugh at her behind their hands. She wanted to die.

Then, miraculously, a face emerged from the blur and it was Bertran! His smile calmed her and although she was still scared, it was so lovely to be able to dance with him and clasp his hand as they crossed the set, that her feet forgot to be frightened and she understood what her mother meant about the music.

When the *saltarello* came to an end and Bertran lifted her by the waist, she let the moment last just a fraction longer for the sake of feeling his arms around her.

'Forgive me, lady,' said Bertran, gently extricating himself. 'It is time for my new song.'

He stood by Perrin, who sang passionately to Lady Clara on Bertran's behalf. It was a strange new *canso*, more about war than love. Elinor scarcely took it in; she was still thinking of how it felt to be held by Bertran. But gradually her blood cooled and she paid more attention to the words he had written.

'*He who loves nobly seeks not to be cured of Love's ill, so sweet it is to suffer.*'

And her heart was pierced with such a pure pain to think that none of Bertran's songs were for her, or ever would be, that when she went to the bed she shared with Alys, she lay awake in the dark for hours weeping silently so as to keep her grief to herself.

CHAPTER TWO

Parting

The sky was still streaked with red when Bertran saddled up his horse to ride out of the castle. Only Perrin was up early enough to say goodbye. Before the troubadour mounted, he undid the brooch from his hat and gave it to his *joglar*.

'A present?' asked Perrin, grinning.

'Not for you,' said Bertran. 'Take it to the Lady Elinor and give it to her privately.'

'A love token?'

'You know that it can't be that. But there would be no great harm if she took it that way,' said Bertran.

'You must be mad!' said Perrin. 'No harm? You know how the *donzela* feels about you. This will just encourage her.'

'I am sorry for her,' said Bertran seriously. 'She has no idea that her life and the lives of all of us are about to change. I may never see her again. Would it hurt for her to nurture the fancies of her heart a little longer? Before her family is plunged into bloodshed and war?'

Perrin bowed his head in obedience and took the brooch. He had no arguments against these. Bertran patted him affectionately on the shoulder.

'Stay safe, my friend,' he said. 'And go east in the spring. It may be that your path should take you to Italy.'

'And you?' asked Perrin, overwhelmed by fear that the poet would be riding into danger.

'My road lies west,' said the troubadour. 'I must take the warning to our brothers and sisters of the storm that is coming.' He embraced Perrin warmly then stood back and placed his two palms together, the fingers pointing upwards – the secret sign of greeting and farewell in their religion. The *joglar* did the same.

Then the poet leapt into his saddle and rode out of the castle of Sévignan.

Elinor was watching, dry-eyed, from a window slit as his horse picked its way down the hillside. It was a picture she would keep in her mind for years.

It took some weeks for the news of Pierre of Castelnau's murder to reach the Pope in Rome. Innocent III was hearing an embassy from Navarre when the messenger was shown in and he pursed his lips at the interruption. But the man was so nervous that Innocent became sure he brought urgent and terrible news.

He hadn't dreamed how terrible though, and he sank his head in his hands as soon as he had understood what had happened.

He gestured to the Navarrese Ambassador to join him in prayer and the two men knelt on the bare floor just as they were.

'May his soul rest in peace,' said the Pope, getting creakily to his feet. And that was the last peaceful thought he had for a long time.

'As for the Count of Toulouse,' he said to the messenger, 'you say he has done nothing to apprehend the murderer?'

'No, Holiness,' said the man. 'The rumour is that he knows the culprit but will not act against him.'

'And there were no witnesses apart from the monks and the ferryman?'

'One, Holiness, a nobleman, but he rode off in pursuit of the attacker and has not been heard of since.'

'And he was?'

'I do not have that information.'

'Send to see what can be found out. I should like to talk to that man.' The Pope sat lost in thought, then suddenly asked, 'And where is Pierre's body now?'

'At Saint-Gilles, Holiness. The monks thought it best to take him back. There was a solemn Requiem Mass said by the Bishop and he has been interred in the Abbey, with full ceremony.'

'He shall be Saint Pierre before long,' vowed the Pope. 'And Raimon of Toulouse shall be excommunicated again.'

Giving orders right and left, he swept out of his apartments to pray at the church in Rome named after the first Saint Peter. But his heart was full of hatred for the heretics and their supporters.

※

It was a simple pewter brooch with a stone set in it that looked like red glass. But it might have been the finest ruby in Europe, so pleased was Elinor to receive it.

It hadn't taken Perrin long to find an opportunity to give it to her; Elinor's sleepless night made her crave something sharp and savoury to eat and she was soon in the kitchen cajoling Hugo the cook into giving her a strip of salted venison. When she left to nibble it in private on the battlements, the *joglar* had seen her and slipped after her to give her Bertran's token.

'But what did he say?' she asked, thrilled.

Perrin improvised. 'He said . . . that he had to go away for a long time and . . . you were not to forget him.'

'Forget him?' said Elinor, hugging the brooch to her, in spite of its spiky fastening. 'I could never do that. But is he to be away for very long? Will he not come in the spring as usual?'

Perrin shook his head. 'I don't think so, lady.'

'Lady Elinor, Lady Elinor!' echoed a shrill voice. It was Lady Clara's maid, puffing her way up to the top of the wall. 'Ah, there you are, my lady. Your mother said I might find you here. She wants to see you at once.'

The maid leaned against the rampart, to get her breath back. She was neither young nor slender and Elinor knew that Lady Clara employed her partly because her mother was vain and the servant provided such a contrast to the lady's own still-admired beauty.

Elinor had jumped guiltily and tried to hide the brooch in her sleeve. But the maid's eyes were sharp, even if her body was sluggish.

'You are discovered, lady,' said Perrin lightly, reaching out and taking the strip of venison from her, his body masking what she was doing with the brooch. Elinor blushed to the roots of her brown hair. The maid looked at the meat with interest and the danger passed.

'I don't see why I shouldn't eat my father's own food,' said

Elinor sulkily, keeping up the pretence. 'Everything in the kitchen is his.'

'Well, there's no time for more eating now,' said the maid firmly. 'Lady Clara is waiting.'

Perrin shrugged as Elinor passed him on her way down the stone stairs and began to chew on the venison strip. *I wonder what the* domna *is on the warpath about now*, he thought.

'Your behaviour last night was quite unacceptable,' said Lady Clara.

In the long history of their battles with each other Elinor had never known her mother to sound so cold. And this time she did not know what she was supposed to have done wrong.

'But I did what you said,' she protested. 'I didn't stumble at all. I listened to the music and let myself enjoy it.'

Her mother sighed with exasperation.

'With Bertran de Miramont! With the troubadour!' she said.

'I . . . I didn't know that was wrong,' said Elinor. 'Is it not allowed to dance with troubadours?'

'Dancing is one thing,' said her mother. 'Flinging your arms round him like the lovesick girl you are is quite another!'

Elinor felt suddenly reckless. She felt the pin of the red brooch pressing into her arm.

'And what if I do love him?' she said boldly. 'He is the nicest, handsomest man I have ever met. And he was kind to me. And he is a nobleman too. What is wrong with loving him?'

Lady Clara looked horrified. 'It is worse than I thought,' she said. 'Has he said anything to you?'

Elinor hesitated. 'No, not exactly. And he has gone.'

Her mother stiffened with shock.

'When? And how do you know?'

'At first light. I saw him from the window. I couldn't sleep. Perrin says he will stay away a long time.' She could not hold her voice quite steady.

'This has to end now,' said Lady Clara. 'Bertran de Miramont is not for you. I shall speak to your father today. It is best you marry straight away.'

'You're just jealous!' Elinor burst out hotly. 'Because I am young and you are old and Bertran has to write his poems for you when it's me he loves!'

'Enough!' said her mother in a voice that cracked like a whip across Elinor's face. Two round red spots burned on Lady Clara's cheeks. Elinor had gone too far. She knew she ought to beg her mother's pardon but her blood was up and she didn't feel sorry. She ran on further, making it worse with every word.

'I suppose it would be all right to like Gui?' she said. 'Or some other loutish knight. But Gui went too fast for me in the *saltarello*. He wanted me to fall. It was Bertran who showed *cortesia*.'

Her mother came and stood right up close to her so that Elinor felt her words hiss breath on to her face.

'You are to forget Bertran de Miramont! He will never marry. Not you or anyone else. The way things are, he will be lucky to be alive this time next year. You are a foolish, moonstruck child dabbling in things you don't understand. Now . . . leave my sight!'

Bertran's path first took him southward, along the River Orb. He had to get to Béziers and pass on his news to the Believers there. The town was under the rule of young Viscount Trencavel, who was sympathetic to the Believers, but he did not live in Béziers. Bertran would have to find someone else to spread the word.

The troubadour rode up the hill into the city and made his way to the cathedral of Saint-Nazaire. He was about to do something very dangerous and needed some advice. Three years ago the Papal Legates had ordered the Bishop, Guilhem, to come down hard on the heretics and he had refused. He was killed for his pains and a new bishop installed. This Bishop, Ermengaud, was still an unknown quantity to Bertran, who had been in Béziers only a few times in recent years, and the troubadour was not going to show him his hand without finding out something about him first.

As soon as he reached the cathedral, Bertran branched off towards the Jewish quarter, where he had a good contact. Nahum was a trader in spices, one of a large number of his people living in the city. The Jews sympathised with Bertran and those of his faith, because they were no more popular with the Church than were the heretics. Nahum would know what sort of man the new Bishop was.

Nahum's house was a warm and welcoming place and Bertran felt himself relax for the first time since he had left Sévignan. He sat in front of the fire with a cup of hot spiced wine in his hand and told the trader his news.

'This will go ill for the Believers,' said Nahum gravely.

'Yes,' said Bertran. 'The Pope is sure to blame Raimon of Toulouse since he parted on such bad terms with the Legate.'

'Would he accuse him of murder?'

'Oh, not the actual act,' said Bertran wearily. 'I saw the murderer myself, remember, and he was no nobleman. But he could have been acting on orders from Toulouse. More likely though, he just hoped to rise in the Count's favour by ridding him of an enemy.'

'What do you think the Pope will do?' asked Nahum, refilling the troubadour's cup.

'Well, he's bound to renew the Count's excommunication. But Toulouse will be lucky to get away with just that. I'm sure he'll try to placate the authorities in some way – perhaps he'll even hand the murderer over. Who knows? But a storm is on the way that can't be averted by anything the Count can do.'

Nahum shook his head. 'Then that assassin – whoever he was – did you no favours at all.'

'No, he's just made everything harder for the Believers,' said Bertran. 'But tell me about the Bishop. Is he likely to be as sympathetic to us, as the Count and Viscount Trencavel are?'

Nahum looked serious. 'I don't think so,' he said. 'From what I've heard of him, he's as fanatically against your religion as Pope Innocent himself is. And I can tell you that he doesn't like my people either.'

'What does the Viscount think?' asked Bertran.

'Oh, he follows the courtesies,' said Nahum. 'But he is worried. I have heard that he was very upset by the death of

Bishop Guilhem. It was a sign that Rome would come down hard on the heretics. And the young Viscount has always been a good friend to my people. He made my cousin Samuel, his bailiff.'

Bertran stretched his long legs towards the fire and sighed.

'Well, I must seek out the leaders of our religion here and warn them what is likely to come. I think I should visit the Bishop too.'

'Be careful,' said Nahum.

'I am always careful,' said the troubadour.

Relations between Elinor and her mother were still strained. Elinor stomped round the castle in a foul mood, refusing to attend dance lessons or to do tapestry. Her only relief from gloomy ideas about the future was the time she spent with the *joglars* and musicians. Huguet was teaching her to play the flute and to her surprise she was rather good at it.

'You have a natural gift,' said Huguet. 'A good ear and a good sense of rhythm.'

Elinor was astonished; that was not something the dancing master had ever discovered about her. She thought perhaps her ease with the instrument might be because no one looked at a musician; they were all but invisible. They sat in corners of great halls, obscure in the flickering torchlight and provided the background to other people as they danced or sang or ate or flirted.

She was beginning to think that, if she had been a boy, it might have been more fun to be a *joglar* than a knight. But it was no good; she wasn't a boy and she would have to marry soon and then the music would stop. With these thoughts the gloom would descend again.

Lady Clara became more and more remote from her daughter's ill humour. She ignored her. All Elinor's frowns and glares and sullen remarks bounced off her elegant composure like rain off armour. And this just made Elinor crosser and more depressed. She now knew just how little power and influence the *donzela* of a castle wielded.

The winter days stretched drearily in front of her with not even the prospect of seeing Bertran in the spring to look forward to. She felt like an animal in hibernation – a toad maybe, crouched in a hole, in a state of suspended animation, just waiting for something to warm her into life.

But when that something came it wasn't pleasant at all. Anything less like a ray of sunshine than Thibaut le Viguier would have been hard to imagine. He was a thin, grey man well into his forties, a widower with three daughters. And he had sons too: Gui, who had so humiliated Elinor in the *saltarello*, was one of them.

She wondered if she had summoned Thibaut into her mother's mind by her comparison of Gui to Bertran. For now Thibaut was at the castle, seemingly to visit his sons but actually, Elinor was sure, to be offered to her as a possible husband. And he had brought his daughters with him.

As soon as the daughters realised what was in the wind, they made themselves as unpleasant to Elinor as possible. They were all older than her, though the youngest was only a few months so. The oldest was married and the middle one was betrothed, so only Blandina would still be living in her father's bastide by the time Thibaut brought his new bride home.

But Elinor realised that she could not bear that situation even for a few months. Thibaut himself did not seem a bad man, though he was more like a grandfather than a husband, but Blandina was a sharp-tongued and vicious girl who was instantly Elinor's enemy.

'Our late mother' was all Blandina's theme. That lady had been a paragon of all the virtues, according to her daughter. A scholar, musician, needlewoman, she had also been an exemplary wife and household manager.

'And to see her dance,' said Blandina pointedly, 'you would think an angel had alighted on the earth, so graceful were her movements.'

Elinor was sure that Blandina had been talking to Gui and that they had been laughing at her together.

'Then she will feel all the more at home in heaven among all the other angels,' Elinor said tartly.

This provoked a fit of weeping in Blandina, who ran to her father to say that Elinor had been cruel to her and irreverent towards her mother's memory. If Thibaut minded this, he gave no sign. He was always courteous and friendly to Elinor but she simply couldn't imagine being his wife and sharing his bed. Then, sometimes, she could and the thought put her off even more.

The next time Blandina tried to provoke her, Elinor said as calmly as she could manage, 'I have no more desire to marry your father than you have to endure me as your step-mother.'

But that made the girl indignant on her father's behalf.

'I suppose you think yourself too good for a Viguier?' she fumed. 'Just because your father owns more land.'

'Not at all,' said Elinor. 'I should merely like to marry

someone closer to me in age. Or perhaps not marry at all.'

And Blandina had gone this time not to her father but to Elinor's.

Lanval sent for her the same afternoon. He looked unusually stern.

'I gather you understand why Thibaut le Viguier has come here?' he said, going straight to the heart of the matter.

'I believe so, Paire,' she said.

'And it does not please you?'

Elinor did not answer but shook her head dumbly.

'Well, it pleases me,' said Lanval. 'I want to see you married as soon as possible and Thibaut has a well-fortified and provisioned bastide. You will be as safe there as here, perhaps safer.'

'This sounds more like war than a marriage proposal,' said Elinor, remembering Bertran's new poem.

Lanval looked up at her sharply. 'You may be right,' he said. 'There are difficult times coming and I want to see you established.'

'But must it be with old Thibaut, Paire?' Elinor pleaded. She knew she was her father's favourite and she had never been made to do anything she didn't like by him before.

But it was no good. On this, the most important event in her life so far, he was obdurate.

'This is not a time for girlish frets and fancies,' he said. 'Thibaut will make a respectable offer, giving a good bride price.'

Elinor couldn't help herself. 'So I am to be sold to him, like a pig in the market?'

'You are to be given to him as his legal wife, to become the *domna* of your own castle,' said her father. 'And you should

33

consider what *you* bring to the marriage that he should be so desirous to marry you. At the moment I think you are getting the better side of the bargain.'

Every word from the father who had never spoken so severely to her before was like a lash from a hunting whip. She bowed her head as if in submission and bit her lip so as not to let him see her real thoughts.

In that moment Elinor decided that she would rather do anything than marry Thibaut le Viguier – anything at all.

CHAPTER THREE

Choices

P ope Innocent, wearing a violet cope, entered his chapel accompanied by the Abbot of Cîteaux. Twelve cardinals bearing lighted tapers surrounded Innocent as he intoned the solemn words of excommunication:

'Wherefore in the name of God the All-powerful, Father, Son, and Holy Ghost, of the Blessed Pierre, Prince of the Apostles, and of all the saints, in virtue of the power which has been given us in binding and loosing in Heaven and on earth, we deprive Raimon, Sixth Count of Toulouse, himself and all his accomplices and all his abettors, of the Communion of the Body and Blood of Our Lord, we separate him from the society of all Christians, we exclude him from the bosom of our Holy Mother the Church in Heaven and on earth, we declare him excommunicated and anathematised and we judge him condemned to eternal fire with Satan and all his angels and all the reprobate, so long as he will not burst the fetters of the demon, do penance and satisfy the Church; we deliver him to Satan to mortify his body, that his soul may be saved on the day of judgement.'

He slammed shut the fat black Bible in his hand. One of the Cardinals rang a bell – a mournful tolling for the Count of Toulouse's lost soul – and then the Pope led all twelve in turning their tapers upside down and dashing them out on the ground. The snuffing out of the light left the chapel in temporary darkness until a priest opened the door and the solemn procession filed out again.

It was not the first time that the Count had been cut off from the sacraments of the Church. It had happened first twelve years ago when he had crossed the old Pope Celestine III. That had been over land disputes and he had been absolved two years later.

But, as Innocent disrobed, he was remembering the more recent occasion, less than a year ago. The Abbot was remembering it too. One of the Count's crimes then had been appointing Jews to high office in his city.

'Our brother Pierre – may God rest his soul,' said the Abbot, 'had not lifted the Count's last excommunication before he was so vilely murdered, had he?'

'No,' the Pope shook his head. 'But it will do no harm to renew it. I want to send a strong message to the Count that he must hand over the murderer and fulfil his promises to root the heretics out of his lands before he enjoys the comforts and favours of the Church again.'

The Abbot had reached Rome only days after the first messenger and told the Pope what little he had been able to find out about Pierre's death. The Abbot was a Legate too and now that his senior partner was dead, it would fall to him to lead the persecution of the Perfects, as the leaders of the heretics of the south were known.

His eyes gleamed at the thought. The heretics needed uprooting just as surely as the Saracens did – more really, because they shared the same land as the French. The Fourth Crusade against the Saracens had been disastrous. But here was a crusade that could be waged and won much nearer home. They wouldn't call it a 'crusade'; instead they would

36

talk of 'the business of faith and peace'. All the Abbot needed was an army and the Pope would get it for him. He and the Pope were of one mind in this.

'I have tried writing to the French King,' continued Innocent. 'Three years ago. And nothing happened. This time I will write directly to the barons of the north, offering a full indulgence if they join us in our campaign.'

Neither man mentioned the even greater incentive to war – that the northern barons would be able to take the rich lands of any heretic nobleman they displaced – though they both knew this would be the best recruiting sergeant they could find.

Once Elinor had decided that she would definitely not marry old le Viguier, no matter what her parents said, she became much calmer. At the same time, she completely lost her appetite, which was noticed by no one but Hugo, who missed her visits to the kitchen. The less she ate, the more clear-headed Elinor became. Although she spoke to no one of her dilemma, she was in no doubt about what her alternatives might be.

They narrowed down to two choices: enter a religious house or kill herself.

Elinor had never thought of becoming a nun; she was far too strong-willed and restless of spirit. But now she had to ask herself whether it would be preferable to spend a lifetime of prayer and deprivation in the company of other women, rather than bringing that lifetime to an end while she was still a girl.

And there was something else which made this option more attractive. Elinor knew, though she couldn't say how, that her father was of a different religion from her mother. It was a secret and somehow dangerous faith and she knew that many people in the castle shared it. Aimeric, her brother, for example, and some of the knights and *joglars*, but not Lady Clara. So the daughters of the family had been brought up in ignorance of what it meant.

But Elinor knew that there was a house of sisters nearby who were always referred to as Perfects and that was not just because they were devout Christians. She had heard the word applied to them and it sounded so peaceful and welcoming. As yet, Elinor had no idea what you had to do to become a Perfect but if it was something her father would approve of then it might soften the blow when she refused old le Viguier.

It was at dusk that she thought about the other way out. How on earth could she, a healthy young girl, bring about her own death, even if that was what she chose to do?

I could starve myself, she thought, looking down at her gown, which had become quite loose on her of recent days. But there was a difference between losing one's appetite and letting oneself waste away till the last breath left the body. Surely that would be a horrible way to die? But what was a good way?

Elinor thought about death by drowning, burning, poison or a sharp dagger to the throat or wrists. She didn't have a dagger and she doubted that the pin on Bertran's brooch would be a sharp enough or deadly enough weapon. To cast herself in the well would pollute the whole castle's water supply and she shuddered at the thought of the dark stone walls enclosing her while her head sank under the surface.

She could escape the castle and walk down to the River Orb and jump in; she couldn't swim. But would it be deep enough and fast enough to take her away from the bank and whirl her to certain death? And what about being bruised and battered by the rocks?

As for poison, Elinor had no idea how to get hold of any. And burning? The only fires in the castle were in the kitchen and the great hall, but pitch-covered torches were lit regularly at those flames. She could steal one and set light to her loose gown. But the very thought made her want to jump in the well after all.

To burn, to feel flames licking at your flesh as they did the poor animals turning on the spit! And those creatures were dead and felt nothing. Elinor could imagine all too vividly the smell of her skin beginning to crackle, her flesh spitting and hissing with melting fat. Her hair would be aflame in seconds – a torturing, blazing crown around her head. Could she bear it? Would she pass out quickly and not suffer too much torment? She dared not hope so.

And so another sleepless night would pass and she would rise with the day and think that it would be better to become a Perfect sister after all.

Bertran did not linger in Béziers. His meeting with the Bishop had been strained on both sides. The troubadour was careful not to reveal that he had witnessed the Legate's murder, portraying himself as a messenger only, reluctantly bringing news.

Bishop Ermengaud had crossed himself and prayed and

Bertran had joined him. But he noticed that the old man had a fanatical glitter in his eyes when he rose from his knees.

'We shall hear soon from Rome, I think,' he said. 'The Pope will not let the Count of Toulouse get away with this crime. He has gone too far this time. This means the end for the heretics.'

Bertran had been glad to leave without having to express an opinion. He had gone straight to the leader of the Believers in the city. The one thing that he had in common with the Bishop was that they both knew the murder marked a change in the persecution of the heretics.

It was vital to spread the word among their other communities in the south. Bertran had some hard riding ahead of him. Puisseguier, Saint Pons, Narbonne, Minerve – all the towns on the way to Carcassonne would have to be visited. And with every day that passed there could be orders from Rome against the Believers, rushing north and west and overtaking him.

But Bertran was welcome at every court. His life as a troubadour was not a disguise but his real profession and even though it was unusual to get a visit from a lone troubadour in winter without a train of *joglars* and *joglaresas* attending him, the many lords and castellans of the Midi would be sure to open their doors to him.

He might have private audiences with a few nobles, like Lanval de Sévignan, who were known to be Believers, but even more people would hear the message through his new song that spoke of war when it appeared to be about love. The heretics of the south were well attuned to every nuance that carried a threat to their religion and their lives.

But there were two problems, only one of which Bertran

was aware of. The Believers were peace-loving and would not willingly take up arms to fight for their rights and their homes and families. The troubadour respected that; he was of the same persuasion himself. But he must encourage them at least to hide a portion of their wealth and goods in far off places so that if they had to flee they would not wander penniless in the world. And also to build up their defences. The hill towns and cities of the south were all fortified with strong walls and, if only the inhabitants had enough warning, could store defences and water enough to withstand a long siege.

The second problem was that, as Bertran rode towards Puisseguier, messengers from the Pope were on their way to Saint-Gilles charged with finding out the name of the unknown witness to Pierre of Castelnau's murder.

'No, really? Is that what it's like?'

Elinor was talking to Miqela, an old serving-woman in the castle. She had been wet-nurse to all the children but now helped with sewing and other light duties. She had a sister who was a Perfect in a sister house nearby and Elinor had come to ask what the life there was like.

'Oc,' said Miqela. 'I wouldn't lie to you, my dove. It is a hard life for a young woman to bear. But like many of us,' she lowered her voice, 'I hope to come to it at the end.'

'What do you mean?' asked Elinor.

They were sitting in the solar, Miqela benefiting from the light while she hemmed a sheet with Elinor threading her needles for her and snipping ends with her little scissors to save her old nurse's eyes.

'Only that I will come to perfection on my deathbed,' said Miqela calmly. 'I hope to receive the *consolamentum* then before I die. But I don't think I could live like Joana before then.'

'No meat,' said Elinor woefully, remembering the turning spits with their fearful but delicious burden. 'No fish, or cheese, or eggs?'

'Nothing that has been the result of any coupling,' nodded Miqela. 'And of course no coupling for the Perfects either, no love, marriage and childbearing. But I think I shall be past all that on my deathbed. Indeed it is many years since it has been behind me! It is the good food I should miss.'

Elinor looked solemn. She had understood about the living a clean life; that was true for all holy sisters not just the Perfects. And wasn't it exactly the carnal knowledge of Thibaut le Viguier she would be fleeing from?

But to be forbidden wine, to pray fifteen times a day, to fast three days out of seven, and for forty days three times a year! Elinor did not see how she could bear all that. It would be better to die swiftly and cleanly than to live out her days in such deprivation.

Miqela looked up at her sharply; her eyesight might be failing but she had known Elinor from birth.

'Don't tell me you are thinking of entering a sister house,' she said. 'I thought it was a wedding gown I was to stitch for you, not the black robe of a Perfect.'

'Oh you heard that, did you?' said Elinor casually. 'It might be that I am to be married, indeed. And no, I am not thinking of joining the sisters. I just wanted to know what it was like.'

Later that day, with her blood pulsing loudly in her ears,

Elinor crept into the kitchen. Food was being served in the great hall but she had absented herself on the grounds of feeling unwell. The room still smelled strongly of roasted meat and Elinor felt her empty stomach rumble. She tore a bit of bread from an unused trencher and stuffed it in her mouth; it tasted better than anything she had eaten for weeks. Her last meal.

She had to hurry before Hugo and the kitchen servants came back for the date sweetmeats and apples dipped in honey that were spread on a table. Swiftly she crossed the room and took one of Hugo's knives, with a horn handle. It was an old one, thin in the blade from having been honed against the whetstone so often. And it was sharp as any dagger.

Alys had been allowed to eat dinner with the local nobility in Elinor's place. She said little but watched and listened. Le Viguier had good manners and was no fool but he was old; she could understand why Elinor would not want to marry him.

And his daughters were cross-grained, froward creatures. Lord Lanval and Lady Clara were polite to them but Alys could see that her parents did not regard the Viguier women as good models for their daughters. Perhaps their mother had been dead too long and they had been allowed too much freedom by their quiet, grey father?

Alys was worried about Elinor. She had seen her wasting away and thought at first it was because she was missing Bertran. But now she was sure that her sister's decline was because she didn't want an old husband and had realised it was her parents' plan to give her one. Alys shuddered and drank some hippocras to disguise her trembling.

Suppose they had such a fate in mind for her too? She had hoped for something better. And what would Elinor do if she were forced to marry old Thibaut? Alys couldn't imagine her sister just giving up and settling down. She had been watching her and had come to some conclusions of her own.

When the dinner came to an end and just a few men were left drinking and listening to the musicians, Alys passed close to Huguet and whispered that she would like to talk to him on the battlements when the evening's music was over.

She passed a cold hour walking up and down on the walls, in spite of her fur-lined cloak. She kept herself warm by blowing on her hands and wrapping her arms round herself. After a long wait, a whistle like a bird's single note told her that Huguet was near.

Alys was suddenly shy. The *joglars* were Elinor's special friends and she felt all at once the scandal of meeting a young man alone in a secret tryst. She was very aware of his presence, even though she was still a little girl, and was glad to be able to pull her hood over her face.

'What can I do for you, my lady?' he said and his warm and friendly voice allayed her fears. Huguet was a friend.

'I am worried about my sister,' she said. 'She is so unhappy I fear she will harm herself in some way.'

'She has certainly looked pale and thin of late,' agreed Huguet. 'May I ask what you think is wrong? What is it that has taken her appetite away? I thought it was – forgive me – some ailment of women.'

Alys sighed. 'It is in a way. If marriage is a woman's

ailment. I'm not sure but I think our parents intend her to marry old Viguier. I know that's what Elinor thinks he has come here for – to ask for her hand.'

'The Lady Elinor and that stick!' said the *joglar*. 'Never! Besides,' he hesitated. 'Forgive me, not my place to mention it but I have always thought your sister looked with favour on Bertran de Miramont?'

Alys smiled inside her hood; did everyone in the castle know of her sister's preference?

'My sister might not be able to act upon her own wishes,' she said. 'If our father says she must marry Thibaut, then what else can she do?'

She heard Huguet gasp.

'No, surely she couldn't . . .' said the *joglar* anxiously.

'What? What are you thinking?' said Alys, his panic infecting her own mood.

'That as I passed the kitchen, Big Hugo was bawling that someone had stolen his boning knife.'

Alys suddenly felt a lot colder.

And then she was flying along the wall to the little chamber she shared with Elinor, Huguet at her heels.

They burst into the room and found Elinor slumped on the bed, the knife in her hand and the front of her chemise stained all red.

CHAPTER FOUR

If Wishes Were Horses

It took a few seconds to realise that Elinor was not dying. She was sobbing but with frustration rather than suffering her death agony. The wounds she had managed to inflict with Hugo's knife were superficial only and soon staunched. Huguet, white-faced, did all that Alys told him, swiftly fetching cold water and cloths and even some spiced wine from the kitchen. He took that opportunity to restore the knife, dropping it under a table so that it might look just mislaid and not stolen.

'I couldn't do it, Alys,' sniffed Elinor, sipping the wine. The colour was returning to her face.

'I'm glad, sister,' said Alys seriously.

They all kept their voices low; if Huguet had been found in the girls' chamber, their reputations would have been ruined. He held his face averted from the tending of the *donzela*'s wounds but he had been shocked to the soles of his feet to realise that she would rather die than be forced into marriage against her will.

'What shall I do?' whispered Elinor. She was calmer now but her situation had not changed and her future seemed just as bleak as before.

Alys felt that their roles had been reversed and she was the older sister now. But however hard she cudgelled her brains, she couldn't think of any advice to give Elinor. In desperation she turned to Huguet.

'What shall she do?'

'I can't marry le Viguier,' repeated Elinor. 'I shan't.'

'Is there no other way?' asked the *joglar*.

'I thought of joining the sisters,' said Elinor. 'You know, the Perfects. But from what I have found out about their lives, I can't imagine that I could endure that existence for long. It would be small improvement on being Thibaut's wife.'

'But is there nowhere else you could go?' asked Huguet, who was well aware of what the life of the Perfects was like and silently agreed that Elinor would not be suited to it.

She shook her head. 'Nowhere. My parents would not let me go anywhere else.'

They were all silent for a few moments. Then Huguet hesitantly put forward an idea.

As he spoke, Elinor and Alys listened intently, the older girl with eyes wide and shining.

'Would it work?' asked Alys.

'Would you dare do it?' asked Huguet.

'I was willing to die, Huguet,' said Elinor. 'I wasn't brave enough to do it to myself but this I could do. It would be less hardship than joining the Holy Sisters and less painful than all the ways I have planned to leave the castle.' Her face brightened. 'And we could find Bertran!'

Huguet sighed. He had wondered how long it would take the *donzela* to think of that.

The barons of the north received messengers throughout March. The Duke of Burgundy, the Count of Nevers and many others who had knights at their disposal, read the Pope's letter.

'Forward, volunteers of the army of God!' it said. *'Fill your souls with godly anger to avenge the insult done to the Lord.'*

The language was flowery but the meaning was clear: the Count of Toulouse had at the least allowed and at worst encouraged the murder of the Pope's faithful Legate while he was going about his lawful business. So the Count must be punished. The reward for any crusader from the north who took up the Cross against Toulouse and the heretics was huge.

First there would be a plenary indulgence from the Pope, which meant that they would be absolved of any sin committed so far and not receive any punishment in this life. All the interest on their debts would be cancelled too and, best of all, if they seized Raimon of Toulouse they could appropriate his lands.

It was customary for a crusader to sign up for forty days so, although the Pope didn't spell it out, the barons and knights of the north knew that they could be back in their own demesnes in a little less than two months, with their saddlebags full of southern booty. And they wouldn't even have had to cross the seas to get it. It was an attractive proposition.

Burgundy and Nevers between them could muster five hundred knights – a good basis for an army. They didn't expect much resistance from the southerners. Wasn't it a part of their unnatural beliefs that fighting was wrong? The lords of the north whipped themselves into a state of holy outrage about Pierre's murder. Rumours abounded about the Count of Toulouse. The memory of Saint Thomas Becket's death was still current in northern Europe and everyone knew that the English King was supposed to have asked 'Will no one rid me of this turbulent priest?' before four of his knights stabbed the Archbishop at his own altar in Canterbury.

And now word was circulating that the Count had publicly said of Pierre's assassin that he was 'the only man loyal enough to rid me of my enemy'. It was open knowledge in the South who the man was, but instead of punishing him, Raimon of Toulouse had praised him. Didn't that make the Count guilty? It was as good as admitting he was a heretic himself. The impious Count should feel the wrath of the Pope through the strong arms of the northern nobles.

But these things took time. First the barons had to get permission from the King, Philippe-Auguste, to leave their lands and set out for the south, and he hadn't been very receptive to the Pope so far. Who was going to pay the expenses of what was a crusade in all but name? An army of many thousand strong would need a patron with a deep purse.

But the seeds of the idea had been planted and it seemed certain that the Pope would have the revenge he wanted.

It was part of the plan that Elinor should now get to know the *joglaresas*. She had always been friendly with Perrin and Huguet, sometimes too friendly, in her mother's view, but she had held apart from Pelegrina, Maria and Bernardina. *Joglaresas* did not have a good reputation; they were loud and flamboyant and most people thought them loose in their morals. But if Elinor was to escape from the castle, these three women had to be in on the plot.

Pelegrina was a Catalan, dark-haired and sullen. Maria was of a sunnier temperament and was the youngest of the three – not much older than Elinor herself. Bernardina was the oldest, a woman in her late twenties who had run away from a violent husband. She had a crooked arm, which he had broken and which had set badly. Bernardina had made a new life for herself, travelling from castle to castle, and her husband had no means of chasing after her.

It was to Bernardina that the plan was first disclosed.

'So you see,' said Perrin, who had accepted Huguet's idea without hesitation, 'the *donzela* must leave the castle with us in the spring. We have to welcome her into our troupe.'

'As a *joglaresa?*' asked Bernardina incredulously. 'She will never pass as one of us.'

'No,' said Perrin. 'As a *joglar*. She will wear boy's clothes and has agreed to cut her hair.'

'That could work, I suppose,' said Bernardina. 'The *donzela* doesn't yet have a woman's figure. But can she sing? Can she play an instrument? We know she is not much of a dancer.'

'I am already teaching her the flute,' said Huguet. 'And I'm sure she will be able to play the tambour.'

'And she has a sweet voice,' said Perrin. 'We must all teach her the songs. She must have the full repertoire of chansons de gestes and *cansos* if she is to pass as a *joglar*.'

'As for the dancing,' said Huguet, 'she is sure to improve. I think she will like to lead better than to follow.'

Maria and Pelegrina took some persuading. The Catalan was forthright in her objections.

'What will happen to us if the disguise fails and she is recognised as a runaway *donzela*? We will all be punished and never be able to return to Sévignan. Why should we risk our livelihood for a spoilt young noblewoman?'

'Listen,' said Perrin. 'We shall all be in danger soon, whether we do this for Lady Elinor or not. Everyone associated with the Perfects, especially the troubadours and their troupes, is suspect as far as the Church is concerned. And what makes you think that Sévignan will be here to come back to, even by next winter?'

'Is it really as bad as that?' asked Maria. They had all heard rumours and they had picked up the hidden message in Bertran de Miramont's new song.

'It could be,' said Perrin. 'Bertran advised me to go east, maybe even as far as Italy. The Midi will not be safe for us much longer.'

'Besides,' said Huguet, 'can't you understand that Elinor does not want to marry Thibaut le Viguier?'

Pelegrina thought about it. The question of marrying a nobleman did not arise in her case; most women of her class didn't bother with marrying at all. That was for the nobles, who had land to leave and property to worry about. But they still had men they liked and men they didn't. There were boisterous young knights like Gui le Viguier and older lords in some of the castles they visited who were free with their hands and difficult to repulse if they were the troupe's paymasters.

The *joglaresa*s had their reputation unfairly; it was not that they willingly gave their favours to any who desired them, but that they were often not in a position to say no. A song, a dance, a tune, or a night in a nobleman's bed were all something to be bought and sold.

'She hates him so much?' asked Maria. She didn't find the old lord attractive herself but he wasn't one of the ones who pawed over her and leered suggestively at her while she danced. And the idea of being the *domna* of a fortified town, with servants to do your will, was not so very terrible in itself.

'She does not wish to marry at all,' said Huguet.

'Huh,' snorted Pelegrina. 'She wishes this and she doesn't wish that. If wishes were horses, beggars would ride. When does anyone care about our wishes? If you are determined to do this thing, we'll have to go along with it, whether we like it or not.'

'But it would be preferable if you were all kind to the *donzela*, when she is dressed as a *joven*, travelling among us. We will be her only friends in the world, her only family.'

'What does Lucatz think?' asked Maria.

Lucatz was the troupe's troubadour, who had been wintering with them in the castle when Bertran had turned up so suddenly. They were rivals and Lucatz had taken the opportunity to visit his ailing mother in Nîmes. He was only recently returned to Sévignan.

Perrin and Huguet exchanged glances; they had decided not to tell Lucatz until the party was well away from the castle and on the road east. It would be possible to keep Elinor out of the way until at least their first stop for the night.

'We have not told him,' said Perrin. 'We shall introduce him to "Esteve" – our new *joglar* – on the road. Then, if he accepts her as a boy, there will be no need to say more.'

Pelegrina said nothing but all three *joglaresas* wondered why they had been entrusted with a secret their troubadour would remain ignorant of.

Bertran had reached Narbonne by the time the Pope's messenger had arrived in Arles to look for the ferryman. The troubadour loved the city of Narbonne, which had a long history of appreciating poetry. One of his predecessors had written poems to Viscountess Ermengarde, who ruled the city for so long.

The present Viscount was Aimery III, a man who had just separated from his wife, causing a scandal in Narbonne. It was claimed she had been married to someone else all along. Such behaviour was not likely to make him popular with Bertran, who thought Aimery's great-aunt Ermengarde must have been turning in her grave, but he knew the Viscount would receive him courteously.

Aimery was not particularly sympathetic to the Believers but Bertran taught his new song to the *joglars* at court and saw that his message had once again been understood.

For those who had ears to hear, the *canso* was both a warning and a call to arms, yet was still on the surface a poem of *fin'amor*, which no one could take exception to.

And while the *joglars* were singing it in Narbonne, the Pope's messenger was in a tavern in Arles, plying Borel the ferryman with strong wine.

'So you saw the whole thing?' asked the messenger.

'I did,' said Borel, who had been bought many a drink in return for his account of the murder. With each telling he embroidered the story for his listeners with some new detail.

'It must have been terrible for you,' said the messenger encouragingly, signalling to the tavern keeper for more wine.

'Not a night has passed since that I haven't dreamed about it,' said Borel. 'The blood, the Legate's single scream as the lance went in, the assassin on his horse, the size of a giant.'

'The assassin or the horse?' checked the messenger.

'The ash-ash-sashin, of course,' slurred Borel.

The messenger called for a trencher of bread and meat for his guest; he thought the ferryman was getting drunk too quickly.

'Do you know who it was?' he asked Borel.

The man tried to tap the side of his nose and missed.

'Best not to mention any names,' he said. 'I didn't know him myself but there are those that do. Guilhem de Porcelet, for one.'

The messenger stowed this information away for future use.

'And I believe there was someone in the boat with you?' he asked.

'That's right. Troubadour,' said Borel.

'Did you know him?'

"Course. Always popping back and forth over the river that one. Been coming to Arles for years.'

'And his name? Do you know that?'

'As well as I know my own. Bernard, no, that's not right, Bertran, that's the fellow. Made off on his horse after the killer as soon as he saw there was nothing to be done for the poor Legate, God rest his soul.'

'So,' said the Pope's man. 'Bertran the troubadour. Is he known by any other name?'

'Miraval. No, hang on, that's the other one. Miramont! Bertran de Miramont. Anyone here will tell you about him. Handsome devil. All the ladies love him.'

'Not a devil, surely? He tried to help Pierre.'

'*Oc*. But he doesn't love the ladies back, you see.'

'You mean he is an . . . unnatural, a sodomite?'

'Nah. Too pure for that or for the ladies. Still he did go after the murderer.'

'But didn't catch him, as far as you know?'

'The rumour is,' said Borel. 'That he lost him in Beaucaire but that was my *amic* Simos told me that. He brought the troubadour back in the ferry a few days later. Simos and me, we take turns on the boat. He's on it now.'

The innkeeper brought Borel's food and the messenger sat back and let his informant enjoy it. He had three useful pieces of news to take back to Rome: that one Guilhem de Porcelet knew the killer, that the witness was Bertran de Miramont and that the handsome troubadour was 'too pure to love the ladies'. It had not been a bad evening's work.

Winter was finally defeated and the days were beginning to stretch out longer again. Warmth returned even to the hills of the Midi and fur-lined cloaks were folded up and laid in cedar-wood chests. Elinor had tried on her *joglar*'s outfit in secret and Alys had agreed she could pass for a boy as soon as her hair was shorn. But they couldn't do that till the day of the escape.

Lucatz and his troupe of *joglar*s normally moved on in April and he had not demurred when Perrin had suggested they might head eastward. He might be jealous of Bertran but he was not fool enough to ignore his advice.

March was coming to an end and Thibaut and his daughters were still at Sévignan. Elinor prayed daily that they would just go back home to their own bastide without any proposal having been made. She had shown him no encouragement. And, in spite of her escape plan, Elinor was in no hurry to leave the only home she had ever known.

But the day came when Lord Lanval summoned her to the solar and she found him sitting with le Viguier. Her father's expression was set and she felt her mind closing down as the terms were at last offered to her.

'My dear,' said Lanval, without any warmth in his voice. 'Our neighbour and friend, Lord Thibaut, has something he wishes to ask you and I must tell you that he does so with my full consent and approval.'

Both men looked at her expectantly and Elinor managed a small curtsey. Her father looked pleased to find her in such a submissive humour.

'Lady Elinor,' said Thibaut and she realised that her father wasn't even going to leave the room. That would make it easier in case her old admirer offered to kiss her, she thought. She could feign shyness and modesty.

'I have long been without the comfort of a wife,' continued Thibaut. 'Of my daughters, one is married, one betrothed and the third likely to be so soon. It will not be long before my castle is without a feminine presence and my court without a lady. You would do me a great honour if you would consent to be that lady.'

He stopped. Was there going to be more? Shouldn't he say that he loved or worshipped her beauty or something similar? But Thibaut's dignified little speech was clearly all that he had prepared.

'Well, Elinor?' said her father. 'You cannot pretend to be surprised.'

'No, indeed, Paire, Lord Thibaut. But forgive me – I am so young. Can I have a day or two to give my answer?'

Her father was frowning again.

'There is nothing to think about, surely? It is a fine and gentlemanly offer, nobly made. You would not insult our guest, Elinor?'

'No, Paire, I would not.' Elinor gave another little curtsey. 'I am . . . most grateful to the Lord Thibaut for his handsome offer. It's just that I should like to talk to my mother and sister before I accept.'

'Your mother is of one mind with me in this matter,' said Lanval but he had been mollified by that word 'before'.

So had Thibaut. 'Shall we say two days then, my dear?' he said. 'Then we could announce our betrothal before I leave Sévignan.'

'Very well,' said Lanval. 'Have your two days of maiden uncertainty. But then come back here and accept Thibaut's most generous offer. I want to have a celebration before our *joglars* all move on.'

Elinor ducked her head and left the room quietly but then rushed back to her chamber, where Alys was waiting.

'Quick, sister,' she said, all out of breath, 'the scissors! I must be gone before the sun sets twice. We must tell Huguet. The time has come for me to be a *joglar*!'

CHAPTER FIVE

Joglar

ord Lanval was not best pleased when Lucatz the troubadour came and asked if the troupe might leave next day. The request for permission was a courtesy; there was nothing the castellan could do to stop them. They had been in Sévignan for months and it was understood that they would move to another bastide in the spring.

But he wanted them to stay to celebrate his daughter's betrothal. He tried to persuade Lucatz to wait a few days longer but the troubadour was politely firm; the *joglars* were already packing up their instruments. Lucatz himself had been surprised by the urgency with which Perrin and Huguet had argued the need to move on immediately. But he did not want to stay in the castle without them and risk missing them on the road.

So with April just beginning and the trees all coming into light green leaf the troubadour, the two *joglars* and three *joglaresas* and a handful of acrobats, jugglers and dancers wound their way down the hill from the castle. Once the townspeople had gone back into their houses, a slight young boy with a heavy pack slipped out of the bailey and took the same road as the troupe.

It was some time before Elinor was missed. No one had

seen the *donzela* for some hours before her mother started to inquire after her. The Lady Clara was planning another session of explaining to her daughter exactly how desirable it was for her to accept Lord le Viguier. But she was nowhere to be found.

The dark hair that Alys had carefully snipped off with Miqela's scissors had been burned in the kitchen fire and one of Elinor's dresses concealed in Alys's chest for future destruction, so that no one would guess she had left in disguise. Her fur-lined cloak had been rolled into her pack against the next winter. There was nothing to suggest that she was anywhere other than roaming the castle and its environs as she so often did. And nothing to suggest that she was dressed in any way differently from normal. Any search party would be looking for a young girl, not a boy.

It wasn't till nightfall that her parents were alarmed and by then it was too dark to take the search outside the castle. And when the dawn broke, after a sleepless night for many in Sévignan, Elinor was many miles away.

The troupe had reached Lodève and settled for the night near a tavern, when a young boy on a dappled pony stopped and asked if he might join them.

'I am Esteve,' he said in a high, unbroken voice. 'And I am a *joglar* like you. I got separated from my troupe.'

Lucatz looked at him dubiously. 'What troupe? Who is your troubadour?' He thought the pony looked a little familiar but he did not recognise the boy.

Indeed her own mother would not have recognised Elinor

in this slender and hollow-eyed youth. She was riding the pony with a man's saddle, which had made her sore and awkward. But she had been happy to find Mackerel tethered by the town gate, as arranged with the *joglars*. He was her own pony and had whickered in recognition as she approached, undeceived by her new appearance. Although it was unusual for a *joglar* to have his own mount – indeed only Lucatz had a horse and the rest of his troupe walked beside the pack ponies – it would make her adaptation to a rougher life a bit easier.

'Guilhem Ademar,' Elinor, who had been coached by Perrin, answered Lucatz's question. 'We were at Albi together.'

'You must have left the court there very early in spring to have come so far by now,' said Lucatz suspiciously. In truth he was rather jealous that Ademar's least *joglar* – for this was just a boy – had his own mount.

The boy said nothing; he had been advised not to elaborate.

'What do you play?' asked Lucatz.

'Flute and tambour,' said Elinor. 'And I can sing all the latest *cansos*.'

'I say we let him join us,' said Perrin. 'Now that Huguet's voice has broken we could do with another singer to take the high line.'

'Very well,' said Lucatz. 'You may travel with us till you can rejoin Ademar's troupe. I'll not have him saying I stole his young *joglar*.'

'Thank you, sir,' said Elinor and then went through introductions to all the people she had already known when she was the *donzela*.

The *joglaresas* were the hardest, flirting with him and teasing him about his absence of beard and other aspects of manhood that he lacked.

'Leave him be, Pelegrina,' said Perrin in the end, quite harshly. 'The lad must be tired. Give him something to eat. And then you can bed down with Huguet and me, son. Take no notice of the women – they treat everyone the same.'

Elinor was grateful, though she hoped perhaps the women's teasing was meant to help keep up her pretence. She ate her bowl of rabbit stew greedily and, after stretching out her bedroll between the two *joglars* who were already her friends, she fell into a deep and refreshing sleep, better than any night she had passed in the castle for weeks. To lie on the ground, under the stars, was a completely new experience and she would never have guessed how free and at the same time how safe she felt.

In the morning, after some fresh bread and small ale from the tavern, the troupe packed up and returned to the road.

'Would you ride while a lady walks?' Bernardina asked the new *joglar*. 'That is not true *cortesia*.'

'See how he colours up like a girl,' jeered Pelegrina. 'Perhaps because he doesn't think we are ladies?'

Elinor stopped the pony and dismounted, bowing awkwardly to the *joglaresas* and offering Mackerel to whichever of them would like to ride. But Lucatz had ridden back to see why they had stopped and ordered the boy back up.

'I don't want them getting soft,' he said. 'How many *joglaresas* do you know who can ride? But then perhaps in Ademar's troupe everyone has their own mount?'

'No, sir,' said Elinor. 'I was given the pony by a lord.' That was true enough.

'Hmm,' said Lucatz. 'We will not enquire into why.' He glared at the *joglaresas*, who were cackling with lewd laughter. 'Now we have delayed long enough. On your way.'

While Lucatz and his troupe travelled slowly east towards Montpellier, Bertran was working his way from court to court in the west. From Narbonne he crossed the River Aude and headed for Minerve, calling at the hill towns in between: Aigne, Aigues-Vives and La Caunette.

After many weeks on horseback he rode unchallenged through the gates in the double curtain wall round the town and over the bridge into Minerve. The River Cesse disappeared into a large natural tunnel, affording a good water supply for the castle. And from here he could see the tall *candela*, the central tower. From here it looked impregnable, standing on a high spur of rock.

The town was built on the site of an old Roman temple to the goddess Minerva, who had given it her name. In ancient times, the locals would have prayed to the warlike goddess to protect them, but what could save them from the battles to come now that the Midi was Christian but the Church itself was about to take up arms against them? Bertran hoped that the town's many natural advantages would hold the answer.

He sang his song himself that night at the court of Viscount Guilhem. There were no other troubadours or *joglars* in the castle so he took his own lute from his saddlebags and sang to all who would listen about the love that was like war, the battles that would be fought and lost or won depending on the readiness of the beloved.

After dinner, he had an interview with the Viscount alone.

'Where will you go next?' asked Guilhem.

'West, to Carcassonne,' said Bertran. 'I must talk to Viscount Trencavel.'

'Do you think he understands the gravity of the situation?'

'I think not,' said Bertran. 'He will see it as a problem only for his uncle in Toulouse. But once the lords of the north take up the Cross against the south, it will not be the Count of Toulouse alone who will suffer.'

'You really think that an army will invade the Midi?' asked Guilhem. 'That the northerners will besiege our castles and bastides?'

'I do indeed believe that, my lord,' said the troubadour.

'But look how we are placed here,' said Guilhem. 'We have the outer walls and the tower and enough men to defend them. Even if they come in their tens of thousands, we could withstand them.'

'Then prepare for that,' urged Bertran. 'Build up your stocks of armour, weapons and food. And make sure that the people are loyal to you and willing to defend the Believers.'

Bertran did not know whether the Viscount of Minerve shared his secret religion; he had given no sign. But he did know that if the Church moved against the south, an army hungry for blood and land would not distinguish between heretics and the faithful.

It took the troupe several more days to reach Montpellier and Lucatz was so keen to be in the city in time for Easter that he hired a cart to carry all those without mounts. The three *joglaresa*s sat in the back with their legs dangling over the edge, chatting and laughing and greatly enjoying the treat. After the long winter in Sévignan, they were out of practice in walking the roads. Perrin and Huguet sat next to the carter on either side, playing on a flute and fiddle to keep him entertained on the journey. The jugglers and dancers huddled up together on the straw in the back of the cart improvising raucous and rude lyrics to the *joglars'* tunes. Lucatz rode well ahead but Esteve kept the pony alongside the cart.

Elinor was getting used to being Esteve the *joglar*. She had hardened to riding in a man's saddle and had not found the change in her life too difficult. It helped that the weather was warm and the nights mild, since the troupe usually slept in the open. Their food was homely and without the refinements that Hugo had applied in the castle kitchen at Sévignan, but Elinor throve on it. Riding in the fresh air and performing at country fairs gave her an appetite much greater than her restricted life in the castle. And now that she was no longer afraid of being made to marry, her heart was light.

She missed Alys, of course, and her brother, but she was not lonely. Perrin and Huguet were as friendly as always and protective too, and the *joglaresa*s, though they kept up a stream of mockery, were not hostile. Lucatz was a bit remote and prickly but he nodded in approval at Esteve's singing and playing. It was hard work, keeping up with the professional musicians but Elinor was thrilled to find that here was something she could do. She even managed a passable dance when surrounded by the rest of the troupe and her fine leg was commented on by many maidens in the villages they passed through.

Of Bertran, she heard nothing. Perrin went extremely

vague when she tried to press him about the troubadour's movements.

'He was going east, that's all I know,' he said but he seemed uneasy and Elinor was sure he knew of some danger to Bertran that he was keeping from her.

As they approached the walls of Montpellier, Elinor looked up with interest. She had never been in such a great city and the furthest she had travelled away from her home before had been to the market in Béziers. Montpellier had a market too, much larger, and that was where Lucatz was heading.

It was like nothing Elinor had ever seen and Huguet had to nudge her knee to stop her looking like a gaping carp at all the sights.

'Surely Esteve has seen a market before,' he whispered. 'They must have them in Albi.'

She tried to seem less impressed but it was difficult. The central square was filled with more stalls than she had ever seen before. It was Holy Saturday and the city was brimming over with visitors as well as the local population, come to spend their money and go to Mass in the cathedral for Easter Day. Lucatz told the carter to tie up at the edge of the market and look after the horses and signalled to his troupe to follow him on foot.

Montpellier was known as the 'golden city' of the Midi because of all its goldsmiths and there were stalls glittering and glinting in the sunshine with all kinds of chains and rings and seals. They sat alongside the wares of glassworkers, parchment-makers, haberdashers and dyers.

In the food part of the market smells of raw fish and eels and game made Elinor's gorge rise but there were also stalls selling sweet spiced bread and tarts and chestnuts and roast mutton. She had never seen such a range of different kinds of food, not even at one of Hugo's best feasts in the castle.

At the far end of the market was a raised platform, not much more than a cart frame on barrels instead of wheels, which Lucatz had his eye on. The troupe followed him slowly, threading their way through the many delights being offered on each side. Perrin bought spiced biscuits for the *joglars* and Elinor thought the mixture of cinnamon, sugar and almonds was the most delicious thing she had ever tasted.

'This is where we'll perform on Monday,' said Lucatz. 'And I will go to the court and see whether the Lady will give us hospitality.'

'So we can explore the market now?' asked Bernardina.

The troubadour frowned. 'Very well. But I shall expect to see all of you in the cathedral for the Easter Vigil tonight. Then I'll let you know where we'll be sleeping. You, Esteve, come with me.'

'Me?' asked Elinor, dumbfounded. She was torn between longing to explore the market and curiosity about what the inside of a grander court than her father's would be like.

'Yes, don't dawdle like a halfwit,' said Lucatz. 'If you behave like a normal person, I think you might impress the Lady.'

As they walked up to the castle, the troubadour stopped to pick up useful pieces of gossip on the way.

'So,' he said, when they had at last left the market and the winding streets around it and were heading up a broader approach to the citadel. 'It appears we have come at a fortunate time.'

He was unlike his usual self, almost gleeful at the prospect

66

of gain to be had in the golden city.

'It seems that the Lady has an heir,' he said. 'The new little *Senhor* was born in February. Jacques they call him and he is but two months old. That means the Lady will be recovered from her lying-in and full of joy and, we hope, largesse.'

'That's good,' said Elinor uncertainly. 'I'm sorry but I know nothing of the Lady of Montpellier. Has she no *Senhor*?'

'She is married to King Pedro of Aragon,' said Lucatz, 'but is Lady of Montpellier in her own right. She got the title back from her half-brother only four years ago.' He lowered his voice. 'But there's a rumour that Pedro is trying to divorce her and marry someone else. He wants Montpellier for himself but I don't think the *domna*, will let him have it easily.'

Elinor was amazed. Here was a woman ruling a city in her own name and defying her husband even though he was a powerful king and Elinor's father's own suzerain. It made her own attempts at independence seem rather puny.

'It's not the first time she has married a scoundrel,' said Lucatz and Elinor was astonished at the casual way he referred to their sovereign lord. 'Maria's first husband married her and gave her two daughters. But the Pope annulled that match because he had two wives alive already!'

By now they had reached the castle, with its silver shield with a red circle on it hanging over the gate. Elinor was a bit disappointed that they were not ushered into the presence of Maria of Montpellier herself. But they were well entertained by her *senescal*, who was courteous and welcoming. Elinor kept very quiet throughout the interview, saying little except for thanking the man for the sweet wine and biscuits and giving her assumed name.

By the time they left, Lucatz was in a very good humour.

'Monday morning in the market and in the evening entertaining at the child's Christening feast,' he said. 'What could be better? I didn't know about the child but I made the right decision leaving Sévignan when we did, even though there was a betrothal feast in the offing.'

Elinor realised with a shock that he was talking about her own possible troth-pledging to old le Viguier. Was it really less than a week ago that she had stood in the solar and heard his proposal?

To cover her confusion, she asked whether the Lady would not have already arranged the entertainment for her son's important day.

'We can't expect to be the only troupe in Montpellier,' said Lucatz. 'You must know that from your time at Albi. But we will have the charm of novelty. I'm sure we will be the crown of the evening. I must tell the other *joglars* to match our songs to the Lady's circumstances.'

The cathedral was ablaze with light. And in the choir stalls sat all the nuns from a nearby convent. Three of them came down into the main aisle, each carrying a candle, a towel and a box.

'What are they doing?' whispered Elinor.

'They are the three Marys,' Perrin whispered back. 'They go to the tomb to anoint the dead body of the Lord.'

The three nuns walked towards the altar, where two choirboys dressed in white, stood like guardian angels and warbled in their high voices: *'Quem queritis?'* – 'Whom do you seek, O servants of Christ?'

'Jesus of Nazareth crucified, O inhabitants of heaven,' sang the nuns.

'He is not here, he is resurrected as it was foretold.

'Go and announce that he is raised from the dead.'

It was surprisingly moving. The priest took up the Host and processed round the cathedral with the two 'angels' on either side of him and the three 'Mary's walking behind.

And then the true Mass began. Perrin and Huguet slipped out and Elinor noticed that two of the *joglaresas* left quietly too. So they were also heretics, she thought. She knew that those who practised her father's religion would not receive the Sacrament.

Elinor strained to see the Lady of Montpellier, who sat in her own special stall at the front of the nave. She was tiny, a dignified and indomitable figure with a very straight back and a mass of dark hair. But she was surrounded by ladies-in-waiting and guards, so that there was not much more than a glimpse of her to be seen, in a cloth of gold robe.

Elinor would get a closer view tomorrow.

CHAPTER SIX

Honeysuckle

Innocent III celebrated Easter in Rome with the usual magnificence and pomp. By the end of Easter Sunday, he was tired and elated in equal measure. When he had disrobed and taken a light meal, he sat down to ponder the news that his messenger who had been sent to the Midi had brought him. The Pope had been thoughtful when he heard his information. What did the troubadour's lack of enthusiasm for women mean? The ferryman had been sure he was not abnormal in his desires and perhaps he was just a clean-living man? As Pope and a celibate Christian himself, he could hardly condemn Bertran for that. But just possibly the troubadour was a heretic, who either was a Perfect already or was planning to become one before he died. That would account for his abstinence from female company.

But the life of a troubadour would not really be compatible with that of a Perfect; he would have to pray too many times a day to be at his lord's beck and call for poetry and he'd have to eat whatever the lord he was serving put before him. So Bertran de Miramont was possibly just a Believer who was on the heretics' side. But wasn't it a bit too much of a coincidence that this troubadour should have been there at the very moment when the Pope's Legate, acting against the heretics, had been murdered?

It was beginning to look like conspiracy. The murderer could have hidden in the wood and waited till he saw the ferry-boat coming, knowing that Pierre and his companions must cross the river by that route. And it could have been pre-arranged that the troubadour would travel in the first morning boat.

Then after the murder, he could have merely pretended to chase after the assassin, making sure that no one else did so. It made perfect sense. He must investigate this Guilhem de Porcelet named by the ferryman. It was clear that both de Porcelet and de Miramont knew something; they must be interrogated with the strictest rigour.

Innocent sighed heavily. He must now send out other men, capable of tracking down the troubadour and carrying out the most severe kind of investigation. This business in the Midi was taking up more and more of his time. But it would be worth it if the heresy could be stamped out.

In Montpellier the *joglars* were having a successful Easter Monday. The market square was thronged with people, even more than on Holy Saturday and the customers, after an hour or two of filling their baskets with cheeses and oatcakes, eggs and honey, were ready for some entertainment.

Lucatz stood at the side of the cart-platform, master-minding the troupe's activities so that jugglers and acrobats were followed by dancers and singers. Perrin, Huguet and Esteve accompanied them all, with scarcely more than a moment to sip at the mugs of ale that market-traders bought for them.

One of the acrobats took round a velvet hat which was filled up often with silver pennies and the occasional larger coin from a rich trader, minted by the lords of Montpellier themselves. Lucatz was well pleased with their haul.

Many of the people who came to watch and listen had a special request for a particular *canso* or one of the longer chansons de gestes but the troubadour held back on most of the longer poems, knowing that they'd have to perform more of those at the court.

By the time they stopped at midday, Lucatz was able to give six pennies to every member of the troupe and the *joglars* got a solidus each.

'He always pays the men more,' grumbled Pelegrina.

'Well, we have had to work the hardest,' said Huguet, before Pelegrina could say anything that would reveal that one of the *joglars* wasn't a male at all.

Elinor wondered if she should share her payment with the women but Perrin saw her thought before it flowered into action and shook his head.

They all had a free afternoon now until they were expected to assemble in the castle for the baby prince's celebration. Elinor had never had so much money of her own to spend. As a nobleman's daughter, everything had been provided for her and even though she had occasionally visited a market, she had never bought anything from a stall with her own coins, earned by her own work. It was an exhilarating feeling.

The first call on her purse was lunch and she went with Perrin and Huguet to a stall where balls of minced chicken and spices were being coated in batter and dropped into pans of sizzling oil. The smell was heavenly and Elinor nearly burned her mouth on the hot savoury fritter.

As she stood and ate her lunch in the middle of the teeming marketplace, hot juices dribbling down her chin, Elinor had never felt happier. She hadn't been born a boy but this was the next best thing, to have all of a boy's freedom and none of a man's responsibilities.

The only tiny cloud in the blue sky of her new travelling life was that she had absolutely no idea what was going to happen to her in future. She had thought no further than finding Bertran and throwing herself on his mercy. Surely he wouldn't have sent her his token if he hadn't loved her? Beyond that she had no idea, not even of marriage to the handsome troubadour. She didn't want to think about it.

'Come on,' said Perrin. 'When you two have finished stuffing your faces, we should go and explore.'

The Lady of Montpellier knew how to put on a good feast. With her marriage in doubt, she now placed all her hopes of a happy future on her baby son, Jacques. He would be *Senhor* of Montpellier after her death, and today's feast was all about proclaiming that fact, which was much more important to her than his inheritance of the throne of Aragon, which was far away over the Pyrenees. All the local nobles had been invited and more than twenty dishes prepared. And the entertainments would be equally splendid. It was a real piece of fortune that a new troubadour had turned up with his young *joglar* and promised to put on a fine show with his troupe at the end of the evening.

Maria of Montpellier put on her blue silk gown and got her maid to brush her hair till it crackled. She had wrested the lordship of the city back from her half-brother a few years ago and now she was enjoying being ruler. Marriage, pregnancy and childbirth had not got in her way. She had her two little daughters, Matilda and Petronilla, living with her in the castle and tonight they would join in the celebrations for their baby brother.

She hoped they would never be in bitter feud with him as she had with her half-brother Guilhem. They certainly seemed to dote on him now. Maria looked fondly down at the infant in his crib. How could anyone not love him? With his tiny pink fingernails and downy black hair? She shook herself and stood up extra straight. The Lady of Montpellier would not achieve her ends by sentiment but by skilful negotiations and political adroitness. She would write to the Pope about her son's inheritance as soon as the Christening celebrations were over.

The great hall of the castle of Montpellier could hardly have been more different from the improvised stage in the market. Lucatz had made sure that all his troupe wore their best clothes, which would have been a problem for Elinor, who had only one boy's outfit, but Huguet lent her a tight purple velvet surcoat and Perrin had bought her a pair of velvet slippers to match.

The *joglaresa*s were magnificent in full-skirted dresses of crimson, green and yellow. They had all washed and curled their hair and every member of the troupe wore brightly coloured ribbons, some of them bought that day in the market.

74

As usual they would not eat till after the performance, but Lucatz told them that the Lady herself had given orders to the kitchen to hold back enough of every dish and course to feast the entertainers well.

They watched the diners from a minstrels' gallery at the far end of the hall from the table where the Lady Maria sat.

'Look at her,' said her namesake, Maria the *joglaresa*. 'Isn't she beautiful? I hope I have a figure like hers after three children.'

'Hah,' said Pelegrina. 'Worry about that when you have a man to give you some.'

'Hush!' said Bernardina. 'Marriage and children aren't all they're cracked up to be. Why, even the Lady herself, with her fine blue gown and her fine baby boy, is at loggerheads with her husband. And he's her liege lord into the bargain.'

'Stop gossiping,' said Perrin. 'We are the Lady's guests tonight and we shan't feel the lack of a lord. Look, I think the *senescal* is about to give the signal for the entertainments to begin.'

The little band of musicians who had been playing in the gallery throughout the dinner now yielded place to another group. Down below in the hall the acrobats and dancers of that troupe began a lively performance accompanied by their instrumentalists above.

'They're good,' said Huguet. 'You have to admit it.'

'Very good,' said Elinor, alarmed. Up in the gallery they had a boy singer of about her age, with a pure treble voice and with a presence to rival Esteve's. To her surprise, Lucatz came and put a hand on her shoulder.

'Don't compare yourself with others, Esteve,' he said kindly. 'I back my troupe against any in the Midi and, until we catch up with Ademar, you are part of my troupe.'

Their time came to perform and they passed the outgoing troupe who waved good-naturedly. Lucatz and the dancers, jugglers and acrobats went down into the great hall and the *joglar*s and *joglaresa*s positioned themselves to play and sing from the front of the gallery. Halfway through, the three *joglaresa*s also went down into the hall, leaping and whooping among the other dancers, swinging their petticoats and clapping their hands.

But they weren't as raucous and rowdy as Elinor had seen them in the villages. This was still Eastertide, after all, and the welcoming of a new soul into the family of the Church.

There was a pause in the dancing and the *senescal* brought a request from the Lady herself that they should perform the lay of Tristan and Iseut. Elinor was surprised. It was a sad story with no happy ending for the lovers but maybe it suited the Lady's view of her present situation, though she had committed no adultery. Rumours had been rife in the market but all agreed it was King Pedro who had been the unfaithful party.

More importantly, this was a *canso* with a large part for the *joglar* with the highest singing register. So Esteve would have to be on the top of his form.

Elinor stepped forwards in her purple surcoat, feeling hot now and far from composed but she had memorised this lay, called '*Chevrefeuille*' or 'Honeysuckle', among others by Marie de France, and as she started, the words began to work a kind of magic on her. Everyone was listening to the story – not to the individual *joglar* who sang it. Elinor or Esteve was just the vessel through which the sad tale passed.

Tristan was sent to woo the Lady Iseut for his uncle, King

Mark, but had the misfortune to fall in love with her himself. His love was returned and the young couple pursued their affair in secret, not wishing for the King to discover it.

Elinor now came to the climax of the poem, where the banished Tristan carved a signal for Iseut into a hazel tree and a honeysuckle became entwined with it. The honeysuckle was so entangled with the hazel that either would die if the other were uprooted. And so it was with the two lovers, 'Ni moi sans vous, ni vous sans moi' – 'Neither me without you nor you without me'.

Elinor thought of Bertran as she sang that part and it gave her voice more poignancy. She didn't exactly feel that she couldn't possibly live without him, like the honeysuckle and the hazel, but she could imagine what it would be like to feel that and for the duration of the song she did. She looked towards the Lady, who was listening to her so intently. Was she thinking of King Pedro? Elinor had gleaned from the gossip in the market that Pedro was fourteen years older than his wife – not as big a gap as between Iseut and King Mark but perhaps she was now yearning for a young Tristan to adore her. The Lady was still only twenty-two years old.

The lay of Chevrefeuille came to an end and Lady Maria led the applause. Elinor bowed and Lucatz clapped her on the back.

'Well done, young *joglar*,' he said. 'You have made our fortune tonight.'

And indeed the *senescal* himself soon brought a goblet of hippocras especially for 'the young *joglar*' together with a velvet bag of coins. Elinor drank the spiced wine gratefully but handed the bag straight to Lucatz, without counting the coins. He appreciated her gesture but his eyes opened wide to see how much silver it contained. He stowed it away in his jacket but nodded to Elinor as if to say, 'don't worry – you'll have some of it back.'

Some weeks after Elinor had brought tears to the eyes of Maria of Montpellier's court as the young *joglar* Esteve, Bertran, quite ignorant of the *donzela*'s new life, at last reached Carcassonne. It was a city even more highly fortified than Minerve. Massive walls were punctuated by semicircular towers dating back to Roman times. There was a double gate to get through between the two suburbs outside the city, before the main road approaching the moated Château Comtal in the northeast corner, which had its own fortifications and towers.

Bertran was shown through all the gates and across the bridge to the château without challenge. The troubadour was a familiar figure in Carcassonne even though the young Viscount had poets and musicians enough of his own. Bertran was not kept waiting long before being shown into the presence of the Viscount himself.

Raimon-Roger Trencavel at twenty-four was younger than Bertran. But he looked tired, his face lined and sad. He brightened a bit when Bertran was shown in and, dispensing with the formalities, clasped the troubadour in his arms.

'Well met, Miramont,' he said. 'It does me good to see you. Sit with me a while and let us drink a cup of wine together and put the world to rights.'

'Ah, sire, if only we *could* put it to rights,' said Bertran. 'But I will willingly drink and talk with you, since there is much to talk about.'

'Have you heard the latest news from the north?' asked Trencavel, when the servants had gone and the two men were drinking companionably in the Viscount's private room.

'Tell me, sire,' said Bertran.

'The Pope has written direct to the nobles, asking them to take up arms against my uncle.'

'I see,' said Bertran. 'What about King Philippe-Auguste?'

'His Holiness has not written to him this time, they say. But I don't imagine he will be happy if his barons take their soldiers and head south to please the Pope.'

'What does your uncle say?' asked Bertran.

'I haven't seen him. But he has brought this trouble on himself. He should never have promised the Legates that he would persecute the Believers. The Pope was bound to keep him to his word.'

The two men were silent for a while, drinking their wine and each thinking his own thoughts.

'You heard about the murder of the Legate?' asked Bertran.

The Viscount nodded. This was a delicate area. He could hardly tell the troubadour that his uncle had been responsible. But the fact was that Trencavel did not know the truth. He and his uncle, the Count of Toulouse, had not been on good terms for some time.

'I was there,' said Bertran. 'I saw the murder and gave chase after the murderer. But I lost him.'

'That is news indeed,' said the Viscount. 'I did not know you had been there.'

'I am not proclaiming the fact,' said Bertran. 'It would have been all right if I had caught the villain but since he escaped me, there might be those, especially in Rome, who think I was in collusion with him.'

'Surely not. You exaggerate the danger. Who would suspect you of such a heinous crime?'

'That is not what matters anyway,' said Bertran. 'It is my belief that, if the Pope is successful in raising a northern army, it will not come only against Toulouse.'

'What do you mean?' asked the Viscount. 'His argument is with my uncle, no one else.'

'His argument is with the people he calls heretics,' said Bertran. 'And with any lord who supports them and is sympathetic to their cause.'

'But that is more or less every lord in the Midi,' objected the Viscount. 'None of our cities and bastides could manage without the Believers – or the Jews come to that.'

'That's what I mean,' said Bertran. 'And why I have been singing of war and battles in every hill town between here and Saint-Gilles. I do believe that, using this murder as an excuse, the Pope will do everything he can to wage war against every court in the south. Anyway, once there is an army on the rampage, they will not be precise about who is a heretic and who is not.'

They were both thinking about this when a servant knocked at the door and came and whispered something in the Viscount's ear.

'And now we have two more pieces of news,' said Raimon-Roger, his face grave. 'The Pope has excommunicated my uncle again.'

'That is surely no surprise,' said Bertran.

'No, indeed, he must be getting used to it,' said the Viscount.

'If he were a heretic, to be banned from the Sacrament would not mean much to him,' said Bertran cautiously.

'Nor if he were just a not very devout man but a rebellious and ambitious spirit, as I know him to be,' said the Viscount, evading the implied question.

Bertran bowed. He was not going to find out, even from this intelligent man that he counted his friend, whether he or his uncle shared the troubadour's religion.

'But I said there was another piece of news,' said the Viscount. 'My servant tells me that there is a Pope's man at the outer gate. He seeks one Bertran de Miramont. He thinks that the troubadour might be here and wishes – this is the precise phrase – to "interrogate him". What shall I do Bertran? It seems you might be right in one of your surmises at least. The Pope is looking for you.'

CHAPTER SEVEN

Two Journeys

The troupe stayed in Montpellier over a week. The Sunday after Easter was the feast day of a Saint Martin who had been a Pope hundreds of years before and Lucatz was insistent that they had to show themselves willing to celebrate the feast.

'Pope Martin was a persecutor of heretics in his day,' he told the *joglars*. 'And there are too many people who believe that we poets and minstrels support the heretics now. We have to show veneration for Saint Martin.'

Elinor caught the look that Perrin and Huguet exchanged and decided she must ask them about it. So when Lucatz had gone off to organise their next performance, she got the two *joglars* on their own in the stables of Montpellier's castle.

'What's going on?' she asked. 'You know something you're not telling me. And there are whispers in the town.'

'Sometimes it is better not to know too much,' said Perrin. 'Then you can plead ignorance if questioned.'

'Questioned!' said Elinor, alarmed. 'What do you mean?'

'You heard what Lucatz said,' said Huguet. 'Travelling companies like ourselves, particularly the troubadours and *joglars*, have been suspected of supporting the Believers and of carrying messages between them.'

'And are you saying that is true?' asked Elinor.

Perrin shifted uneasily. 'Sometimes and in some cases, perhaps,' he said.

'And something has happened? Something that makes our situation more dangerous?' asked Elinor.

'We'd better tell her,' said Huguet, looking at Perrin, who nodded briefly.

'There was a murder a few months ago,' said Perrin seriously. 'The man who died was Pierre of Castelnau and he was archdeacon of Maguelonne here – a local man.'

'Why was he murdered?'

'He was the Pope's Legate,' said Huguet. 'His official ambassador appointed to suppress the Believers. And he had just come away from a meeting with Count Raimon of Toulouse.'

'That's why the people of Montpellier are angry,' said Perrin. 'They feel that one of their own has been cut down.'

'And the Pope blames the Count of Toulouse,' said Huguet.

'But how does that make it dangerous for us?' asked Elinor. She felt at a loss, at sea in a world she didn't understand.

'Bertran thinks the Pope will take vengeance, not just on the Count but on the entire south,' said Perrin.

'Bertran said that? When?'

'When he came to Sévignan,' said Huguet. 'That's why he arrived in winter. He was visiting all the bastides sympathetic to the Believers, to warn them.'

Elinor was gradually beginning to understand. 'My father . . .' she said. Fear made her mouth dry. Was this why he had been so anxious to marry her off? Because he thought their castle would be attacked by the Pope? She forced her terror down and tried to listen carefully to what the *joglars* were telling her.

Perrin was nodding. 'I see you know about Lord Lanval's religion,' he said. 'And I think you guess that Huguet and I – and Bertran – share it.'

'But what can the Pope do?' asked Elinor. 'And why should he attack Sévignan if it was the Count of Toulouse who ordered the murder?' She stowed away in her mind the revelation of Bertran's dangerous religion.

'He can raise an army,' said Huguet grimly.

'He hasn't managed to do so yet – though he has tried,' said Perrin. 'But this time he has the best excuse ever to go to the French King and ask for help in defeating what he sees as heresy in the south. He's always wanted to eliminate us.'

'And if an army comes, they won't stop at Toulouse,' said Huguet. 'And they won't stop at heretics either.'

Elinor's head was whirling with all these new ideas and facts. If Bertran was really a Believer of her father's religion, she could understand better what her mother had meant when she said he would never marry. Elinor didn't know much about them but she did know that all the Believers aspired to be Perfects before they died. And a Perfect must be celibate, without earthly ties.

'But where is Bertran now?' she asked. 'And how did he know about the murder?'

'He saw it,' said Perrin. 'And wherever he is, we must all pray he is not in danger.'

The unexpected visitor from the Pope to Viscount Trencavel's court was the Bishop of Couserans. The Legate was very nervous about the task he had been assigned. But Innocent had been quite clear: 'Find Bertran de Miramont, question him and bring him to Saint-Gilles for further interrogation.'

The Viscount rose and came forward to kiss the Bishop's ring.

'A thousand apologies, Your Grace,' said the Viscount. 'My foolish servant did not make clear to me how distinguished a visitor we had. May I introduce my friend, Bertran de Miramont?'

The Bishop had been one of the party with Pierre of Castelnau when he was killed and as soon as he was shown into Raimon-Roger's presence, he had recognised the troubadour. It put him in a quandary, because he remembered very well how eagerly the man had mounted his horse and ridden after the murderer. It was hard to believe he had been part of a plan to kill the Legate.

The Bishop noticed that the troubadour did not offer him the same homage but the man bowed courteously enough.

The Viscount sent a servant away to fetch the best wine from the château's cellar and the Legate seemed mollified, after his lukewarm welcome at the gate.

But the Bishop's mind was in turmoil. This encounter was all very well and polite, but it did make it awkward for him to question Bertran as a possible criminal.

He cleared his throat. 'I have been sent by His Holiness, Pope Innocent the Third, to continue his work in the Midi and to root out heresy,' he began. 'You have heard of the heinous murder of my fellow Legate, Pierre of Castelnau?'

'Indeed I have,' said the Viscount not looking at Bertran.

'I was there, Your Grace,' said the troubadour. 'You might

not remember, so sudden and terrible was the deed, but I gave chase to the assassin.'

This was better; the man was volunteering information.

'Yes,' said the Bishop. 'I do remember you. What happened afterwards? Did you catch up with the man?'

'I am afraid not,' said Bertran. 'He had a good start on me since my horse had to be got off the ferry-boat. I rode hard after the man but lost him near Beaucaire.'

'Do you know the man's name?'

'No, Your Grace. I should of course have passed that information on if I had found it out.'

'And have you heard the name Guilhem de Porcelet?'

'I have heard it, Your Grace, but know nothing of him save that he owns lands near Arles.'

'The Pope has received information that this man knows who the real killer is,' said the Bishop. 'And he wishes me to find him.'

'I'm sorry that I cannot help you, Your Grace,' said the troubadour. 'Perhaps you would find out more in Beaucaire or Saint-Gilles?'

The Bishop looked relieved. 'Yes, I might. And that will be convenient, for my next mission is to go eastwards.' He coughed and stammered before saying, 'However, I have to ask you to accompany me there. The Pope has asked me to take you to Saint-Gilles.'

There was nothing menacing about this Legate but Bertran understood that he was, in the politest way possible, being taken prisoner.

From the moment that the *joglars* took her into their confidence, Elinor became more thoughtful. This adventure, which had started as an escape for her and had brought moments of longed-for freedom and exhilaration, had become something different, a flight from more than marriage.

Her thoughts turned increasingly to her old home and the dangers that her family might be facing. Sévignan was a well-defended hill town, with thick strong walls and battlements and a good company of knights and warriors, including her father and brother. It had its own wells and enough storerooms and barns that could be stocked to withstand a siege. She had grown up feeling safe and secure within its walls.

But what if an army of thousands or even tens of thousands, as the *joglars* seemed to think possible, were to arrive, with equally experienced soldiers and the siege engines and catapults that she had heard about? She wished now that she had paid more attention to Aimeric's talk of battles.

And what could the women do in such a situation? Would there be any role for Lady Clara or Alys during a siege or while the men went out to fight? Images flitted across her mind of bloody and broken bodies. Of course; that's what the women would do: tend the wounded and dying. It made Elinor shiver, even in the warm southern sun.

Many times she thought of going back but it was impossible. A lone girl, even one dressed as boy, would not be safe in these turbulent times in the south. And Perrin had told her, very seriously, that Bertran would not want her to do anything but continue her escape. He knew the power of that name with her.

Bertran. She had loved him for so long that he was a part

of her mind; her first thought in the morning and her last at night. He was her idea of the perfect man – like the heroes of the *cansos de gesta* she had been brought up on and the northern lays – her Alexander, Roland or Tristan. The irony did not escape her; 'perfect' was what Bertran aspired to be and that meant there could be no future for her with him, except as a loyal friend.

Then if that is all I can be to him, I will be that, she thought. *For I must be something to him – at least if I am ever to see him again.*

At last the troupe left Montpellier, richer by far than when they had arrived. Their road took them towards Lunel and the journey was long, without the luxury of a cart, even although Lucatz could now afford it. Their steps were accompanied by the low level grumbling of the *joglaresa*s, who didn't want to walk and complained that they had to associate with acrobats and jugglers.

Lunel was not a hill town; it sat at the foot of the Cévennes Mountains and was surrounded by scrubland. But it had a fine Saturday market and that meant rich pickings for the troupe. It was May before they got there and the weather had turned very warm.

By now, Esteve had been accepted into the troupe and there was no more talk of finding his old troubadour. Lucatz valued his high clear voice and his knowledge of all the popular songs; he didn't know that the other *joglar*s coached him every day, as they walked beside his pony.

The *joglaresa*s were the only other members of the troupe who knew Elinor's secret.

Once, when they were camped at a little village on the way to Lunel, Pelegrina had probed her about her plans.

'What will you do when you become a woman?' she asked. 'When you start to bleed every month and grow breasts? Will you wait for Lucatz to notice or will you look for another troupe as a *joglaresa*?'

Elinor had been horrified. Joining another troupe was a step too far. She looked at the Catalan, who was biting into a peach with evident enjoyment.

'I don't know, Pelegrina. I really don't know,' she said. 'I can't think further than this summer.'

Pelegrina shrugged and threw the stone of the peach into the trees. 'Fair enough. It doesn't do to look too far into the future. And if the rumours we hear are true, we could all be dead before you come to womanhood.'

It was not a cheerful prospect, though Elinor recognised it could be true. Every day, she thrust such gloomy thoughts down and taught herself to live in the moment, enjoying the sun, her food, the applause when she performed as Esteve – and her memories of Bertran. From then on she looked backwards more often than to the future.

What she would have thought if she had known Bertran was on his way back through the south and not so far away was another matter.

The troubadour and the Bishop had spent one night under Viscount Trencavel's roof and then set off for the east. Bertran was allowed to ride his own horse. He was not even bound, but the Legate had his own small band of guards to accompany them and, if Bertran had tried to escape, they would have caught him straight away.

As it was, the two men fell into the habit of riding alongside each other; they were the best educated and highest born of the company and it was natural that they should enjoy each other's conversation, as long as they kept off the dangerous subjects of religion and politics. No one passing them on the road would have guessed that they were captor and prisoner.

Their route back to Saint-Gilles was more direct than the one Bertran had taken when travelling the other way. He had been aiming for the hill towns, so that he could talk to the lords of the bastides and advise them to prepare for war. Now they took the low road and passed through Lunel within a day of the arrival of the troupe from Sévignan.

But Bertran did not see them. Civilised as his custody was, he was not likely to be allowed to attend a market and hear *joglars* perform. But the music did reach his ears from a distance and he wondered about the clear treble voice he heard over the rebecs and fiddles. Something about it touched him deeply.

The troubadour was under no illusions about what might happen to him at Saint-Gilles. *I wish I could write a new poem for that voice*, he thought. Something with no word of war in it, to be worthy of that innocence and purity.

But the Legate's group travelled on towards Saint-Gilles without the troubadour's knowing that it was his friends who performed in the market square of Lunel.

They reached Saint-Gilles all too quickly and Bertran was taken to the castle. And this was where the courtesies came to an end. With great embarrassment, the Bishop informed him that he was to be escorted to the prison under the castle, to await further questioning when another representative should arrive from Rome to join them.

As the key turned in the door of his cell, for the first time Bertran felt fully the reality of his situation. He was a heretic, under suspicion of involvement in a Papal Legate's murder, and he wondered if he would ever see the light of day again.

***

'Here, in Saint-Gilles?' said Elinor, her eyes wide. It was the first news of Bertran since they had set out and now Perrin was telling her that the troubadour was in the same city where the troupe had just arrived.

But his face was serious as he imparted the news.

'He is in the castle dungeon,' he said. 'A prisoner of the Pope's man. At least that's what I believe.'

'A prisoner!' said Elinor. 'But on what charge?'

'We don't know,' said Perrin. 'But I doubt whether the exact charge is important. It will be to do with the Legate's murder, I am sure of that.'

'Can we visit him?' asked Elinor.

'Perhaps,' said Perrin. 'The man who gave me the information was a Believer like us – best you don't know his name. This city is a dangerous place. All he said was a troubadour had been brought into the city a few days ago by the Pope's Legate, a bishop, and he was taken straight to the castle.'

'The rumour is,' said Huguet, 'that another interrogator is coming from Rome.'

Elinor had heard what 'interrogators from Rome' were likely to do and she could not bear to think of it happening to Bertran.

'We must go to the castle,' she said. 'Immediately.'

'Hold on,' said Perrin. 'We can't just turn up at the dungeons and offer to entertain the guards.'

'Why not?' said Elinor. 'That seems a very good idea. Then we could rescue him while they are distracted.'

Both the *joglar*s were startled. Much as they valued the troubadour and as appalled as they were by his situation, their ideas had not stretched to rescue, only to comforting him in his distress.

'You teach us our duty, lady,' said Perrin. 'But if we really do intend a rescue, it needs more planning. We can't just rush in at hazard and expect to leave with a prisoner.'

He was right but it did not take Elinor long to come up with a plan, one that would involve the *joglaresas* too. The tricky thing was how to carry it out without Lucatz's knowledge.

The guards at the castle prison were old hands. They had looked after many prisoners in their time and were inured to cries of both pain and grief. But the troubadour was quiet and gave no trouble. He hadn't had any visitors since his arrival, which was good news for him, because the only visitor he was likely to receive would probably not wish him any good.

So it was a surprise to them when suddenly the outer room of the guardhouse was filled up with a gay troupe of singers and dancers. They came out of the night and into the prison bringing with them a couple of flagons of wine.

'It is our tradition,' said Perrin, who had made the tradition up with Elinor a few hours earlier. 'Whenever a troubadour or a *joglar* is in prison, if there is a troupe like ours anywhere near, we come to entertain his jailers. That way we hope our friend will receive better treatment.'

It was a dull life stuck inside the castle's thick stone walls all day and there was no doubt that the *joglaresas* in particular brought a touch of colour to the grey world of the prison. And free wine made the jailers even more cooperative. They did not notice that all their wine came from one flagon while the troupe drank sparingly from the other.

The *joglars* played and sang for them and the women danced, whisking their long bright skirts round the room. By the time the two jailers had drunk deep, they were willing enough to take a brooch to the troubadour as one of the *joglaresas* asked.

'We think we might know him,' she said. 'If he recognises this token, he is our friend.' It felt strange to Elinor to be in a woman's dress again. Her boy's haircut was hidden by a white coif but her legs felt awkward with all the extra material swirling round them and she had to stop herself striding as if she were in her breeches.

One of the two guards set off to Bertran's cell with the brooch, a bit unsteady on his legs. The other, older one, sat happily with Pelegrina on one knee and Maria on the other. His friend was soon back with the brooch.

'He says he knows it,' said the jailer, 'but that he gave it to a lady.'

'That's right,' said Elinor. 'Am I not a lady?'

The jailers thought this was a fine joke and laughed loudly. But Elinor was more agitated than she showed. Not only did this prove the prisoner was Bertran; he knew that friends from Sévignan were near.

'Have another drink,' said Perrin.

'Can we see him?' said Maria, twisting a lock of the older guard's greasy hair round her finger.

The two men looked at each other.

'Well, what harm is there in it?' said the older one. 'He's not a dangerous criminal and why shouldn't he hear some music?'

The younger one still had Bertran's brooch in his hand. He closed his fingers round the red stone. 'I reckon we should have something for breaking our orders,' he said. 'My girl would like this trinket.'

'So would my wife come to that,' said the older man. 'But we can decide that later. Take them to see their friend but don't leave them with him for long.'

'We'll stay here and keep you company,' said Perrin. 'Let the girls go.'

So the four *joglaresas*, whispering and giggling, went with the young jailer to Bertran's cell. But Elinor lagged back and swiftly stripped off her coif and her dress, rolling them into a bundle. She had her *joglar*'s clothes on underneath. Slowly, she crept back along the passage to where Perrin and Huguet drank with the older guard.

'I must just step outside for a moment,' said Huguet. 'Too much wine. I'll be straight back.'

The jailer assumed he was just going outside to relieve himself and Huguet passed Elinor in the passageway. She handed him the bundle of her clothes, which he stowed in his pack. Then he went to stand watch outside the guardhouse door while she, as Esteve the *joglar*, slipped back into the inner guardroom.

If the jailer noticed any difference, he didn't say anything. Elinor and Huguet were much of a height and size, since he was short for a boy and not much older than her. Elinor was careful to say little and even the younger jailer didn't seem to notice when he came back. He hadn't registered either that he had let only three women into Bertran's cell, even though four had gone down to it with him.

Both men were much the worse for all the doctored wine they had drunk and the man coming back from the cell saw what he expected to see: his fellow-jailer drinking with two *joglars*, a man and a boy.

In the cell, an astonished Bertran was being made to put on the outer layer of clothes that Bernardina quickly stripped off. She was the largest of the *joglaresas* and had looked even bigger when wearing two layers of clothes. Bertran was not a very heavily built man but the woman's clothes were a squeeze.

'Good job you don't wear a beard,' said Pelegrina, efficiently tying a brightly-patterned scarf round his head, while Bernardina bundled his hat under her apron.

'Is Perrin here?' asked Bertran, scarcely able to believe he was being rescued.

'We are all here,' said Maria, applying rouge to Bertran's lips. 'But it's the Lady Elinor who thought up the plan.'

'Please God she was right about it,' said Bernardina fervently.

'Elinor?' said the troubadour. *Could she really be here?*

'Now,' said Pelegrina. 'This is the difficult bit. When the jailer comes to let us out, you must bow your head and weep into this kerchief. That way he won't look carefully at your face. Try to slouch a bit, to conceal your height.'

Maria and Pelegrina were stuffing their petticoats under the blanket on Bertran's straw pallet, to look like the figure of a man. It was dark and the flickering light from the jailer's torch, together with his drink-fuddled brain, was what they were trusting to.

'Ready?' asked Bernardina.

Then Maria called out for the jailer.

By the time he came, his feet wavering down the stone steps, the powder they had put in one of the flagons of wine was taking its effect. He let the four *joglaresas* out of the cell, just as he had thought he let four in to visit the prisoner. And one of them was making such a lamentation he could scarcely think straight.

'She's upset,' said Pelegrina. 'He's her sweetheart.'

That was right, thought the jailer, one of them had carried the troubadour's love token. Pretty thing it was. Where had he put it? Blowed if he was going to let old Victor have it for his harridan of a wife. The prisoner was quiet enough; maybe he was weeping too, on his pallet, for his *joglaresa*. Well, they were all good-looking women, even if he couldn't at the moment tell one from another.

The troupe burst out of the prison, singing raucously, as if they had all had a bit too much to drink. Huguet joined them and they weaved their way across the castle yard, arms linked.

And no one who had seen them go in an hour before had any notion that there was now an extra member in their midst.

Part Two

Trobairitz

Kill them all; God will know his own.

Attributed to the Abbot of Cîteaux at the siege of Béziers
and still quoted as fact throughout the Languedoc.

CHAPTER EIGHT

Flight

Lucatz was woken from a deep sleep by Perrin, shaking him and whispering urgently, 'We must leave – now!'

The troubadour started to protest but one look at the *joglar's* face told him that this was serious. Muttering and grumbling, he bundled together his instruments and song sheets while Perrin roused the rest of the troupe.

The urgency in the *joglar's* voice and the near panic of the *joglaresas* infected the whole group and they were soon on their way, silently leading the packhorses out of the city gate. It was eerie travelling by night; they headed north, not south towards the ferry point on the river to Arles, since there would be no boats in the hours of darkness. Instead they went in the direction of Beaucaire aiming for beyond it to the only bridge across the Rhône, at Avignon.

There was no sound but the clinking of the horses' harness and their shod hooves on the rough road. The troupe travelled all night and arrived in Beaucaire at daylight, tired and, for the most part, completely at a loss as to why they had left Saint-Gilles without even having performed there.

Lucatz bought breakfast for everyone at a tavern and the troupe then rested in a meadow to the north of the city.

'All right,' said the troubadour. 'Now tell me what's going

on. What was that all about? We lost the chance of good money in Saint-Gilles.'

'We would have lost more than that if we'd stayed,' said Perrin.

'By now the city guards will be looking for us,' said Huguet. 'At least, they will be looking for a troupe like ours. They knew no names.'

Lucatz sighed. Some *joglars* could be troublesome, he knew, getting involved in fights, love triangles, theft even. But he'd never had any bother with Perrin and Huguet, and Esteve was too new and too young to cause problems – or so he thought.

'What did you do?' he asked. 'Or is it better if I don't know? I see no bruises so I assume you weren't brawling at least.'

'We neither received nor caused injuries,' said Perrin. 'But we did break someone out of prison.'

'And we had to give him all our money to buy a new horse,' said Huguet wistfully.

Lucatz looked exasperated.

'I'm not going to ask any more about it,' he said. 'I have a feeling there is something going on here that it is better for me to know nothing about. But tell me why we are on the way to Avignon instead of Arles?'

'I'm afraid the prisoner was being detained on the Pope's orders,' said Perrin. 'And the further away from Saint-Gilles we can be the better. They will expect us to have taken the ferry or perhaps to have headed back west. But it will be safest if we can carry on travelling east and Avignon is a big town. There will be lots of people there.'

'And what has happened to this prisoner?' asked Lucatz.

'Or is that something else it is better for me not to know?'

'He is no longer with us,' said Perrin. 'And yes, it is better that you know no more than that.'

Lucatz looked at his *joglar*s for a long time. They had never asked anything of him before and he was aware of their connection with the Believers. In the end, he decided to let it go.

'Was Esteve involved too?' was all he asked.

The *joglar*s nodded. 'He and all the *joglaresa*s,' said Perrin. 'No one else.'

'Just the six of you then,' said Lucatz sarcastically. 'Ah well, I suppose I should be grateful for small mercies.'

Elinor lay wide awake while all around her the troupe caught up on their lost night of sleep. She didn't think she would ever forget the rescue of Bertran – or what had happened afterwards.

They had been confident that the jailers wouldn't discover Bertran's escape till morning but that left them with only the hours of darkness to get clear of Saint-Gilles. Bertran had stripped off his woman's disguise, wiping his lips clear of make-up with the bright scarf. Bernardina solemnly handed him back his hat and there was Bertran the troubadour again, as handsome as ever, and free.

'Thank you all,' he said softly. 'I owe you more than I can ever repay. But someone mentioned the Lady Elinor – where is she?'

Elinor had stepped forward so that the light from the cresset by the castle gate shone on her face. Bertran gave a sharp intake of breath.

'Is it you, lady? I should not have known you.'

'That was the idea,' said Perrin. 'The *donzela* travels with us as the *joglar* Esteve.'

'There is no time to hear that story,' said Bertran. 'We must separate without delay. Every minute I spend in your company brings you danger.'

'Won't you come with us?' asked Elinor, heartbroken at the thought of Bertran's being taken from her so soon when she had only just found him again.

The troubadour shook his head. 'No. I am an outlaw now. I shall change my clothes, grow a beard and assume a new name. No longer shall I be a poet, able to gain entrance to any court. From now on, I shall be Jules, no more than a spy.'

Then he had remembered his horse. They all decided it would be too dangerous to try to spring the steed out of the castle stable as well as his master from its prison. That was when they had all turned out their pockets. Elinor had gladly given all the money she had earned in Montpellier.

'Where can you buy a horse at this time of night?' she asked quietly.

'I shall take the road to Nîmes,' he said, 'and buy a horse in the first village I come to. Some new clothes too.'

For the first hour or so of the night, Bertran's road was going to be the same as the troupe's but he had a start on them and they had not overtaken him. Elinor had ridden wearily, feeling as low as she had before leaving Sévignan.

She had found Bertran again only to lose him and now she was tired, fearful and penniless. Her journey east felt pointless; where was she travelling to? Up till now she had been buoyed up by the thought of what she was fleeing from, together with a vague hope of meeting her troubadour.

Then she remembered that she didn't even have his token any more. A tear trickled down her cheek and she brushed it away with the back of her hand. She felt a pat on her knee. It was Huguet. He was holding out his hand to her, cupping something that winked and glittered in the moonlight: Bertran's brooch!

'How . . . ?' she began to ask but Huguet put his fingers to his lips.

'Pelegrina,' he whispered. 'She picked the young jailer's pocket before we left.'

Elinor would never have believed that the Catalan would have done something so thoughtful – and now she couldn't even pay her for it. And all the *joglaresa*s were as penniless as Elinor; they too had contributed all they had to Bertran's needs.

But it had lightened her heart to have the brooch with the red stone back. Now she lay twisting it in her fingers and thinking of the days when Bertran was no more than a handsome poet and she the simple *donzela* of the castle, until she too fell asleep.

In Sévignan they had not forgotten the older daughter of the castle. When Lord Lanval had realised she was really gone and apparently by her own will, he set his face into grim acceptance. He knew that he and Elinor's mother had driven her away by their insistence on a marriage she was opposed to.

Thibaut le Viguier had left the bastide in a bad mood; he

had abandoned his own castle for too long and with no reward but the information that he should go home and prepare for war. Blandina was equally disgruntled. She had lost the chance to push Elinor around in her own castle and, by what she had seen at Sévignan, it would have been good sport.

As soon as they were gone, Elinor's brother Aimeric had volunteered to lead the search for his sister.

'Don't worry, Father,' he said. 'I'll be discreet.'

'Begin with the sister houses,' said Lanval. 'Both the Perfects and the Church's own convents. She might have taken refuge in one of them.'

'And if I find her?'

Lanval hesitated. His instincts told him to say 'Then bring her home, of course!' But perhaps she would be safer in a religious house?

'If you find her in a Church convent, leave her there,' he said reluctantly. 'But she might not be safe with the Perfects. See if you can persuade her into a convent recognised by the Pope or, failing that, bring her home.'

Aimeric had been gone two months and there had been no word from him. The castellan and his wife had only one child left within their walls.

They hadn't asked Alys what she knew about Elinor's disappearance. She was grateful that she didn't have to tell any lies but secretly hurt that it hadn't occurred to her parents that she and Elinor might have been close enough for confidences between them.

As the days lengthened and spring turned into summer, Alys felt desperately lonely. She had no one to talk to and no one to ask for news of her sister. And then, months after

Lucatz and his troupe had left the castle, some more *joglars* arrived from the east.

Eagerly, Alys volunteered to serve them refreshments. And it was not long before her questions about a troupe led by a tall, thin troubadour with three *joglars* and three *joglaresas* bore fruit.

'*Oc*, we saw them,' said one of the *joglars* to the others. 'You remember, in Montpellier? That light-voiced boy who got so much silver from the lady? He sang after our Enric.'

'Oh,' said another. 'The boy who sang the lay of Tristan and Iseut? We weren't best pleased when they turned up.'

'Did you hear his name?' asked Alys. 'The boy who sang the lay?'

'Ah, is it your sweetheart then?' teased one of the *joglaresas*. 'He looked too young to have a lady love.'

'Why, the *donzela* is not more than a child herself,' said the first *joglar*. 'I think the lad was called Esteve.'

Alys's heart jumped. It really had been her sister; the plan had worked!

'Did you hear where they were going next?' she asked.

'On to Saint-Gilles, I think,' said the *joglar*. 'East, anyway. That's one of the reasons we came west. They were a bit too good and we didn't want the competition.'

She couldn't tell her parents but Alys hugged the information to herself. Elinor was safe and she was moving away from danger.

All that summer the troupe worked their way east. They travelled on from Avignon up into the Vaucluse mountains, through Sénanque, Forcalquier and Digne. It did not take them long to recoup the cost of Bertran's new horse, even though there were no more great halls like the castle at Montpellier. There were enough villages and hill towns to fill their purses and Lucatz's saddlebags. People seemed to need music and song more than ever, as if it might be the last summer when the south was happy. Elinor was astonished by the landscape they travelled through. The mountains were higher than the hills in which she had grown up and as they travelled further east into the Alps they got even higher. And the weather was unusually warm, even for the Midi.

The summer sun beat hot upon them but it was often accompanied by a fierce wind that cooled them on their travels. As they reached the far eastern part of Provensa, the autumn was beginning to draw in and the wind grew colder. Elinor was glad to have her fur-lined cloak with her.

They had been anxious at the beginning of their journey, sure that someone would follow them from Saint-Gilles, unable to believe that they had got away with their risky actions. But as the summer progressed and no one had stopped them on their journey, the troupe relaxed. Even Lucatz, who had taken a long time to recover any sort of good humour after their night flight, had forgiven the *joglars* for their sudden and ignominious departure.

The trees were changing colour as they entered Saint-Jacques, a prosperous bastide in the lower Alps. Not that there were many trees in this landscape. Sturdy holm oaks were all that withstood the relentless wind.

Saint-Jacques had belonged to a crusader, Lord Jaufre, who had not come back from the disastrous Fourth Crusade in 1204. His lands, his flocks and herds and his castle at the heart of the fortified town, were now all in the hands of his widow, the Lady Iseut.

Her reputation had reached the troupe as they travelled away from Avignon. That she was beautiful and gracious was only to be expected; report never named a lady as anything else. But she was also admired for her learning and her justice. She was a *trobairitz*, a female troubadour, but not one who wandered from court to court. Iseut de Saint-Jacques was a poet, one who composed her verses sometimes in debate poems, called *tensos*, with other *trobairitz*, like the Countess of Provence and Maria de Ventadorn.

'It would be a good place to winter,' said Lucatz, gazing up at the strong walls and imposing tower of Saint-Jacques as the troupe approached the town.

'Thinking of winter already?' asked Perrin.

'I'm not as young as I was,' said the troubadour. 'And this wind bites through my cloak to my very bones. If the Lady of Saint-Jacques were inclined to give her patronage to a fellow-poet through till spring, I should not demur.'

Elinor looked up too. If Lucatz succeeded, this would be her home for months. A wave of nostalgia swept over her for the castle at Sévignan, its kitchens and its stables, even for the boisterous knights and *noiretz* who had teased her so. She wondered if she would ever see any of them again.

In mid-September, while Lucatz's troupe was getting established with the Lady Iseut, the crusade against the Believers was officially called. The Abbot of Cîteaux used his position as both a senior churchman and the Pope's Legate to make it official at the General Chapter of the Cistercian Order.

But the Pope's letter six months earlier had already done most of the work; all over the north barons had been counting up the men and arms they could rely on, armour was being repaired, weapons forged and stores calculated.

The northern barons wouldn't go to war in winter, but it was becoming clear that by the following summer the Pope's army would be able to mass in force against the south and particularly against Toulouse, whose Count had been responsible for a lot of the trouble.

Bertran was at the Chapter in Cîteaux, disguised as a monk. He wore the white robes and had allowed his hair to be tonsured. He moved through the crowds unnoticed and unrecognised. But when the Chapter was over he cast aside his disguise, clamped a hat over his telltale shaven patch and rode hard for Toulouse.

Count Raimon was an extraordinary man by any standards and Bertran regarded him warily. He had inherited his titles, which included Duke of Narbonne and Marquis of Provence, fourteen years earlier.

Known for his ruthlessness about domestic and dynastic matters, Raimon was hardly likely to be the sort of man that Bertran would admire. Yet he had been a staunch friend of the Believers till now, risking the Pope's displeasure on more than one occasion. And he was a great defender of the rights of his people to remain free from taxation by the church.

The Count listened to sermons by the Believers and always had a least one Perfect in his retinue. Many of his nobles, his allies and supporters were of that religion. As the Count had protested to Pierre before the murder, no one could have possibly exterminated what were now considered heretical beliefs as thoroughly as the Pope required him to do.

So it was with a mixture of hope and caution that Bertran approached the Count in Toulouse. As Trencavel's liege lord, the Count also had Bertran's allegiance and the troubadour had often been at the court in Toulouse. He entered the rose-coloured city through its eastern gate and made his way to the Count's château. The streets were full of the Count of Toulouse's coat of arms – a gold cross on a red background, and it made Bertran smile wryly. Would the Count still use it when the barons of the north took up the sign of the Cross to go to war against Toulouse?

But at the château he was disappointed; the Count was not there.

'The Count of Toulouse, Your Majesty,' announced the footman.

King Philippe-Auguste shifted irritably in his ornate chair. It was the last name he wanted to have announced. He was heartily sick of Raimon of Toulouse, heresy and, well . . . He stopped short at thinking he was sick of the Pope himself, but he could have done without the distraction of another appeal from the south.

'Show him in, man,' he said.

Raimon entered bowing low. He was already an old man at fifty-two and some ten years older than the King, but he was vigorous in mind and body and hopeful of persuading Philippe-Auguste to his side.

'Your Majesty,' said Raimon. He had no need of quite so

much formal courtesy; Philippe-Auguste was King of France but had no power over the south, whose allegiance was mainly to Pedro of Aragon. But Raimon was on a delicate mission and courtesy hurt no one.

'To what do I owe the honour of this visit?' asked the King.

'It will be no surprise to you, Majesty, that I come about the Pope's "crusade", as men are calling it,' said the Count. 'He is waging a personal vendetta against me and perhaps against all the nobles in Western Europe. I fear his ambition is growing too great, saving His Holiness.'

'I have had my own troubles with Rome,' admitted the King. 'I'm sure you know the Pope refuses my request to annul my marriage to that Ingeborg who insists she is my queen.'

'What even though Your Majesty has since married the beautiful Agnes?'

The Count was very well aware of the King's marital problems, which were similar to his own eventful domestic life, and he was banking on the King's annoyance with the Pope to get him to forbid the crusade to the south.

'Even so,' said the King, brooding on the injustice. 'Ingeborg insists the marriage was consummated and the Pope chooses to believe an ignorant girl over an experienced widower and father like myself.'

'Perverse, perverse. But so are many of his decisions nowadays,' said the Count.

'Like this crusade?' asked the King.

This is going well, thought the Count and continued, 'He has taken it into his head that I am responsible for the death of his Legate, Pierre of Castelnau.'

'And of course you were not?' asked the King ironically.

'Of course I did not run his Legate through with my lance,' smiled Raimon. 'I admit I was very angry with the man. He was insufferably arrogant and rude. But, no, I did not kill him.'

The King didn't enquire if the Count had ordered the death. There were things that nobility and royalty did not ask each other.

'Then it is a pity,' said the King.

'A pity, Your Majesty?'

'That I have already given my leave for my barons to march south,' said Philippe-Auguste. 'I do not want to anger the Pope. I am still hoping for my annulment. So I'm afraid I really can't withdraw my permission now.'

CHAPTER NINE

Amistat

The Lady Iseut turned out to be just as gracious and beautiful as report had made her. She was now only twenty-three, a presumed widow, though no specific news had ever arrived of Jaufre's death. Her husband had gone crusading a year after their marriage and she had lost the only baby conceived before he left.

So she had been ruling her own demesne for six years. She had made it a haven for poets, composers, musicians and artists and a place where her fellow *trobairitz* were welcome.

When Lucatz's troupe arrived at Saint-Jacques, there were already several musicians at court and another *trobairitz* called Azalais de Tarascon. Iseut invited the whole troupe to dinner, not to perform, but out of good fellowship and in consideration of their weariness after travel.

'Lucatz was right,' whispered Maria to Elinor. 'This will be an excellent bastide to winter in.'

Lady Iseut presided over the table in a dress of light blue satin, which perfectly complemented her fair colouring and her copious and curling hair, so pale it was almost white. Her friend was a perfect foil for her, black-browed and as dark-skinned as Pelegrina the Catalan *joglaresa*, and dressed in scarlet. But Elinor noticed that a costly diamond brooch pinned a blue feather to her gown, as if to proclaim her part of some society or clan.

'Come, my friends,' said Lady Iseut. 'Tell us of your travels. We have had no news from as far west as Sévignan for a long time. Were your last lord and lady well when you left them?'

'They were indeed, lady,' said the troubadour. 'And about to celebrate the betrothal of their elder daughter.'

Elinor felt herself stiffen and prayed she would not blush. She fancied that the Lady's friend, Azalais, had been looking at her rather intently and she felt seen-through already.

'And we have ourselves taken part in christening celebrations in Montpellier,' added Lucatz. 'The Lady Maria's young son.'

'How delightful,' said Iseut. 'So Lady Maria has a son? She is fortunate indeed.'

'Though not in her marriage, I believe,' said Lucatz.

Elinor would not have believed Lucatz was such a gossip but he was soon telling the ladies all about Maria de Montpellier's unfortunate situation. And then about their other encounters in Provensa and the Alps, though not a word of what had happened at Saint-Gilles.

Iseut and Azalais listened eagerly to all the news. Then the Lady from Tarascon asked, 'And what of the other events we have heard rumours of? Some say that there is to be some action taken against Raimon of Toulouse?'

It was Perrin who answered this question.

'We do indeed believe that there might be trouble throughout the south. And not just in Toulouse.'

'You really think the northerners will want to fight our cities?'

'And smaller bastides too,' added Huguet. 'Our information is that none will be safe.'

Elinor could see that the Lady was reluctant to believe that. Her town was well fortified and her lands down in the valley fertile. It was clear from her table that she was rich in grain, meat and cheese.

Iseut turned to Azalais, with a troubled face.

'Surely we are safe here in Saint-Jacques? Who would attack our walls because of a quarrel with Toulouse?'

'That depends on whether your ladyship is sympathetic to the Believers,' said Azalais, in a low voice.

'And maybe it will not depend even on that,' whispered Perrin. 'The men from the north may march under the banner of a holy war to crush heretics but will actually be more interested in acquiring land – no matter whose it is.'

Lady Iseut clapped her hands. 'Enough of war,' she said. 'For now, we are safe in Saint-Jacques and can speak of happier matters. As you see, I have a few court musicians but nothing to compare with your company. They will play for us now and perhaps you could tell us about your new songs and poems?'

The rest of the evening was passed in music and discussion of poetry but Elinor noticed that the Lady of Saint-Jacques now wore a small frown making a line between her fair brows. She was sure that their news of war from the north had deeply disconcerted her.

From Paris, Raimon of Toulouse travelled to Germany to see Otto of Brunswick, one of the two claimants to be Holy Roman Emperor. The Count was still fuming from his interview with the French King.

How could Philippe-Auguste have yielded to the Pope so easily? It was understandable that the King's long-desired release from the wife he found repellent had been held out as a reward for his cooperation with Rome but the Count was certain that the Pope would not give Philippe-Auguste what he wanted once the crusade had been launched.

But for now Raimon must see what succour he might hope for from Otto IV. The would-be Emperor was an ally through King John of England, who had been the Count's brother-in-law at one time, and he had always been good at reminding others of alliances. In fact, until this wretched business with the Pope and the heretics, he had enjoyed his position as Count of Toulouse and overlord of such fine cities as Carcassonne, Béziers and Nîmes.

When he wanted something done, people leapt to obey his command. And when he wanted something not done, whatever it was ceased without question. But everything had changed once Innocent III had been elected Pope. Since then, the Pontiff had been a thorn in his side and, as the Count had told Philippe-Auguste, he suspected there was more to it than a hatred of seeing the Church defied by heretics.

The court of Otto of Brunswick was even more magnificent than that of the French King. Raimon was kept waiting for a little in an anteroom, so gilded and damasked, so mirrored and bedecked with candelabra holding such a wealth of the best beeswax candles that it would have served as a throne room in any other palace of Europe.

After a short wait, while he wondered which of these innovations he might employ in the château at Toulouse,

Raimon was shown into the royal presence. Otto was as sumptuous in his own person as was his palace. He wore crimson velvet and a cloth of gold cloak, his fingers bejewelled with many rings and an elaborate gold circlet on his head.

Though the Count had been able to speak French with Philippe-Auguste, the only language he and Otto had in common was Latin.

'*Salve, Imperator,*' said the Count, kissing Otto's hand.

'Ah, not that yet,' said Otto, all smiles. 'My rival, Philip, seems to have met an untimely end but now Fredrik von Hohenstaufen claims to have more right to the title than I do.'

'The problems of inheritance,' said the Count, shaking his head. 'And even when the title is secure, the problems don't end there. I have lately come from the King of France. I sought his help in my, ah, difficulties with His Holiness the Pope.'

'*Your* difficulties?' said Otto. 'I thought he had "difficulties" enough of his own with Pope Innocent.'

'Indeed, that is what he said,' acknowledged Raimon ruefully.

'So he refused you?' said Otto.

'I'm afraid so,' said the Count. 'May I tell you what I asked of him?'

'That he would refuse permission for his knights and nobles to take up the Cross against the south?' said Otto.

The Count was crestfallen. If Otto knew and had not already offered his help, he was not likely to act on Raimon's personal entreaty.

'Saving Your Majesty,' he began hesitantly, 'and His Holiness, I suspect that it is not simply "the south" that

Innocent wants to punish. He is waging a personal vendetta against me – you know he has excommunicated me again?'

'I was not aware that you had been received back into the Church since last time,' said Otto.

'Indeed, I had not,' said Raimon, struggling to maintain an expression of sorrow and regret. But his anger soon got the better of him. 'I say that this Pope has decided that I am his enemy.'

'It is a dangerous thing to have a Pope for an enemy,' said Otto. 'Kings and emperors are one thing, but the Pope . . . ! It pits the whole of Christendom against you. I myself have need of Innocent's support in my claim against Fredrik, particularly since Philippe-Auguste is on Fredrik's side.'

He looked at Raimon speculatively for a long moment. Then he held out his beringed hand for him to kiss again.

'*Vale*, my son,' he said to the Count, who was nearly twenty years older than him. 'There is nothing I can do to help you. *Quem Papae oderunt nemo audet adiuvare.*'

And Raimon left Brunswick with that farewell ringing in his ears: '*Whom Popes hate, let no one dare to help.*'

Lady Iseut was as generous a patron as Lucatz could wish for. But as autumn wore on into the colder months, Elinor became aware of the sadness that hung over the bastide of Saint-Jacques.

Iseut was a good '*Senhor*' – as good as any man – but, in spite of the competence with which she ran her household, her vassals and her farms, whenever her face was in repose, it wore an expression of deep sorrow.

From the *joglaresas'* gossip with the castle servants, Elinor understood that the Lady was still in mourning for her husband, Jaufre. He had gone off on the crusade to the Holy Land six years before and she had never seen him again. After two years, the survivors had started to straggle back and news had gradually filtered through the Midi of what a disaster it had been.

But of Lord Jaufre there was no word. For the first two years of his absence, once recovered from the loss of her child, Iseut had enjoyed taking over the reins. But she had always believed that her husband would return from the war and resume the Seigneury.

It was a whole year after the end of the crusade before Iseut really understood that Jaufre was not coming back. What had helped to convince her was the string of suitors who wanted to pay court to the rich young widow of Saint-Jacques.

'But she wouldn't have any of them,' said Maria. 'Isn't that romantic?'

'More fool her, then,' said Pelegrina. 'I don't see what's romantic about living on your own when you could marry again.'

'But she's not on her own, is she?' said Bernardina. 'She has her special friend, the *trobairitz*.'

'Huh!' snorted Pelegrina. 'That wouldn't make up to me for losing a husband.'

'I don't know,' said Bernardina, whose own experience of marriage had left her a less high opinion of men. 'The lady from Tarascon seems very fond of the Lady here.'

'She's not like that,' said Pelegrina. 'Azalais may be – but not the Lady Iseut. She needs a man.'

The suitors had eventually given up but Elinor noticed one visitor who was often at the Lady's court. Berenger de Digne was older than Iseut, around thirty, and reminded Elinor a little of Bertran. He was tall and dark-haired with intense dark brown eyes and he was clearly devoted to the Lady of Saint-Jacques.

When Elinor asked the *joglaresas* about him, Maria said that he had wanted to marry Iseut before she chose Jaufre and was now her most loyal friend and local ally.

The winter months passed and the troupe celebrated Christmas at Saint-Jacques. When Elinor's jacket started to feel tight on her she thought it was because of the unaccustomed feasting. Then, the night after Epiphany, she woke on the pallet she shared with Huguet feeling a nagging insistent pain tugging at her lower back.

A moment or two to shake off the fog of sleep and she realised what it must be. Elinor crawled over to where the *joglaresas* slept and found Bernardina in the dark.

'I'm sorry to wake you,' she whispered, 'but the blood has come and I don't know what to do.'

Towards the end of the month a group of pilgrims arrived at Saint-Jacques. It was only a short detour off the Pilgrim Way, the Via Domitia that went all the way from the Alps to Compostela. This was a party of Piedmontese on their return journey. They sought hospitality, which Lady Iseut was happy to provide, and they brought news. They had come from Saint-Gilles.

Even within a year, Pierre of Castelnau had become

revered as if he were a saint. On the anniversary of his murder, his body had been exhumed.

'It was unbelievable,' said the pilgrims' leader, a priest called Taddeo. 'His blessed body was completely uncorrupted, the flesh as fair as the day that monster pierced it with his lance.'

'Who dug it up?' asked Azalais.

'The Cistercians, my lady,' said Taddeo stiffly. 'It is already a source of miracles, as well as being one in itself. Why, one of our party was cured of a rheum just by gazing on the sacred corpse!'

'Not by Saint Jacques, on your pilgrimage then?' asked the lady of Tarascon, who was inclined to be sceptical.

'Alas, no,' said Taddeo and turned his full attention to Lady Iseut, who seemed to show a more reverent attitude to his tale.

Elinor was listening closely from the musicians' place near the dinner table and saw that the *joglars* were equally attentive. This was that same Pierre whose murder Bertran had witnessed.

Where the troubadour was now was unknown to all of them; there had been no news since he had separated from them in Saint-Gilles.

The Lady signalled to Lucatz to begin the entertainment and he nodded to the *joglars* to start playing. Any further conversation of the pilgrims was lost to Elinor as she played the flute and sang.

In deference to the pilgrims, their songs were less secular than usual, leaving aside the chansons de gestes and heroic or romantic tales. They sang instead of Our Lady and Our Saviour, ending with the song of the white almond tree.

'White the blossom as the snow,
Rich the fruits that on it grow,
Bitter in each twelve is one,
Rendered sweet by Mary's son . . .'

It had been recently written by the Lady Iseut herself and the *joglars* sang it to honour her. In her role as Esteve, Elinor sang it in her sweet high treble. The Lady was listening intently with her eyes closed but her companion was watching the young *joglar* closely.

Elinor had learned the song well but, as she sang it for the pilgrims, she felt as if she understood it for the first time: even at the heart of joy you must expect a bitter note, but through love even that sharp tang could yield sweetness. There was something about this realisation, about the reasons that Iseut had written this song, about finding and losing Bertran and understanding that her future did not lie with him, that made Elinor weep.

She tried to make her tears seem like those of an over-wrought boy, wiping them impatiently away with the back of her hand. But she noticed the lady of Tarascon looking at her oddly. This had been happening a lot since that night a few weeks ago when Bernardina had confirmed to Elinor that she had now become a woman.

Elinor did not want to be a woman. She was appalled by the treachery of her body that could turn her into something against her will.

'*Dolcment, donzela,*' Bernardina had said when she shed her first tears. 'It is the burden you were born for. Without it, you could not bear children.'

'But I don't want children!' Elinor had protested. It was

121

true. She was scared of childbirth, which took so many women out of the world and killed so many babies too. Human beings seemed so much worse at it than animals, who only rarely died from reproducing.

Running away from home was one thing; even getting involved in the dangerous politics of the time through rescuing Bertran had been an adventure to savour. But this most recent event had been a change too far. What would she do once her growing breasts could no longer be confined within Huguet's old jerkin? Or her hips split the seams of his old breeches?

So Esteve wept, because he would soon be Esteve no longer. And what he would or could be was a mystery.

And Azalais of Tarascon watched the young *joglar*, satisfied that, however unlikely it might seem, she was right about him. The time had come to tell Lady Iseut what she suspected.

CHAPTER TEN

Cortesia

The pilgrims were gone long before the snows came in February and perhaps were already back in their homes in Piedmont.

Before he left, Taddeo had told Iseut that if ever she needed to leave her bastide, Piedmont was the place to seek sanctuary.

'Leave Saint-Jacques?' she had exclaimed. 'Why would I ever do such a thing?'

The priest looked very serious as he told her that he had heard rumours that no bastide in the Midi would be safe for long.

'They caught one of those *ribaut*s who killed Pierre of Castelnau, at Saint-Gilles,' he said. 'But a gang of ruffians tied up the guards and set him free. It will not be long before the Pope wreaks his revenge for the blessed Pierre and then you might have reason to leave.'

'That can have nothing to do with me,' said Iseut firmly, unaware that the 'gang of ruffians' was under her roof. 'I deplore the taking of a life, whoever did it.'

'Indeed, of course,' said Taddeo. 'And I'm sure you would not shelter heretics either. But if you do ever need a safe place further away from the Rhône, remember that troubadours are well received in Piedmont, particularly at the court of Monferrato.'

Even trobairitz? thought Iseut but she merely thanked him and wished the pilgrims well on their way back home.

It was perhaps as well that Elinor did not hear this conversation, though by now Perrin had told her that their way lay east towards Monferrato, where the Marchese was sympathetic to the Believers.

But when the snows came and she had bled for the second time, she received a message to go and see the Lady in private. Lucatz was put out when she told him; for Elinor had soon learned that nothing must be done without his knowledge and approval, since the night of Bertran's rescue.

'I expect she wants me to learn a new poem, sire,' said Elinor. It had happened before.

'Yes, but she has not asked to see you without me before,' said Lucatz.

'Cannot you come with me?' asked Elinor, who did not at all want to have a private audience with the Lady.

Lucatz shook his head. 'No, not if I am not asked for. That would not be *cortesia*.'

But he was pleased that the boy had asked. It showed the right spirit.

'I will tell you what she said,' promised Elinor, little knowing how hard that would be.

When she got to Lady Iseut's private room, where she kept accounts and record, Elinor was surprised to find Azalais there with her. The lady of Tarascon was first to speak.

'Esteve,' she said thoughtfully. 'A good name for a boy. It is a shame that your sweet voice will soon crack. How old are you?'

'Nearly fourteen, lady,' said Elinor. She could feel the throb of her own blood in her neck.

'Then it will not be long.'

There was a charged silence in the room. Elinor noticed that Iseut was as pale as she feared herself flushed.

'At least, not if Esteve were really a boy.'

It had been said now. The thing that Elinor had feared. Her secret was out. She saw little point in denying it. She had taken off her cap when she entered the room and now ran her fingers through her shaggy hair, which Huguet had kept trimmed for her every few weeks. But she remained silent; there was nothing to say.

'Why did you deceive me?' asked Iseut.

'Oh not you, my lady,' she found her voice at last. 'I mean not just you. It was everyone. I had to leave my bastide and it was the safest way for me to travel.'

'Does Lucatz know?' asked Iseut.

'No. Only the other *joglars* and the *joglaresas*.'

'I find it hard to believe that a young woman of quality – for you are of noble birth, aren't you? – would leave her home and roam the country dressed as a boy in a company of travelling musicians,' said Azalais. But even as she said it, she had a wistful look, as if she wouldn't have minded doing such a thing herself.

'It was my only choice,' said Elinor. 'My father wanted me to marry an old man and I couldn't bear it.'

Now both ladies were looking more sympathetic.

'Who are you really?' asked Iseut.

'Elinor of Sévignan. I am daughter of Lord Lanval and Lady Clara.'

'And they do not know where you are?' asked Iseut. 'They

must be mad with worry in these dangerous times.'

Elinor bowed her head; it was true, but she hadn't understood that when she left. The resentment had gradually faded on her journey. It was as the Lady's poem said: bitter things could be made sweet by love. Her parents had loved her and everything they had tried to do was to protect her. Where they had gone wrong was in not explaining it her.

'You must have known you could not get away with it for ever,' said Azalais. 'You are already bursting out of your disguise.'

Elinor's cheeks burned. 'I, I did not think further ahead than escaping from my father's choice of a husband for me,' she said.

'And now?' asked Iseut. 'Azalais is right. I do not think your disguise will help you for much longer. Can you still be Esteve the *joglar* when Lucatz moves on in a few months' time?'

Elinor hung her head miserably; she knew they were both right. It had kept her awake for many a night.

'I shall go back to Tarascon in the spring,' said Azalais. 'You may come with me if you wish. You could be transformed back into a young woman by the time we reached there. I could say you were another *trobairitz* I had met in the mountains.'

'Or you could stay here with me as my companion when Azalais leaves,' said Iseut. 'I am sure that with a dress and a coif no one would recognise you as the boy *joglar* once your troupe had gone.'

Elinor felt the tension in the air and realised that the two women had discussed these options before she had been sent for. Again she was being asked to choose and she knew that this time it was about more than where she lived. She had to choose her words carefully. Two pairs of eyes, one dark, one grey, were watching her closely.

'I had a . . . friend,' she said at last, 'who advised me to travel east. I don't know how far he meant. But I do know that he thought there was danger in my old home. He would not recommend retracing my journey even as far west as Tarascon.'

Azalais relaxed a fraction. 'So you will stay here,' she said flatly. 'I thought that would be your choice. Even before I knew you had a "friend". So it was only the age of your suitor that troubled you. You are not against marriage in general?'

'No, not in general,' said Elinor. 'But you misunderstand me. It was not that sort of friend.' Her face belied her words.

'Your reasons are your own,' said Iseut. 'I am glad you want to stay at Saint-Jacques.'

Elinor realised that she did want to stay up here in the mountains, where the air was clear and sharp and where murder and revenge were just words. Even though she would miss her friends in the troupe more than she dared to think about now. She admired the Lady, who was such a good '*Senhor*'. Iseut reminded Elinor of Maria of Montpellier. Another woman ruling her own lands and vassals, who did not need a man to advise or protect her. Perhaps Elinor could be like her one day?

'But what shall I tell Lucatz?' was all she said.

Bertran de Miramont had waited at Toulouse for Raimon's return. He was unrecognisable now either as a Cistercian monk or a troubadour. He had grown a dark beard and moustache and there was no trace of his former tonsure. His little stock of money had dwindled, even though he had lived as frugally as a monk since the rescue at Saint-Gilles. But he was loath to sell the horse he had bought then; it was his last connection with the *joglars* and *joglaresas* who had rescued him – not to mention with Elinor. And it was his passport to a quick getaway if he was traced to the 'rose city.'

So he had posed as a scholar called Jules, fallen on hard times and taken on work as a scribe and clerk. It was enough to pay for his board and lodgings and his religion made him an abstemious man. The only item of value he possessed he had given to Elinor.

Elinor. As his situation seemed more and more desperate, Bertran thought more often of the *donzela* he thought he had left for ever in Sévignan. He knew she was in love with him, or that at least that she believed herself so. That was why he had left her the token and with it a small hope; it was all that people had in such critical times.

Besides, as he grew closer to death, Bertran was trying to divest himself of possessions. He would die a true Perfect, and he must prepare for that. So what of love? He could perhaps have put Elinor out of his mind if he had not seen her again so unexpectedly in Saint-Gilles and been told that the escape plan was her doing.

But why had she been dressed as a boy – a *joglar*? He regretted now that he had not spared the time to hear her story, but it seemed that she had left her family with the help of Perrin and Huguet. In a way, as long as they continued east, it was safer for her than staying at Sévignan. Her father was a well-known Believer and Bertran was sure Lanval would feel the wrath of the crusade that would soon muster in the north.

But what would happen to Elinor in future? She couldn't maintain her disguise as a boy for ever and he couldn't imagine what she would do next, even if the troupe did reach Italy. But he did find himself imagining all sorts of things. He tried to stop himself; this was not the right way for a Believer to be thinking.

For all that he had sung and written of love, Bertran did not have love affairs. He kept women at a distance, even though many had tried to win the heart of the troubadour. But Elinor had somehow crept behind his defences. She was so young, so determined and so idealistic. Seeing her at Saint-Gilles in her disguise had made him realise that. Whatever had made her leave her home, she had risked a great deal; rescuing him was all of a piece with that.

Bertran, living in disguise himself in Toulouse, without friends to talk to, felt Elinor's position even more strongly. And he had little to take his mind off it till the Count returned.

Raimon of Toulouse came back into the city as unpredictable and sore as a wounded lion. Philippe-Auguste had turned him down and so had Otto. He had even been to see the Abbot of Cîteaux, who was the Pope's Legate, and begged forgiveness for his sins. The Abbot had also refused him. Then in a last-ditch attempt to forestall the Pope's rage, he had gone, cap in hand, to his nephew and vassal Viscount Trencavel at Carcassonne.

Young Trencavel had been polite; he was the model of *cortesia* at all times. But he did not feel he always had to follow the same line as his ambitious and hot-tempered uncle. He declined the alliance. The Count had left Carcassonne thwarted for the fourth time and this last refusal had hurt more than the other three. It had been his last chance to form an alliance and make a concerted defence against the Pope's war. Now he had no choice but to submit to whatever penance Innocent demanded of him. And it would not be long in coming.

'She wants you to stay here?' said Lucatz, stupefied. 'Whatever for?'

'The Lady wants me to stay at Saint-Jacques until I can rejoin my old troubadour,' said Elinor. She felt very uncomfortable about lying, but hadn't she lied to Lucatz from the beginning?

'And that is what you want?' said the troubadour. He was clearly hurt.

'I think it would be best,' mumbled Elinor.

'Then there is no more to be said. I must find myself another *joglar* with an unbroken voice,' said Lucatz.

'I shall still be your *joglar* till you move on in the spring,' said Elinor.

'Hmm? Oh, yes, yes,' said Lucatz vaguely. Elinor realised he was already mentally recasting the troupe's repertoire without her. Until he did find a new *joglar*, they would not be able to perform the songs she had made so much her own.

She was glad of the sanctuary that Lady Iseut had offered her but she couldn't help feeling a pang at the thought of the troupe moving on without her. Huguet and Perrin would go back to their original bond of two and the *joglaresa*s would go on gossiping, joking and one day teasing a new boy. If she could have stayed as Esteve, she would not have left the troupe; she would have been content to be a *joglar* for ever. But nature had forced this solution on her.

And she would be forgotten. She wondered if even her family still thought about her. She dared not hope that Bertran did. But then a small, fluttering optimism hinted that her new life might have its adventures too. Iseut was going to teach her to be a *trobairitz*. She would have something else that she could do. And having sung both Iseut's and Azalais' songs, she had a shrewd idea that she could work out how to write them.

Telling the *joglar*s and *joglaresa*s was hard, harder than the interview she had first had with Lucatz. But they were all understanding.

'It is for the best,' said Pelegrina. 'You couldn't hide your womanhood for ever.'

'And it's not right for a lady like you to travel the roads,' said Maria. 'It's all right for us; we're used to it.'

'I was getting used to it too,' said Elinor, trying not to cry.

'We will miss you,' said Bernardina simply.

'Will you be all right?' asked Perrin. He was anxious; he felt responsible for the *donzela*.

'I think it is the best solution,' said Elinor. 'If the ladies here have discovered my secret, then so would others.'

'We'll come back and see you,' promised Huguet.

'If we can,' added Perrin.

'Where do you think you will go?' asked Elinor.

'I don't know if Lucatz will agree to go all the way across the border into Piedmont,' said Perrin. 'But we won't return west while the land is so troubled. We'll await word from

Bertran. I'm sure he will get a message to us somehow.'

'Would you like us to tell him where you are, lady?' asked Huguet in a low voice.

Elinor could only nod.

The remaining cold weeks flew past. Lady Iseut gave some grand banquets and invited some of the nobles who the *joglaresas* said had been her suitors. The troupe sang, danced and played for them and Esteve gave some of his best performances.

Lord Berenger was often there at Saint-Jacques. Elinor was sure that he still wanted to live by the Lady's side. And she was equally sure that Azalais didn't like or approve of this. The lady of Tarascon had become much sharper in her manner ever since the day of Elinor's interview and she was now inclined to be critical of the young *joglar*'s performance.

Then Elinor overheard a conversation at the nobles' table about Azalais' return to her home on the Rhône.

'I might not stay there long,' said Azalais. 'I'm thinking of going into Piedmont myself. I have been there before and there are many *trobairitz* there.'

Lady Iseut looked at her with troubled grey eyes. 'If that is what you want,' she said. 'I hope you will be happy wherever you go. And that we may still correspond?'

'Of course,' said Azalais. And the conversation moved on.

When the arrangements were made for Elinor's transformation, it was Lady Iseut who told her what to do; her friend took no more interest once Elinor had chosen to stay at Saint-Jacques.

The troupe moved on in early April, as they had done the year before; but what a different parting this one was! This time Elinor set off with them, as Esteve, riding on Mackerel, turning back in her saddle to wave at the townspeople who had turned out to see them off. It would not be long before more entertainers came to Saint-Jacques; the Lady's reputation ensured that. But a bastide always felt a little sad when their wintering troupe left in spring.

Iseut's *senescal*, Nicolas, had been taken into their confidence. He was waiting beyond the first stand of trees, with a pony and cart. The troupe drew to a halt. Lucatz had been surprised that the young *joglar* had ridden out with them but he expected him to turn and ride back to the town. Elinor had already said her farewells to Perrin and the others and her heart was heavy as they exchanged one last embrace.

Then the troupe set off down the mountain towards the next valley and the road east. It took them some time to pass out of sight, since they had to travel at the pace of the slowest walker. But eventually they were hidden by an outcrop of rock and Nicolas took out a bundle from the trunk on the cart and gave it to Elinor. She changed quickly behind a bush, even though the *senescal* was looking studiously away.

The dress was of yellow silk and the coif to cover her hair was red and beautifully embroidered. Iseut had forgotten nothing: stockings, yellow slippers with red embroidery, a purse to hang at her girdle and a cross to put round her neck. Elinor could not bring herself to put it on. Instead she pinned Bertran's red brooch on to the front of her dress.

When she was completely changed, she called out to Nicolas and gave him the bundle. Next Mackerel had to be disguised. His mane and tail were plaited with red and yellow ribbons. It didn't make any difference to his distinctive dappled patterns, but no one would be expecting the *joglar*'s pony to return to the bastide, tied behind Nicolas' cart.

Then came the hardest part: The *senescal* had to drive Elinor into the bastide in the cart. When people asked who the young lady was, they were to be told that this was one Elinor, a talented young *trobairitz* who had come to study with the Lady. The deception was made easier by both Iseut and Azalais greeting her warmly as soon as she arrived. They had already told the servants that such a visitor was expected.

So when Elinor entered Saint-Jacques for the second time, it was as a beautiful dark poet, clothed in red and yellow, the colours of her native country, come to make the bastide her home. That night Iseut ordered the drawbridge raised for the first time since the troupe arrived in the autumn. Elinor heard the chains clanking and wondered if she was a guest or a prisoner.

CHAPTER ELEVEN

Dolor

N ow Elinor's new life began. She had her own name back and with it her gender and her social status. *Trobairitz*, like the troubadours, came from noble families. They did not travel from court to court like their male counterparts but were in correspondence with other poets, male and female, in both the south and the north.

Azalais did not stay long after Elinor's 'arrival', just long enough not to arouse suspicion. And Elinor soon slipped into her place as Iseut's friend and confidante. At dinner she sat beside the Lady at the nobles' table and if any entertainer came to the great hall, she sat and listened to them as she had once been listened to.

Her life as a wandering musician was over and she was sometimes sad, especially when a young *joglar* came to Saint-Jacques and sang one of the songs she had made her own. But now she felt the pleasures of composition and they were quite different from those of performance.

Elinor was so glad that she had been taught to read and write; not all her contemporaries had been. For younger sons, in particular, these were considered unnecessary skills, unless they were destined for the church. But Lanval and Clara had insisted on all three of their children being civilised, as they saw it, through such arts.

Bertran had once told her that he was a younger son, but his parents had been as enlightened as Elinor's; they believed that everyone who could learn should be literate and had brought up three sons and four daughters in those beliefs.

At Saint-Jacques Elinor's education added the skill of composing verse. They began by Iseut showing her the first poem she had written. It was a *'planh'* or lament for her husband and Elinor felt honoured to read it.

It was very different from anything in the repertoire of Lucatz and his troupe. When the *joglars* sang of *'dolor'* they meant the sorrow of unrequited love, which the beloved could turn to *'joi'* in a moment by a kind look or word. It was nothing like the raw pain of a young widow lamenting that she would never see her true love again.

'To what melody should it be sung?' Elinor asked Iseut. 'I should like to learn it.'

'It has never been sung,' said the Lady. 'It is too personal for public performance. But the tune of any *planh* would serve. It is the words that matter after all.'

Elinor resolved that she would find the perfect sad melody to fit the lament and would one day sing it to her patron in thanks for her trust in showing it to her.

Iseut gave herself a little shake and moved on to explain other verse forms to her willing pupil.

'Here is a debate poem I wrote with Azalais,' she said.

Elinor did not like this one quite so much. The two women had argued back and forth about who could be trusted better, men or women, and it seemed a little dry. But she liked the other *tenso* Iseut showed her better. It had been written in alternating verses between a woman, Maria de Ventadorn, and a troubadour called Gui D'Uissel.

Maria was married to the Viscount of Ventadorn but it was clear from her poem that she had a deep attraction to Gui.

'Were they lovers?' asked Elinor, feeling bold even to use the word.

Iseut looked shocked. 'Only in their poetry,' she said. 'There are many ways in which women and men can express love for each other. It does not always have to be in the flesh.'

'Have you written any poems with a man?' asked Elinor.

'No,' said Iseut. 'I am still very inexperienced as a poet, even though I am daring to set myself up as your teacher. And I do not . . . have a special friend in that way.'

She looked so embarrassed that Elinor tried to change the subject. She picked up another poem from the manuscripts on the Lady's table.

'Tell me about this poet,' she said.

'Ah, that is the Countess of Dia,' said Iseut. 'She was married to the Count of Valentinois, but he has been dead these twenty years. She is an old lady now, but in her youth she wrote a *tenso* with the famous troubadour Raimbaut of Orange.'

'And what is this one?'

'It is a love poem,' said Iseut. 'Listen: "*I'm very happy, for the man I love is so fine. May God with joy richly repay the man who helped us meet.*" She sounds happy, doesn't she?'

'Look at this verse,' said Elinor, poring over the parchment and reading the elaborate black writing with some difficulty. 'She says, "*The lady who knows about valour should place her affection in a courteous and worthy knight . . . and she should dare to love him face to face.*" It sounds as if she thinks we should all have lovers, even if we have husbands.'

'Lovers on parchment only, as I said before.'

'Will you never take another husband, my lady?' asked Elinor softly.

'I can't be sure,' said Iseut. 'I was not like these other poets. I had no need for any other love besides my husband's. We were married such a short time before he left. Perhaps by now I would have tired of him and wanted to write of love to another man – but I don't think so.'

Who knew what would have happened if Jaufre had come back from the crusade? Iseut's eyes were very bright. Whatever Elinor read in these poems seemed to lead back to the same dangerous territory.

'Lord Berenger seems very fond of you,' she ventured.

Lady Iseut shook aside her melancholy and laughed.

'Yes, and I am very fond of my little dog, Minou. But I shan't marry him.'

'Minou or Lord Berenger?' Elinor dared to ask and now both women laughed.

***

While Elinor learned how to be a *trobairitz*, the world outside the safety of the bastide at Saint-Jacques was moving ever closer to war. The Pope was no less bent on teaching the Count of Toulouse a lesson but he listened to Raimon when he asked if a less unbending legate than the Abbot of Cîteaux could be appointed to deal with him. If he was going to have to surrender, he didn't want the Abbot dictating the terms.

Innocent heard his embassy and appointed two new Legates just to accept Raimon's surrender. But it didn't mean he had given up his idea of a war against the south. If the Count came over to the Pope's side, Innocent would just have to find another opponent.

The Abbot went to Paris with one of the new Legates, Milo, on 1st May, while all the south and north were bathed in sunshine, to ask Philippe-Auguste to let his son, Louis, lead the crusade. The King refused but promised a large contingent of knights.

And the muster of the army was fixed at last: for June 24th at Lyon.

'Who will lead the crusade, if not Louis?' asked Milo, on their way back to Rome.

The Abbot was inscrutable. 'I'm sure we shall find someone,' he said. 'Since our cause is so unassailably just.'

'He will lead it himself,' said the Count when rumours reached Toulouse of the King's decision.

'Who?' asked Bertran.

'The Abbot,' said Raimon. 'He wants this even more than the Pope does.'

'But why?' asked Bertran. 'Why does he hate the south so much? It's not just because he considers the Believers to be heretics, I think.'

'Let me tell you something about the Pope's precious Legate, the Abbot of Cîteaux,' said the Count venomously. 'He's a distant kinsman of mine.'

Bertran was astonished.

'He is descended from the Dukes of Narbonne – oh, only a minor branch, of course. But he means to get the Duchy for himself – you wait and see. The Abbot will lead the crusade – he has always meant to. He will do anything to win the south for the northerners. And then, if he succeeds in stripping me of all my titles, just by chance there will be a candidate on hand for one of them – the Duke of Narbonne!'

Bertran was shocked. 'You mean he would launch an entire crusade against the Believers just for his own personal gain?'

'The higher a monkey climbs, the more you see his arse,' said Raimon, 'as peasants say in the Midi.'

'I can't believe it,' said Bertran.

'Perhaps not a monkey. The man is a wolf,' said Raimon. 'He would do anything.'

Iseut had a maid called Garsenda who was not deceived by Elinor. She was a sharp-eyed, sharp-featured girl from Arles who soon spread her gossip among the other servants of the castle.

'There was no talk of another poet-lady coming till the Lady knew the *joglars* were going, was there? And then, by coincidence, as soon as they were out of the grounds, the Lady Elinor turns up.'

The other servants acknowledged that was true.

'And why did the Lady Azalais depart as soon as "Elinor" arrived? Her nose was put out of joint, wasn't it?'

But Garsenda, although she thought she had unearthed a great secret, had got the wrong end of the stick. She had seen Elinor without her coif and recognised her as Esteve the *joglar*. But since she had always believed completely in the boy *joglar*, she now thought that Lady Iseut was harbouring a young lover disguised as a woman.

And she decided to tell her suspicions to Lord Berenger

the next time he visited the court. Garsenda thought the information worth money but the Lord just laughed. Then he looked thoughtful and frowned, but he dismissed her without pressing any coins in her hand and the maid was disgruntled.

Iseut and Elinor were quite unaware of the gossip about them that was spreading throughout the bastide. But they heard other news, from the southwest.

'Raimon of Toulouse is going to submit to the Pope,' Iseut told Elinor one day after Berenger had been to see her.

'That's good, isn't it?' asked Elinor. 'If he submits, then the Pope will not go ahead with the army and the war.'

'Berenger doesn't trust him,' said Iseut. 'The Count gave himself up to the Pope's two new Legates in Valence. He said he was willing to take the Cross himself.'

'Against the south?' asked Elinor.

'Exactly,' said Iseut. 'Can you trust a man who would take the Cross against his own people? He might have made things up with the Pope but they'll find someone else to wage war against.'

'It won't come to that, surely?' said Elinor. 'Does Berenger think we are in danger here?'

Iseut was silent. 'He hasn't said so in so many words. But I think he is worried, yes. He has advised me to be well prepared for a siege, just in case the army comes this way.'

Bertran was one of the sixteen vassals who accompanied the Count back to Saint-Gilles in late June to do the penance devised for him. But they were outnumbered easily by the three archbishops and nineteen bishops who had gathered to watch, along with a vast crowd of locals. One vassal who had refused to go with the Count was his nephew Viscount Trencavel. He was still at odds with his uncle and didn't want to support him.

It was as good as a play to the people who came from a distance round Saint-Gilles to see the spectacle. This was their lord, barefoot, bareheaded and stripped to the waist, on his knees in front of the three abbey doors. But to his vassals it was a penance just to witness him so humiliated.

The very sculptures on the facade seemed to mock him, showing as they did scenes of all the aspects of Christianity denied by the Believers: the Holy Trinity, the Mass and Christ's Crucifixion in twenty scenes. These were all beliefs that the heretics refused to believe or participate in. And over and over again depictions of killings – Cain and Abel, Saint Michael and the dragon, Samson and the lion.

But as the Count knelt on the steps and read out the list of his faults, there was no mention of murder. Even though everything the Pope and his Legates had done for nearly a year and a half had been to avenge the murder of Pierre of Castelnau, they had not got the Count to admit to responsibility for the crime.

Indeed he had sworn to Bertran that he had not had anything to do with it and the troubadour believed him. He had been a vassal of the Count of Toulouse's and of his father before him all his life and, though he had no illusions about what either man was capable of, he did not think the Count likely to have done anything so stupid.

As the Count had told the Pope repeatedly, if he'd wanted to kill his Legate he could have done it in his own court, many times, and if he had wanted to order it he would not have had the act take place so close to Saint-Gilles. It made no sense.

As soon as the Count had finished reading out his list and sworn his obedience to the Pope and his Legates, Milo tied his stole round the Count's neck and dragged him into the church and towards the altar, whipping him with a bundle of birch twigs as they went. It was a sobering sight, the stripping and beating of such a great man – Duke of Narbonne, Count of Toulouse, Marquis of Provence and overlord of the south.

I can't bear it, thought Bertran. The other vassals were also suffering. Their allegiance was to their lord, not to a pope hundreds of miles south in Rome. Even if they were not all heretics, they did not respect the rules of the Church more than the man and the titles they had been brought up to revere.

Bertran had brooded over whether to come with the Count to Saint-Gilles; he was worried about being recognised and had known how hard it would be to see the Count dishonoured. And he knew there was worse to come. But he wanted to support his lord. When the beating was over, and Mass had been said, there was such a crush at the church doors that Raimon's only way out was through the crypt.

Milo liked that solution; it was where Pierre of Castelnau's tomb was. The Count was pulled half-naked and bleeding to do further penance in front of the body of the man he was supposed to have slain. Pierre was treated already as a martyr and revered as if he were a saint; Count Raimon was a villain in comparison. He crawled to the underground exit from the crypt, where his vassals threw a robe around him and escorted him to his castle. The show was over.

Less than a week later, the northern army mustered at Lyon. It was the Feast of John the Baptist, the city's patron saint, and there were crowds of people: pilgrims, traders and pickpockets. Nearly twenty thousand knights, wearing yellow silk crosses on their chests, assembled in a field outside the town.

There were men of every sort, from lords, archbishops and bishops to mercenaries and quartermasters. The host stretched for four miles as it marched down the banks of the Rhône, with its barges floating down the river beside it, carrying all the supplies needed for the forty days of fighting and besieging.

And ahead of the warriors a huge siege train of sappers, carpenters and military engineers had been sent to Avignon to await the army. They carried the mangonels and trebuchets that would hurl stones and carrion at the walls of the heretics' castles.

And who was leading this mighty army? Not the King's son but a group of fanatical men – the Archbishop of Sens, the Bishops of Autun, Clermont and Nevers and the Duke of Burgundy all rode at the head. But over them all was the Abbot of Cîteaux, who had been appointed by Pope Innocent to lead the crusade, just as the Count had predicted.

The mighty army reached Valence on the 2nd of July and the Count was there to meet them. Before he went to the Abbot's tent, he said goodbye to his old friend Bertran de Miramont, who had begged him not to do what he was set on doing.

'It's the only way,' he said simply, taking his twelve-year-old son by the hand. 'I shall take up the Cross, join the army and battle the heretics. It's the only way to save any of my lands at all.'

'You really think your lands will be spared?' asked Bertran. 'That you will have a Toulouse to be lord of in the end or a title to call your own?'

'I am sure of nothing,' said the Count bleakly. 'But it is my only chance. I am venturing everything on this throw of the dice. Including my son and heir. Are you certain you will not come with me?'

'No, Sire,' said Bertran, making a deep bow to his lord, since he expected never to see him again. 'I cannot take up arms against my own people.' It was the closest he had ever come to admitting to the Count that he was himself a Believer in what the Pope called heresy.

'Where will you go?' asked Raimon.

'To your nephew in Béziers,' said Bertran. 'I must warn him of the size and ferocity of the army. And I must tell him of your decision.'

'He won't understand,' said the Count. 'He'll probably think I'm a traitor. But I offered him an alliance some time ago and he washed his hands of me. There is nothing left for me to try.'

He let Bertran kiss his hand and then clasped the troubadour warmly in his arms before waving him on his way.

'Who will sing of this war in years to come?' he mused aloud to his little son, before taking him to the Abbot to offer him as a hostage.

'I give you my most precious jewel,' he said to the Abbot. 'Worth more than all my castles and lands. This is my only son. Take him as an earnest of my good faith. I have come to join the crusade.'

CHAPTER TWELVE

Siege

'*I*t took more than two hours for the French army to pass,' wrote Azalais from Tarascon. '*I have never seen so many people in one place. It was terrifying.*'

Iseut was reading her letter to Elinor. But events were moving faster than a messenger could ride and by the time the women heard about the huge forces from the north, the killing had already begun: Tonneins and Casseneuil in the west, where the crusaders burned their first heretics, men and women who refused to convert. In the east the army passed through Beaucaire and Nîmes and arrived at Montpellier without hindrance.

But the women of Saint-Jacques did not know any of this. Elinor was tortured by fear; if the mighty army was going to pass on to Béziers it would be very close to her home town. But if it changed course and decided to go east, their fastness in the mountains would be under threat.

Azalais had watched the army go by from the east bank of the Rhône, as it passed through Beaucaire, so it looked as if Saint-Jacques was safe for the moment. But that meant Sévignan was more at risk. It was dreadful not knowing. Elinor felt she could cope with a force of armed men turning up to besiege Iseut's castle better than she could bear the long wait for news.

It was hard to live through every day never knowing when a messenger might arrive with something horrible to tell them. Iseut had been through this before, waiting for news from the Fourth Crusade, so she was better able to support the daily burden of running the demesne while ignorant of what was happening elsewhere.

This helped Elinor too. The Lady was an excellent manager. She had flocks of sheep and herds of goats in the higher lands and fig trees and vines down in the valley. Her lands covered fields of wheat and barley and flax for cloth and orchards of plums, cherries, pears and sweet chestnuts.

All the shepherds and goatherds were dependent on the Lady of the castle, as were the farmers, cheese-makers, bakers, carpenters, weavers and poultry men. And then there were the household knights, the squires, the burghers and the many servants of the castle. They all looked to the Lady to manage their affairs, feed and house them.

Iseut had never had much time to spend on her poetry and music and now she had less for sitting around wondering what was going on west of the Rhône. She involved Elinor in more and more of the daily decisions and tasks. Nicolas the *senescal* was her right-hand man but, as time went by, Iseut came to rely on Elinor's opinion too.

This was specially useful since a certain coolness seemed to have sprung up on Lord Berenger's part. Iseut was sure that he had taken a dislike to her new companion. It made her smile at first because he had not been at all jealous of Azalais; if anything, it had been the other way round.

But it really hurt that he was now holding himself aloof from her, at a time when he himself had said she might be in danger. The Lady did not spend much time looking in her hand glass but if she had, she would have seen a permanent line between her brows that used not to be there. It came from frowning over her accounts and trying not to think of the war. Or about Lord Berenger.

When Viscount Trencavel heard that his uncle had taken the Cross, he knew the game was up. Bertran's message brought the worst news he had heard for some time.

'I must do the same as the Count,' he told Bertran, who had gained entry to the château only by saying that he came hotfoot from Count Raimon and the French army. The gate-keepers didn't recognise him as the troubadour that had so often visited the Viscount.

'I must go to the Abbot at Montpellier and offer to surrender on the same terms as Toulouse,' said Trencavel. 'Only I shall stop short of giving him my son as hostage.'

Bertran bowed. He did not think that the Abbot would accept the Viscount's offer, not now he was marching at the head of an army that could find such rich pickings in the south. But he understood why the Viscount needed to try.

'May I come with you, my lord?' he asked.

'Thank you,' said young Trencavel. 'You have always been a good friend.'

They set out straight away and arrived two days later. The sight of the French army camped at Montpellier struck fear into both men. It was unnatural; no company of men and weapons so great had ever assembled in the south in their lifetimes. They found their way to the Abbot's tent, passing by one with the red and gold banner of Raimon of Toulouse.

The Viscount said he couldn't face his uncle yet.

When they were shown into the Legate's presence, Trencavel introduced his companion just as 'Jules'. Bertran was not confident that he would not be recognised with his new beard and he pulled his hat down over his eyes as soon as it was polite to put it back on.

In fact the Abbot scarcely looked even at the Viscount, let alone his companion.

'It is far too late for such gestures,' he said haughtily, waving aside the Viscount's offer. 'You have seen the forces ranged against you. I suggest you go back to your little castle and prepare to defend yourself.'

'Ranged against *me*, my lord Abbot?' asked the Viscount, trying hard to control his temper. 'Why, what am I supposed to have done? I thought it was my uncle you had a grievance against.'

'Your uncle has seen the error of his ways,' said another man, coming forward. He was big with a shock of dark hair and a fanatical gleam in his eye. Both Trencavel and Bertran were surprised that the Legate let this unknown speak.

'Might I know who addresses me?' asked the Viscount.

'This is the Earl of Leicester in England,' said the Legate, in a bored voice. 'He is Simon de Montfort, from the Île de France, and one of our most distinguished soldiers.'

'You, like the Count of Toulouse, have encouraged heretics and Jews in your lands,' said de Montfort. 'My lord Abbot is correct. You should prepare for war.'

'But I came here to offer surrender,' said the Viscount. 'On the same terms as the Count of Toulouse.'

But it was no good. Neither the Abbot nor de Montfort would listen. The two visitors were firmly shown out of the leaders' presence.

Trencavel and Bertran stood together outside the tent, stunned by what they had heard.

'It is hard to stop a thrown stone,' said Bertran. 'They were never going to turn the army back.'

'I must assemble my vassals,' said the young Viscount. 'Carcassonne is the best mustering point – it is well stocked and prepared for siege. But I must now ride back to Béziers. After what they said about the Jews I must get them to Carcassonne too.' He ran both hands through his hair. 'These are dark days, Bertran.'

'What can I do?' asked Bertran.

'Come back to Béziers with me,' he said. 'And help me save the Jews.'

'Surely, sire. And what about the Believers?' asked Bertran.

'I think they will be safe enough there,' said Trencavel. 'Béziers itself is well provisioned; but I want the Jews under my protection. We must pray that this storm will pass over us all and blow itself out in the west without too much blood-shed.'

Bertran went with him to organise messengers throughout the region to rouse the vassals. But meeting Simon de Montfort had unsettled him. The Count of Toulouse had said that the Abbot of Cîteaux was a wolf; it seemed he was not the only one in the French army.

At Sévignan, Elinor had not been forgotten. But the news from the north had made all other considerations secondary.

Her brother, Aimeric, had returned with no news after scouring the countryside for miles around. No one had seen a young girl of Elinor's description and she was in none of the sister houses, whether of the Church or the Believers.

And of course he had not asked about young boys.

Her family prayed for Elinor every day.

'All we can do is hope that she is safe and that we will see her again when these terrible times are over,' said Lord Lanval.

Then he forced all thoughts of his older daughter under in order to concentrate on the safety of his bastide. He had seriously considered leaving their hill town but the same thoughts came round again and again: where would they go? How much property and valuables could they take with them? And, most importantly, shouldn't they stay to protect their dependents?

As the news of the French muster filtered down to the family in the castle, Lanval sent out messengers to more and more people nearby to come and take shelter within its strong walls. The town was full of extra people and animals. Grain was stored in warehouses, vegetables harvested and kept in wooden crates or watered in racks. Pigs and sheep were slaughtered and the meat salted, and there were large numbers of chickens scratching round the streets of the bastide.

The knights and armourers were all busy, forging, mending, sharpening and grinding. The mood was high; the young men like Aimeric and Gui had never seen any more action than a few local skirmishes. They had no idea what real siege and warfare would be like but they were, if not looking forward to it, excited and full of energy.

The older men looked grim; they were under no illusions about the force from the north. Lord Lanval took charge of everything about the defences and Lady Clara kept Alys and the women servants busy, preparing bandages and medicines. The herb-women were occupied with grinding, distilling, mixing and bottling cures and remedies.

The water supply was a major problem in any siege and in addition to keeping the wells in good repair, Lord Lanval ordered barrels to be filled from the streams around the castles, to ensure that they did not run out. As the water grew stale it would be drawn off into buckets which were kept constantly filled against outbreaks of fire, and the barrels would be topped up with fresh water.

And the walls were being repaired, great blocks of stone being hauled in from the countryside around to fill gaps, and smaller pieces brought in by the basket. Soon the walls of Sévignan were as strong and complete as they had ever been.

Beacons were built to be lit when and if the French force came into view, to summon any last dependents from outlying areas to come and shelter in the bastide. Church bells would be rung and drums beaten and trumpets blasted, not only calling in the last stragglers but reminding any fighting men of the Midi who had not already given their allegiance to hasten to the defence of the walls.

Watches were kept in each tower at the corners of the walls, by sharp-eyed sentries during the day and those with the most acute hearing at night. Every night the gates were closed at dusk and this was signalled by the ringing of another bell, in case people had lost track of time and were still labouring in the fields. It also signalled that anyone not authorised to stay overnight should leave, but as time went by, there were fewer visitors.

There were not many who wanted to be caught out in the open away from their own defended towns after dark. Rumour was spreading about the French army: twenty thousand, forty thousand, a hundred thousand. And news filtered through about the burnings at Casseneuil. By the time the force reached Montpellier, everyone was prepared for the worst.

Word of the Count of Toulouse's defection was brought to Lanval, as it was to many lords over the Midi, and he bowed his head in despair. If the army could not lay siege to Toulouse, there was more likelihood that other, smaller towns would be attacked. All over the Midi, bastides were being repaired and stocked, just as Sévignan was.

'Well,' said Lord Lanval, wearily to his wife one evening in late July. 'We are as ready as we are ever going to be – let the Frenchmen come!'

'Oh don't say so, my love,' said Clara. 'If only they would pass by us.'

'Then it would be to go on and sack another town,' said Lanval.

'Why can't they just go back, now that Raimon has surrendered?' Clara asked bitterly. 'Their argument is with him, not us.'

Lanval had summoned all his family members and closest advisors together with his knights, to a meeting in the great hall.

'The French force's argument with us, since my wife has raised it, is that we are sympathetic to what the Pope calls heretics.' He looked round at his senior knights. 'We cannot claim to be guilt-free of that charge, as I think you know, though I would dispute the Pope's term. It seems that the Church cannot bear to be disagreed with on matters of doctrine. The Pope hates the Believers and the French love our lands and property. So we are caught like an almond in a pair of nutcrackers.'

His use of 'we' was as close as he dared come to admitting he was one of the 'heretics' the Pope so hated.

'What I have summoned you here to say is that if we are offered peace on terms of surrendering up any Perfects or Believers in Sévignan to the "mercy" of the French army, I shall not accept those terms. My mind is made up on this. We have heard what French mercy consists of and it is sword and fire. If any man here disagrees with my decision there is still time to take shelter and give aid in another bastide, where the decision might be different.'

He looked round the hall expectantly, but no one stirred or spoke.

'You understand that if it comes to that, we shall be subjected to the full force of the besiegers?' Lanval added.

Still no movement.

'Well, then there is no more to be said. We will stand firm and protect the Believers and our lands. But if we should overcome we will show mercy to the invader. And may the Divine Spirit be with us.'

Bertran and the Viscount rode back to Béziers through the night and they were there before dawn. But Trencavel did not rest. He called for Samuel, his bailiff, to gather all the Jews in the city together. There were so many Jews in Béziers that the city was known as 'Petite Jerusalem'. 'They must come with me to Carcassonne,' he said. 'I can protect them even better there.'

'But are you afraid for the city?' asked Samuel. 'I thought we were well garrisoned and well provisioned here?'

'We are indeed,' said Trencavel. 'But I myself must get back to my château – my wife and child are there. And I should like to keep the Jews under my personal protection. The French are even more set against them than against the Believers.'

The Viscount summoned the citizens and asked them to defend the city as best they could.

'Hold up the crusaders for as long as you can, while I fortify Carcassonne,' he begged them. 'You control their access to the bridge across the Orb and the longer you can delay them, the better for us.' He did not speak of victory.

Bertran himself went to his friend Nahum's house and found the spice-trader ready, with his portable goods packed up.

'We have been expecting to leave for some time,' he told the troubadour. 'We were just waiting to know when and where. You will find many of my people likewise prepared.'

As they left, Nahum locked his front door and pocketed the big iron key. It pierced Bertran to the heart to think that his old friend had faith that he would one day return to his family's home. But there was no time to give way to such feelings. The several hundred Jews had to be assembled and got on their way to the bigger town and the stragglers outside Béziers had to be brought within the walls. Just as in Sévignan, the bell tolled out to warn any remaining country people to hasten to safety.

Bertran didn't know it but there were other friends in the city. The *joglars*, Perrin and Huguet, had parted company with Lucatz and the rest of the troupe earlier that summer. Lucatz had decided to carry on into Italy but by then the troupe had heard the news about the northern force and they felt drawn back to their old haunts, in spite of the danger.

There was no hard feeling; troupes of performing players were often fluid, changing with the seasons or other vagaries of the wandering life. New *joglars* could be picked up along the way, before the troupe settled again for the winter. Lucatz said goodbye to them with his blessing. The *joglaresas* were more uneasy. They had a stronger sense of what their friends were heading back to and were themselves grateful to put as much distance between them and the Rhône as possible.

Perrin and Huguet dug ditches and carried in supplies with the citizens of Béziers, confident in the strength of its walls. It had been a very hot summer and the humid air that hung over the marshes and saltpans to the south had brought swarms of flies and mosquitoes.

On 21st July the vast French army crossed the River Hérault and entered Trencavel lands. The soldiers suffered from the biting insects more than the locals did and were made irritable by the itching and stinging. This open scrubland with its crops of barley or fields lying fallow and yellowed in the sun was so different from their forested lands in the north that it seemed indeed a foreign country.

At Servian, only eight miles from Béziers, the village surrendered without a fight. There were few heretics there and their Lord, Etienne, was anxious for the army to pass through quickly.

The Abbot of Cîteaux sent the new Bishop of Béziers,

Renaut de Montpeyroux, who had travelled with the force from Montpellier, to parley with the citizens. Renaut was an old man and he rode in on a mule. He carried with him a list with two hundred and twenty-two names on it. These were the people, men and women, who had been identified as heretics, a small proportion of a city of about twenty thousand inhabitants.

Renaut went to the cathedral of Saint-Nazaire and spoke to the Consuls of the town.

'If you yield up the people on this list, the army will leave you and your property alone,' he said. 'Or if everyone vacates the city, leaving just the names on the list, the soldiers will not harm you. But if you don't hand the heretics over to the army that has come in God's name, then your safety cannot be guaranteed.'

The Bishop was booed out of the cathedral. 'We would rather drown in the salty sea,' said the Consuls.

They might have had their disputes with the Trencavel family in the past but they were fiercely independent and would not give up fellow citizens so easily. They had good defences and provisions and they expected reinforcements from Carcassonne before long. Only a handful of them chose to go back to the army with Bishop Renaut, who beat a hasty retreat on his mule.

Perrin and Huguet were among many who watched the Bishop go back to the lines. To the southeast of the city, under the rocky outcrop where the cathedral stood, the French army began to dig in for a long siege.

CHAPTER THIRTEEN

The Nightingale of Carcassonne

At Carcassonne there was furious activity; the bells rang constantly to gather in people and animals from the surrounding countryside. The Viscount was everywhere, overseeing repairs and the building of extra defences, but Viscountess Agnes and her little son Roger kept to the château.

Trencavel ordered the stones torn down from the refectory of the cathedral and the wooden stalls sawn up to build more galleries round the towers, which would hold the archers. Outside the castle, the fields were being burned, animals slaughtered and the water mills destroyed so that the crusaders would have nowhere to grind their grain.

It was a grim countryside that would greet the French army when it arrived from Béziers, as the Viscount knew it surely would. And across this burned and inhospitable land two small figures came limping. One was a boy of about fifteen, who asked to be admitted to the Viscount. The other was a silent child, of no more than six, clutching a wooden dagger.

'You can't see the Viscount,' said the gatekeeper, not unkindly. 'He's busy. Can't you see we've got a city to defend? The French are coming.'

'I know,' said the boy. 'I have come from Béziers.'

That changed everything. The gatekeeper sent a messenger to find Trencavel and the smaller boy was carried off by his wife, to be washed and fed. He did not want to let go of the older boy's hand at first, but the gatekeeper's wife was a plump and motherly woman, who cooed over him and coaxed him away with promises of sweetmeats.

The messenger returned and took the weary youth to the château, where the Viscount called for him to come to his private room. Bertran was with him and, as soon as the exhausted boy was shown in, he gasped.

'Huguet! What are you doing here? I thought you safely on your way to Italy.'

'You know him?' asked the Viscount.

'He was my youngest *joglar*,' said Bertran, taking the boy in his arms. Huguet was at the end of his strength, shaking now and ashen, tears seeping from his eyelids without his making a sound.

'He looks as if he's going to faint,' said the Viscount. 'Give him some wine.'

The two men stood over the boy feeding him sops of bread soaked in wine until he had revived enough to drink from a cup.

'The messenger said you come from Béziers,' said the Viscount urgently. 'I don't want to press you but I must know what happened there. You can see we are preparing for siege here. What must we expect?'

'Death,' said Huguet. His eyes were wide and unfocused. He recognised Bertran but saw him as if from far away, part of a life that had gone for ever. 'The French bring nothing but death.'

Bertran knew that the young *joglar* would not have ever seen warfare before and understood that he was in a state of shock. He signalled to Trencavel to let him take over the questioning.

'Take your time, Huguet,' he said gently. 'Tell us first how you happened to be there. What about the rest of the troupe?' A flash of fear crossed Bertran's face.

'Esteve is in the east, with the Lady of Saint-Jacques,' said Huguet, understanding. With what he had to tell, he was glad there was that one tiny fragment of good news to pass on. 'I came back with Perrin . . .'

He gave a huge sob and buried his face in his hands. Bertran waited, appalled.

'The Bishop came with a list,' Huguet continued, when he could. 'But the citizens would not give up the Believers. While he was talking to them, Perrin and I met a man and woman who had lost their child in the press of people coming to take shelter in the town. The woman was distraught and begging the father to go out and look for him. But the gates were closed and he was torn because they had four other children and he didn't want to leave them and his wife in case he couldn't get back. But he didn't want to lose his little boy either. He kept saying that the child was bound to be somewhere in the town. Then the woman started screaming and Perrin said he'd go.'

Huguet stopped to drink more wine to steady his voice.

'I said, I said, "Let me go – they won't attack a boy like me." I really thought they wouldn't.'

'That was very brave of you,' said the Viscount. 'Did you find the child?'

'Did they attack you?' asked Bertran. 'Are you hurt?'

160

'Not in my body,' said Huguet. 'And yes, my lord, I did find the child. I went with the Bishop, pretending to be among the few cowards who chose to leave the town with him. And I found the child curled up with his toy dagger in some bushes outside the walls.'

'That was a miracle,' said the Viscount. 'Did you restore him to his parents? Where are the rest of the citizens?'

Huguet looked at Bertran, not at the Viscount, and shook his head.

'There are none, my lord. I brought the child here. Your gatekeeper's wife is looking after him.'

'What do you mean, none?' asked the Viscount, but Bertran stopped him.

'Tell us what happened, Huguet,' he said. 'Tell us what you saw.'

'Right after the Bishop left and I found the child,' said Huguet. 'There was a sortie from the walls.'

'Madness,' muttered Trencavel.

'Young men, not more than about thirty of them,' said Huguet. 'A crusader came up on to the bridge over the Orb and taunted the citizens. So this band of youths ran out of the city down to the river, screaming and waving white pennants and shooting arrows into the French army. They beat the crusader and threw him in the river. I took the child and hid him among the trees, away from the fighting . . .'

He paused.

'It was like a torch thrown into a barrel of pitch,' he said.

'The army fought back to avenge their man?' asked the Viscount.

'Not the soldiers, Sire,' said Huguet. 'At least not at first. It was the camp followers, who were setting up tents and digging trenches. When they saw the crusader in the water, they took tent-poles and clubs and rushed the gates. The wicket gate had been left open and they forced their way in. Within minutes they had opened the main gates and the bells were ringing to call everyone into the churches . . .'

'What were the French soldiers doing?' asked Bertran.

'I saw them arming themselves and mounting their horses,' said Huguet. 'They poured into the city through the gates and up ladders. There seemed to be no defenders to stop them.'

Viscount Trencavel was pacing up and down the room now.

'And then . . . ?' asked Bertran.

'And then . . . I wanted to get further away from the walls but there was no shelter other than the copse we were hiding in. The child was crying – he was scared by the screaming and yelling. We had to stay where we were. I sang to him and eventually he fell asleep. But I kept watch. I am glad he did not see what I saw, hear what I heard.'

'So,' said Trencavel. 'We have come to it. What did you mean when you said there are no citizens?'

'They killed them all,' said Huguet expressionlessly. 'There's no one left. Only me. And the child.'

'How can you know?' began the Viscount but Bertran raised a hand to stop him.

'Just tell us what you saw,' he said.

'The army stormed the town but only after the camp followers got in first,' said Huguet. 'I heard screams and then, and then, there were flames and smoke. The roof of the cathedral fell in. I could see it from where I was.'

'The citizens would have been sheltering in it,' said

Trencavel. 'And the French set fire to it?'

'I was hiding in the copse for hours,' said Huguet. 'And then it was all chaos and shouting. I think the leaders were worried that everything was being destroyed and there'd be no loot for them. The *ribauts* were out of control, like drunken men. And then the whole town went up in flames.'

'But they must have taken some prisoners?' said the Viscount. 'Didn't they let those who were not Believers go free?' His fists were clenched.

Huguet shook his head. 'There were no prisoners,' he said. 'I waited and waited and there was nothing but flames and screams and shouting and then the smell . . . No one came out of the walls alive, except the French. They couldn't bear the heat from the fire and came down to the meadows by the river.'

'There were twenty thousand people in the city,' said the Viscount flatly.

'Twenty thousand and Perrin,' said Huguet. And then he was weeping uncontrollably. Bertran took him in his arms again and rocked him while the Viscount continued pacing, dangerously quiet.

'This is what we must expect here, then,' Trencavel said at last. 'No mercy from the French. No prisoners. No distinction between those they claim to be fighting and citizens who have never been anything other than faithful to the Church these . . . animals represent.'

'They are worse than animals,' said Bertran. 'No animal kills on such a scale, without reason.'

The Viscount stopped and knelt by Huguet.

'I am sorry about your friend,' he said. 'I had friends in Béziers too. I'm glad I saved the Jews, at least, if only to suffer

163

the same fate here. Did you see where the army went next?' he asked. 'Or do they remain outside the town, resting on their laurels?'

'They went towards the sea,' said Huguet. 'There was nothing left for them to eat and no one left for them to kill. I waited till they had gone and then walked here with the child.'

'You must be famished,' said the Viscount. 'Bertran, take him to the kitchens and feed him and then find him a bed. Then join me at the defences. I must send a message to Pedro of Aragon. It sounds as if the army is marching first towards Narbonne. As for you, young man, you have told me what I had to know. If a miracle happens and we survive the army here at Carcassonne, I will see you rewarded. Meanwhile, accept the thanks of a poor man, who once was viscount of the beautiful city of Béziers.'

He gave Huguet a ring from his hand and kissed him on his grimy forehead. Then he left the room.

Bertran continued to cradle the young *joglar*.

'Why didn't you stay in the east?' he whispered. 'I tried so hard to get you all away.'

'Perrin wasn't just my friend,' said Huguet. 'He was . . .'

'I know,' said Bertran. 'Hush now, I understand. Let's find you something to eat.'

'Why do I feel hunger and the need to satisfy it, when we're all going to die?' asked Huguet wearily. 'The Perfects are right. I was always a Believer, but now I'm sure. The world *was* made by an evil spirit. How else can you explain what the French are doing to us?'

'We are all going to die,' agreed Bertran. 'But not necessarily soon. We must not give way to the sin of despair. You

164

must stay strong and for that you must take food. Do it for me. And for Perrin. He must not have died in vain.'

And then they both wept. It seemed as if they stood together alone at the very end of the world.

It took over a week for the Lady of Saint-Jacques to hear what had happened at Béziers and would be even longer before they heard news from Carcassonne.

Their informant was again Azalais:

'No one here can believe the massacre at Béziers,' she wrote. 'We were so glad the army turned away from us and crossed the river. But now we know what they intended to do we can feel no relief – only horror that men of flesh and blood could do such deeds.

'They say that every man, woman and child was slain, either put to the sword or burned alive. Priests holding crosses and babies clinging to their mothers, heretics and faithful alike. There is a terrible rumour that the White Abbot who leads the army, that one they call Arnaut-Aimery, gave the order to spare no one. He said it was up to God to sort out the faithful from the wicked, once they were all dead.

'Can you imagine such evil? And in a churchman too! But it has worked, at least in their terms. Narbonne has surrendered, giving up heretics and all they own, the Jews' property too. And they've offered to pay money towards the Frenchmen's expenses!

'The last news I have is that they are marching to Carcassonne, where the Viscount is waiting for them. Heaven help them all.'

'My family's bastide is between Béziers and Carcassonne,'

said Elinor, stricken by the news. She could envisage only too clearly Sévignan in flames and Alys or Big Hugo with a French sword in their ribs. 'What can we do?'

'There is nothing we can do for them,' said Iseut. 'Or for the defenders at Carcassonne. Except pray for them. But we have to think what we must do to save ourselves.'

'You think they will come here?' asked Elinor. 'Won't they go on from Carcassonne to Toulouse?'

'You forget,' said Iseut. 'The Count of Toulouse now fights alongside the French. They won't attack the rose-coloured city.'

'So they might come back this way?'

'Who knows what they might do?' said Iseut. 'Who would have thought they would do as they did at Béziers? But I'm not prepared to sit here like a deer caught in a net waiting for the Frenchmen to come and slit my throat.'

But she did not tell Elinor what else she would do.

The main body of the French army arrived at Carcassonne on the 1st of August. Their advance guard had been there four days, digging in for a long siege, such as they had fully expected at Béziers. But now they were flushed with success. After the massacre at Béziers and the easy yielding of Narbonne, they had found nearly a hundred strongholds between there and Carcassonne standing empty with their gates open.

The French were able to replenish their dwindling supplies from the full granaries and fruit-stores they encountered on their march.

'There must be many landless lords wandering the Midi,'

said the Abbot of Cîteaux to Simon de Montfort.

De Montfort had become his right-hand man, showing great fearlessness and calm at Béziers and winning respect from all the leaders of the host.

'Then may they long remain so,' said de Montfort. He was beginning to see just what rich pickings were to be had from this war. All the empty strongholds had been confiscated.

Outside the great walled city, the suburbs were not well fortified and were soon overrun. Carcassonne was impressively walled and towered but it had a weakness and the French were quick to take advantage of it; it was built too far from the River Aude and relied for its water on the deep wells inside the walls.

So the first act of the army was to take the suburb of Saint-Vincent, which lay between the city and the river. But the Viscount didn't give in without a fight; he led a sortie himself and fought valiantly but they had to withdraw back to the safety of the walls and leave the suburb in French hands.

There were not just soldiers and camp followers in the French army; there was a large contingent of clergy, to bless the fighting force as they went about their work. They had adopted '*Veni Sancte Spiritus*' – 'Come Holy Ghost' – as the anthem of the crusade and they sang it lustily as the army took the other two suburbs by storm. They needed siege engines and mines to bring down the walls of the suburb in the south but, a week after they arrived, the French were masters of that too. And still the '*Veni Sancte Spiritus*' rang out.

It chilled the blood of the defenders inside the city.

'They really do believe that God is on their side, don't

they?' said Huguet to Bertran.

The boy was greatly recovered in body though still overwhelmed by grief for what he had seen and suffered. He had no skills as a fighter but he could not keep away from the walls. Bertran did not like to take up arms himself; he had done what he could by passing information and urging the south to defend itself.

But now that it had come to what he thought would be the last stand against the French, he had armed himself and was prepared to kill in order to save his liege lord and the people who relied on him who had fled to the city for its protection.

'They have their anthem,' he said, suddenly thinking of a role for the *joglar*. 'Let us have one of our own. They dare to call on a spirit of Good but we know they act for the love of property and possession. You carry no weapon but you have a great gift still to offer the defenders. Sing to them. Sing all round the city. Sing to raise men's hearts and to make them think of what is at stake here. Sing to remind them of what they are fighting to defend. Are we to be free men and women or to put our necks under the foot of the northerners?'

Huguet's face lit up. He didn't know yet what he could sing but he knew that Bertran was right. He could encourage men on the battlements and give them heart even in the face of the huge French force.

And now there was a lull in the fighting; King Pedro of Aragon had arrived. The King came with a hundred knights to visit the crusaders' encampment. He was Viscount Trencavel's suzerain and he had come as a mediator between the Viscount and the righteous anger of the Church.

A lookout on the walls hurried to the Viscount with the news.

'He has come to save us all,' said Trencavel and made a welcome ready for Pedro while the Frenchmen allowed him into the city to parley.

But his relief was short-lived. Pedro was angry that the Viscount hadn't come to terms with the Legates earlier and given up his patronage of the heretics.

'Why did you not listen to my advice?' he demanded. 'I can't help you now – a hundred knights are as nothing against tens of thousands of Frenchmen. You had better surrender.'

The Viscount did not protest that Pedro could have brought more knights if he had wanted. The King of Aragon had been his last hope.

'You can't win this battle,' said Pedro, who had been talking to the leaders of the army. 'Your city is full of refugees, your wells are running dry and the northerners are lying in the shade of the trees, eating fruit. They have taken control of the salt pans and are trading salt for bread with the locals, so your destruction of the watermills makes no difference.'

Trencavel bowed his head. If Pedro would not help him, he must discuss terms. His face was grey and he looked far older than his twenty-four years.

Within a short time a message came from the French army to say that, if the Viscount wanted to leave the city, he could do so, with eleven companions, each being allowed as many possessions as they could carry. When Pedro heard the terms, he muttered under his breath, 'You are more likely to see a donkey fly than Trencavel accepting such conditions.'

He was right. The Viscount refused and King Pedro went back to Aragon.

Another week of siege passed and at every assault the

crossbowmen of the city repulsed the French knights while Huguet went from battlement to battlement singing songs of encouragement. The defenders called him *Lo rossinhol de la ciutat* – the nightingale of the town, because everywhere he went, his sweet notes rallied the spirits of the men of Carcassonne.

The Abbot was worried; they had a meeting of leaders at which it was decided that one of them would become the new viscount when Trencavel was finally defeated. But what would he have to rule over if the same happened as at Béziers?

'Then offer the Viscount a safe conduct into the camp for another parley,' suggested Simon de Montfort. 'Tell him that we will spare all the citizens this time, if they leave wearing nothing but their small-clothes and carrying no valuables.'

'How would that help us subdue the Viscount?' objected the Abbot.

'I said "offer him a safe conduct" not abide by it,' said de Montfort quietly.

The two men understood one another. The terms were swiftly transmitted to the castle and Trencavel came out to parley under the walls; he had only nine companions with him.

He was escorted to the tent of the Duke of Nevers. And there he was put in chains, the word of the Frenchmen having been completely broken.

Next morning, the 14th of August, the citizens of Carcassonne left their homes, the men shoeless in hose and breeches, the women in their shifts. It took all day to empty the city and then the Viscount was led back in and thrown into a dungeon under his own castle. He was never seen alive again.

CHAPTER FOURTEEN

Planh

'They are arguing over the fleece before they've got a lamb,' said one of the French guards outside the leaders' tent.

'What fleece?' said his friend.

'They are in there quarrelling over who's going to be the next Viscount of Carcassonne.'

'While the real one's still alive?'

'And how long do you think that's going to be the case?' said the first guard. 'Nah! They'll pick one of them to give the castle to and then they'll get rid of young Trencavel. It's the way of war, isn't it?'

'I don't reckon it was right to break the safe conduct though,' said his friend. 'He came out under the flag of truce.'

The guard shrugged. 'What do you expect after Béziers? I'm sick of the whole thing. Can't wait till our forty days are up and we can get back home.'

Inside the tent, the Abbot offered the Viscountcy of Béziers, Albi and Carcassonne to the Duke of Burgundy.

'It would be a dishonour to accept the title while Viscount Trencavel lives,' he said.

The Abbot was seething inwardly but then offered the Viscountcy to the Count of Nevers.

'You must excuse me,' said Nevers diplomatically, 'but I

have enough land in France from my father.'

'It would be a disgrace to accept the fief,' said the Count of Saint Pol, when the Abbot turned to him.

It seemed as if none of the northerners wanted to be associated with the city they had razed to the ground and the one they were in the process of plundering. They knew very well that a great treachery was being committed against Viscount Trencavel. The Abbot was chairing the jury of seven key men and he looked at Simon de Montfort. Surely this ambitious but not over-rich lord would not turn down such a fancy title?

'What say you, my Lord de Montfort?' he asked.

The Abbot was a good judge of men.

'Surely there are others more worthy of this great honour?' said de Montfort, looking round at the group of nobles; he knew he was of lesser degree than any there. They remained silent. 'But if you insist . . .' he said at last.

So de Montfort modestly accepted the title of the young man who was now in the dungeons of his own castle. The Viscountess Agnes and her little son had been released to the care of the Count of Foix. The new Viscount, de Montfort, had a wife too and several sons, one of them almost grown up enough to fight alongside their father.

Inside the city, soldiers had piled up heaps of possessions and valuables, while the citizens continued to troop out through the gate.

But a small contingent, led by Bertran, had left by another route the previous night. Under the northern wall of the city was the entrance to a cavern, which opened on to an underground passage three leagues long. From the outside it looked like a store for keeping wine or cheese cool but

Raimon-Roger had told the troubadour about it and urged him to use it as a last resort if things went ill for the city.

It was a long, nerve-wracking walk in the dark, with no certainty that there wouldn't be soldiers waiting at the far end. Or armed pursuers following them from the entrance in the city. Those who left with Bertran had abandoned all their worldly possessions and fled only with their lives, but they were spared the humiliation of being driven out wearing nothing but their undergarments. And they did not trust the Abbot and the other leaders not to kill them, since he had broken his word to the Viscount.

Huguet was among the group who crawled silently through the tunnel not knowing if they were creeping towards or away from certain death. He wished he could have sung something to raise their spirits but, even if it had been safe to make such a sound when their escape had to be kept secret, the songs he knew all seemed to have fled from his mind.

There was nothing except cold and darkness and the feeling of rock pressing down on him. He thought about Perrin and wondered, as he had a hundred times whether he had been killed by sword or fire. Which would be a better death? Huguet grimaced in the dark at his own question. What was a good death? His fellow-believers said it was one where you received the *consolamentum* at the end but where had the consolation been for the Believers of Béziers?

He felt the Viscount's ring in the dark. There was another good man gone to certain death because of the Legate's treachery. Huguet felt as if he had been crawling along a tunnel for a long time, much longer than he had been escaping from Carcassonne. But he couldn't give way to these thoughts; he was responsible for someone else now.

The child he had saved from outside Béziers had not spoken a word since they arrived in the city. Huguet didn't even know his name. But he had visited him every day in the gatekeeper's house and seen him growing stronger with good food and some cosseting. Huguet had decided to call him Peire, in honour of the dead *joglar*.

With the people all about to leave the city, Peire could have gone with the gatekeeper and his wife. But to what? Huguet had come in the hours of dark and talked it over with the boy's protectors.

'I don't think he'd leave without you anyway,' said the gatekeeper's wife. 'And we'll have enough troubles without another mouth to feed. I think he'll be better off with you.'

And she woke the boy up and dressed him warmly, giving them both food for the journey, crying over them and over Carcassonne.

And now Peire walked silently beside Huguet, his little pack on his shoulders, holding on to the older boy's hand and gripping in the other the wooden dagger that was all that was left of his old life.

'I can't just sit here waiting for news to come to us,' said Iseut. 'I have been through that once in my life and it did not turn out well.'

Rumours were flying all over the south but real news was hard to come by. Iseut sent out her own messengers in the end and when they returned to Saint-Jacques, their faces told their story before they made any report.

'Many places have surrendered, my lady,' said one.

'Or been abandoned,' added the other.

'What places?' asked Iseut.

'Fanjeaux, Castres, Mirepoix, Saverdun, Foix . . .'

It was a litany of names of some of the most important towns in the region. But they were all well to the west of the Rhône.

'And Carcassonne?' asked Elinor.

'The army let the people leave but the city is in French hands and the Viscount has disappeared. People say he is a prisoner there.'

'There is one further piece of news, my lady,' said the second messenger. 'The French let the knights go too, and there are rumours of a fighting force gathering in some of the hill towns. Termes, Minerve and Cabaret, particularly.'

'That is the best thing you have told us so far,' said Iseut. 'What are the French doing?'

'Mostly dispersing. Their forty days were up by the time they took Carcassonne, so the army is dwindling.'

Elinor wondered what was going through the lady's mind. They hardly saw Berenger any more and there was no one else to advise them. They were completely reliant on whatever news came off the Pilgrims' Way or was brought by messengers. Elinor thought as she often had before how much more she had known of what was going on in the world when she was living on the road. Cities like Montpellier had been centres for information, even if that information was not entirely accurate.

But after some weeks of this state of inaction and ignorance, everything changed.

A new message came that the French army, heading back

north so that the landowners could attend to their own harvests, had split into many separate groups, some leaderless and all uncontrolled. Their successes in the south had gone to their heads and now they had dropped all pretence of marching to eradicate heresy. They were burning and pillaging as they went. And some had crossed the Rhône.

The danger was coming nearer; what should they do? Continue to wait and hope that the rabble army would pass Saint-Jacques? Iseut was so tense that the little frown line between her brows had deepened.

And then Digne was taken. The French were less than a day away.

They could get no news of Berenger or the fate of everyone else in the town. But there was nothing they could do to help them; they had to look to their own safety.

'There is no time to waste,' said Iseut, resolute at last. 'We are leaving.'

Elinor had thought the lady would offer her vassals the protection of her castle. But instead she summoned them all to the castle and then gave them all her animals. One animal from each flock was slaughtered for food and the rest handed over.

'I don't know how long you'll have to enjoy them,' she said. 'But from now on the herds and flocks are yours. You can choose whether to stay in your homes or herd the animals eastwards. Go with my blessing and my thanks.'

The peasants were so baffled it took them a long time to understand. But news had filtered through about Digne and they made their decisions accordingly. About two-thirds started herding their animals – an undreamed of richness – down the valley and headed off to a new life.

Back at the castle, Iseut was busy releasing servants, packing stores and saddling up horses.

'We will go alone,' she told Elinor. 'Just you, me, my *senescal* and two pack ponies. That way we can travel light and get as far away from the French army as possible.'

Nicolas the *senescal* was directing servants to dig holes to hide silver plate and any other large valuables.

'It's not worth it,' said Iseut, who seemed to have become almost indifferent about possessions. 'Even if the French don't find them, their hiding-place will be known. Do you really think if we ever come back here we will find such buried treasure still in the same spot?'

But Nicolas went doggedly on with his task and Iseut made Garsenda sew jewellery and gold coins into the hems of her and Elinor's dresses and cloaks.

The maid gave Elinor some vicious looks as she went about her task. Because the end of everything she had ever known was coming and the world was turning upside down, she dared to speak her mind.

'I know your secret,' she hissed at Elinor. 'Coward! Why don't you stop sheltering behind a woman's skirts and show your true colours. Be a man again!'

It was dawn before Bertran and his followers emerged from the tunnel. They stood in the warm early morning air, sniffing the breeze, unable to believe that they had made it through without capture. It seemed strange to Huguet that the sun still rose in the same way as it always had when everything the little group had ever known had come to an end.

Bertran tried to organise the raggle-taggle company into some sort of credible rebel group. His goal was to get them to Termes, one of the heavily fortified towns where they might meet up with other Carcassonnians and join up to resist the French.

But he hadn't had much choice about who left the city by the underground route. He'd had to pass the word round stealthily and without its leaking to the besiegers that he was leading out a company who rejected the French terms. So perhaps that was one thing the little group had in common: that they were all natural rebels. But they were a mixture of Believers and Church followers, united by the idea that what the army had been doing in the south was wrong.

The story of Béziers had soon run round Carcassonne once Huguet had brought the appalling news. He was treated with great respect and kindness and the little boy he had rescued was soon adopted as a kind of mascot by the Carcassonne refugees. There was always a willing pair of broad shoulders to carry Peire or someone to encourage him to eat or to play fivestones with him.

It took weeks but, by the time Elinor and Iseut were fleeing Saint-Jacques, the group of refugees led by Bertran had arrived in Termes. They had taken a roundabout route, hiding in scrubby copses by day and walking through the night, to get round Carcassonne to the south, avoiding the occupying army, and reach Termes.

Termes was a powerful castle sited on top of a large natural hill in the Corbières and its lord owed allegiance to the Viscount of Carcassonne. There was a citadel within town walls with a suburb next to it which had its own defensive walls. The entrance to the castle was secured by an ingenious 'dog-leg' construction, which was easily defended against invaders by a handful of men. And it was protected by a separate forward outpost.

It was there that the group from Carcassonne presented themselves and asked for protection. Immediately they were enfolded into the garrison and welcomed as heroes, though they had seen no fighting.

For the first time since the slaughter at Béziers, Huguet felt himself relax a little. Termes was well garrisoned and guarded. Many knights from Carcassonne had made their way there, weaponless and unhorsed but still fit and determined to harry and overcome the French. And since the army was dispersing, it became easier to believe that the south could fight back.

The Lord of Termes was a brave man, sympathetic to the Believers and horrified by what had happened in just a few weeks at Béziers and Carcassonne.

'And Viscount Trencavel is in prison?' he asked Bertran. 'But not dead?'

'I think we must regard him as if dead, my lord,' said Bertran, the weariness of the many nights keeping vigil in the city and the long march afterwards catching up with him. He had been responsible for the whole group and had feared attack night and day. Now that he was once again in a fortified city, he felt at first the reassurance of thick walls, well-armed defenders and a sympathetic lord. Yet none of these things had saved Béziers or Carcassonne. He sat with the Lord, his head and shoulders bowed in grief and felt the temptation of despair, which had not once visited him on the road to Termes.

And then a young voice rang out:

'And they killed all those who had sheltered in the minster
For neither cross, crucifix or altar could protect them;
And the crazy penniless soldiery killed the clerics
And women and children, so I did not believe any escaped.
May God receive their souls, if it please Him, in Paradise.'

It was a *planh* sung by Huguet the *joglar*, who had been composing the words on the long walk from Carcassonne. And at the end of it, the boy Peire, who could not be separated from his rescuer, said, 'Are my maire and paire in Paradise, Huguet?' They were his first words since his rescue from Béziers.

'They are,' said the *joglar*. 'I am sure of it. But we are here, with the lord of this city, who will look after us. Make your bow to him.'

The little boy bowed and, as if someone had taught him how, he held out his wooden dagger, hilt forward, to the Lord of Termes.

The Lord and Bertran, who had just before been talking like two survivors facing the end of days, stood and smiled. The lament and the little boy's gesture had brought back hope.

And all the court, filled with landless knights and beaten soldiers and refugees from captured castles, clapped, as the Lord took the wooden dagger and thanked the boy before handing it back to him. And he let Peire know that he took his offer of fealty just as seriously as he had made it.

At the bastide of Saint-Jacques, all was chaos. People were

streaming out of the castles, their arms piled high with gifts from the Lady. Tapestries, dresses, cloaks, boots, every pan and dish and chopper from the kitchens. Some struggled under the burden of pieces of furniture, others had equipped themselves with handcarts to carry away the larger objects. It was like very slow and courteous pillaging, with the owner willingly bidding the looters to take whatever they wanted.

'I wish them joy of my possessions,' said Iseut, standing with Elinor on the battlements and watching the trail of townspeople winding down into the valley. 'I do not think they will enjoy their booty for long. But I'd rather see the things leave the castle in their hands than plundered by the French.'

Garsenda too had left, carrying a huge bundle of clothes. Elinor was sure that she had taken a few small gems too but Iseut had told her calmly that it didn't matter.

'We are taking only what we can exchange for goods and food,' she said. 'I don't see a future of our bedecking ourselves with jewels and other finery.'

'Garsenda would have me back in my boy's clothes,' said Elinor.

'She knew?' asked Iseut, diverted, even on the precipice of ruin, by this little piece of gossip.

'Sort of,' said Elinor. 'She thinks I really am a boy and your secret lover!'

It seemed strange to find something to laugh about at such a time but the two women smiled to think of the maid's suspicions.

'I did think she might be right in a way,' said Elinor. 'That perhaps I should resume boy's clothes for our journey, so that it looks as if you have two guards.'

'It is too late for disguises, Elinor,' said Iseut, taking both her hands. 'And indeed I think you would make an unconvincing boy now. I think Garsenda must have very poor vision.'

It was true that over the summer Elinor's hair had grown to a respectably ladylike length and her figure had filled out. But she would have willingly tried to be Esteve the *joglar* again if it would have helped in their escape.

The stables were almost empty, Iseut having given horses and harness to all her knights.

'Take yourselves west to Termes or Cabaret, if you will,' she had told them. 'You may find other brave men there to fight alongside. My way lies east, to Italy.'

There were protests at first, because no one wanted to leave their liege lady, who had looked after them so well when their lord had failed to come back from the Holy Land. But there was no time to argue; the Lady was determined.

By nightfall, the castle was silent and bare; all that was left was the wood and kindling for the hearths and kitchen fires. It was time for them to leave.

'Pile the wood in my hall, Nicolas,' said Iseut.

The *senescal* was going to refuse, seeing what she intended. But at a look from the Lady, he did as he was told, carrying logs and kindling as though he were one of the most menial servants in the castle. When it was all heaped up at one end, where the long table used to be when Esteve and the troupe had come to sing at the court of Saint-Jacques, Iseut took a burning torch from the wall and calmly thrust it into the pyre.

The flames soon caught at some tattered tapestries that the pillagers had left, and leapt up to the wooden rafters.

Everything was bone dry from the long hot summer and the fire soon took hold.

'We should leave, my lady,' said Nicolas urgently.

But Lady Iseut stood and watched her great hall burning as if in a dream. Here she had sat as a girl beside Jaufre at their wedding feast, here heard the music of the troubadours, here danced at many celebrations and later presided sadly while the nobility of the countryside had wooed her without success.

Nicolas looked desperately at Elinor. She went over to Iseut and touched her on the arm.

'Time to go, lady,' she said.

Iseut shook herself out of her reverie and wrapped her cloak around her.

'It will soon be warm enough here,' she said with a bright, forced smile. 'But our journey will be a cold one.'

And the Lady of Saint-Jacques walked out of her castle for ever and mounted her horse alongside Elinor on Mackerel. Minou travelled in a basket tied to Iseut's pommel. The little train wound its way down from the castle and did not look back.

They did not see – as the Frenchmen did, bivouacked only a few miles to the west – the flames and smoke and, at the end, the very stones of the castle glowing blood red against the night sky. The stragglers from the Abbot's crusaders could only watch and curse. By the time they reached the castle, which they had heard held great riches, there was nothing but a heap of charred stones and ash.

And by then Iseut and Elinor were far away.

Part Three

Domna

The Albigensian Crusade . . . crushed Occitan culture and language. Most troubadours fled, especially to Spain and Italy.

From *Music in the Castle* by Alberto Gallo (1995)

CHAPTER FIFTEEN

The Road to Monferrato

Their journey was painfully slow, even on horseback. At first they travelled night and day, hardly resting or eating, anxious to put as much distance between themselves and the French invaders as they could. It took weeks to pick their way through the Alps and it was late September before they reached the plain.

There for the first time Lady Iseut consented to spend the night at an inn. Nicolas carried the saddlebags to the women's chamber and himself slept on the threshold outside their door. But there was no raid and no thieves. The landlord seemed hurt by the suggestion. There were no French soldiers here in the borderlands.

When Iseut and Elinor had slept for twelve straight hours, they devoured a good breakfast, glad not to have to delve further into their own dwindling supplies.

Although they had both agreed that Elinor had grown beyond a boy's disguise, Iseut had reluctantly consented to let her young friend play the maid.

'People will wonder else, my lady,' Elinor had said. 'To see a noblewoman travelling without a female attendant. It might cause talk.'

'It irks me,' said Iseut. 'Since you are as high-born as I am.'

'What does that matter in such times? I don't mind

combing your hair or brushing the mud from your hems.'

'Then I shall do the same for you in private. After all, I am no longer the *Senhor* of a great demesne. All I own is in our saddlebags and what is sewn into our dresses. That is all my wealth now.'

'And all mine too,' said Elinor. 'Which is given to me by you. I came to Saint-Jacques without anything but my flute and a head full of songs. That is still all my dowry.'

'And a fine one it would be for any man, together with your youth and beauty – and courage,' said Iseut. 'Who knows what the future will bring you?'

'Not marriage,' said Elinor. 'I can't imagine a world of courtship and dowries for me ever again. I know it was what I was running away from, but I long to hear news of Sévignan now. If I could be sure the castle was still standing and my family alive, it would be all I could hope for from the future.'

'Well, while we are journeying to wherever we end up by the winter, you shall be the maid. But never call me Lady again except in public. I am Iseut to you and we are the same – two poor pilgrims on the road, in search of Grace.'

They left the inn and took the way to Cuneo, reaching it before the next dusk.

Cuneo was a new town, built only ten years earlier, at the junction of two rivers. It was wedged in the 'V' between them and that was what its name meant: 'a wedge'. The little party from Saint-Jacques halted wearily outside an inn overlooking the point where the rivers met in the south of the town.

'We shall stay two nights,' said Iseut firmly. 'I want to see what information can be picked up here.'

They supped on peasant fare – rabbit stew with herbs and coarse black bread, followed by small red pears and goat cheese. Nothing either woman had eaten in a castle had ever tasted so fine. The tensions of the last few months were beginning to ebb away and Elinor felt safe for the first time since she had decided to stay in Saint-Jacques in the spring. It seemed so long since she had left the troupe as Esteve and doubled back in her red and yellow dress as Elinor again.

'I wonder where they all are now,' she said. 'Lucatz and the troupe.'

'Perhaps we will find them now we are in Italy,' said Iseut. I think we should try to find a court sympathetic to trouba-dours and *trobairitz*. Then we might earn our keep as poets.'

It was a novel idea. The *trobairitz* of the Midi were not like the troubadours; they did not travel from court to court with their latest compositions. But there was no reason why they should not, now that times were different.

Next day they went to the marketplace, which, as with all markets, was a good place for news. They were definitely in Italy now, the voices around them different, but still just understandable by those who spoke the language of Oc. There was even a small group of *joglars*, who made Elinor's heart contract, but there was none she recognised among them.

'What news?' asked Lady Iseut, after she had bought spiced white bread for them and a drink made of plums from one of the stalls.

'The cost of flour has gone up something shocking,' said the baker.

Elinor turned away to hide her smile. Cities might fall and burn, people be slaughtered wholesale, but for a fat country baker with bread to sell, nothing would be as important as the price of flour.

Iseut was sympathetic. 'That's bad news for you,' she said. 'You have to put your prices up to match and then risk losing custom.'

'Ah well,' shrugged the baker, feeling better now someone understood his problems. 'People will always need bread no matter how much I have to charge. They won't find any baker who sells it cheaper.'

'Has there been a bad harvest in Piedmont then?' asked Iseut.

'Not so's you'd notice,' said the baker. 'But I used to buy in some flour from over in the Languedoc and they've got it very bad over there – mills broken down and destroyed and so on.'

'By the northerners?' asked Iseut.

'Mainly by the defenders, or so I've heard. To stop the Frenchies grinding their wheat for the army's bread. For all the good it did them.'

'Yes, news from the west is bad,' agreed Iseut.

'And likely to get worse,' said the baker. 'They say that Count Raimon's been excommunicated again, even though he let them whip him at Saint-Gilles.'

Elinor whispered to Iseut.

'Is there any news of the Viscount Trencavel?' the Lady asked.

'No one's seen him since the French took Carcassonne apparently. But they've given his titles to one of them. So I reckon he's had it.'

Iseut nodded and they finished their bread, letting him serve others. It didn't do to ask too many questions of the same person. Elinor wandered away, drawn to the *joglars* even though she didn't know any of them. She recognised one of their songs and it filled her with a painful pleasure, remembering her time on the road.

When the song was over, she tossed a few small coins into the hat held out.

'Thank you kindly, my lady,' said one, a man too old really for the travelling life. He must have been at least fifty and had a face so full of wrinkles it was hard to decipher his features among them.

'Just Miss,' said Elinor. 'My lady is over there.'

'Ah, do you think she'd like to hear a song or two?' asked the *joglar*. For if the maid gave copper, surely the Lady would carry silver?

'Perhaps,' said Elinor. 'She is fond of music. We used to have a troupe at her castle last winter. I don't suppose you have come across them? Lucatz was the name of the troubadour and he was taking them into Italy in the spring.'

'Not heard of a Lucatz,' said the *joglar*. 'Me and my boys don't go far. We don't need our own troubadour, see? We just learn all the old songs and play around Cuneo.'

'Do you ever play at court?' asked Elinor.

'Not much,' said the wizened little man. 'But we used to go as far as Alba. There's a court there – maybe your troupe has ended up at it?'

At Termes, the defenders spent their time partly mending and maintaining the walls and partly in sending out raiding parties to see if they could capture any Frenchmen or at least steal their weapons and horses. Bertran was often one of the party; the Lord of Termes had marked him out as a leader of men.

More often than French soldiers, they met nobles and knights who had been deprived of their lands. There was a word for them now – the *faidits*. They had nothing more to lose and readily offered their service to the Lord of Termes.

It was from one of them that Bertran learned the fate of Sévignan. It was Gui le Viguier.

He still had his horse and sword but had lost his shield and helm in the fierce fighting to defend the castle at Sévignan. His sword arm had sustained a bad break and set awkwardly so he couldn't straighten it. But he could hold his horse's reins in it and was training himself to fight with his left. He had wounds to his chest too, which needed seeing to. The healer would have a job to fix him up.

'Lord Lanval stayed to fight, then?' asked Bertran. 'He did not leave his gates open like so many lords in the Languedoc?'

Gui snorted but it ended in a cough.

'No, the Lord of Sévignan didn't give up without a fight,' he said. 'Or his son.'

'Aimeric was there on the walls with you?' asked Bertran.

'You know the family then,' said Gui, who had not recognised the troubadour under his beard.

Bertran inclined his head.

'Yes, Aimeric was there. He was my best friend.' Gui fiercely brushed his good arm across his eyes. 'The French killed him with a crossbow bolt, right in front of his father, God rot them. Just get me patched up and I'll avenge him on the next northern bastard I can find.'

Bertran was still for a moment in honour of Aimeric, whom he had cradled as a baby and composed a song for in celebration of his birth.

'What happened to the rest of the family?' he asked,

bracing himself for the worst.

'The French broke the walls down with their siege engines,' said Gui in a flat expressionless voice. 'But the leader – what do they call him?'

'The Abbot?' asked Bertran.

Gui frowned. 'No, that wasn't it. Not a churchman. Simon de somewhere. He said, "Give me your heretics and the rest can go." Lord Lanval didn't believe him and anyway he wouldn't give up good people to be burned. He refused.'

Bertran was silent, knowing Lanval's beliefs.

'What happened?' he asked.

'They had already built the pyre,' said Gui. 'So Lord Lanval said, "I am what you would call a heretic. I will go into the fire myself, if you will free my family and household." We couldn't believe it.'

'He is a brave man,' said Bertran.

'Was,' said Gui.

'So he did burn?'

'He walked out of the castle gate and up on to the pyre. It was alight by then.'

'What of the family? Did the French keep their promise?'

'Lady Clara and Lanval's daughter were distraught, hanging on to his sleeves and screaming and begging him not to do it,' said Gui, who was clearly reliving the moment. 'But then something extraordinary happened. An old nursemaid hobbled out and tried to climb on the pyre too. "You'll not die alone, my lord," she said. And after her at least two dozen, servants, traders, knights. Do you remember Hugo the cook? He was one.'

Bertran felt sick. 'They all went to their deaths?'

'Every one. I think even the French were ashamed.'

'What happened to Lady Clara and her daughter?'

'We wouldn't let them watch. We took them from the walls and huddled them in our cloaks so that they wouldn't hear the screams and smell the burning flesh. And when it was all over, we opened the gates and let the French in. They let us go. They even let us take our horses and weapons. I think they were as stunned as we were.'

He stopped to drink some of the posset the healer had made for him.

'The *senescal* took Alys on his own horse and led Lady Clara away. She could hardly hold the reins – she was like a corpse herself.'

'Where did they go?'

'To the east. That's all I know.'

'Without any guard?'

'She wouldn't have one,' said Gui. 'Don't think they were short of offers. But she said, "No, go and fight the French. Kill as many as you can and avenge the Believers of Sévignan." And she left on the road for Béziers. She said there was nothing left for the army to take from there so her way would be clear.'

'May God go with them,' said Bertran.

'Well, He certainly wasn't at Sévignan,' said Gui bitterly.

'He is the God of spirit, not matter,' said Bertran. 'It was an evil god who burned your lord and his faithful followers.'

'So you are one too?' said Gui. 'No, don't tell me. I don't want to know. I wouldn't hand you over to the crusaders whatever you believe.'

There was silence between them for a while.

'Lady Elinor had the right idea,' said Gui at last, startling Bertran out of his dark thoughts.

'Lady Elinor?' he said, as if talking of a distant view of the sea.

'She left Sévignan rather than marry my father. But she got out last spring before the army was raised. I hope she's somewhere safe out of this nightmare. She's the *Senhor* of Sévignan now, even though the French occupy it and, if I ever saw her again, I'd kneel to her and beg her pardon for ever having teased her.'

Bertran thought back to the time he had rescued Elinor from dancing the *saltarello* with this same knight. It was a scene from another life, another world.

Riding slowly through Piedmont in October brought balm to Elinor's and Iseut's wounded spirits. The country of the plain was wonderfully gentle, with soft rolling hills around and they travelled on to Alba at an undemanding pace. It was true that Iseut had no idea where they would end up but she had always at the back of her mind the words of the pilgrim priest Taddeo, who had mentioned Monferrato as a court where poetry was highly honoured.

If they could get to Chivasso, where the Marchese kept court in his castle, before winter set in, she had a hazy idea of throwing herself on his mercy; surely three weary travellers would not tax his hospitality too much? But at other times she feared that her plan would not work and she had no alternative strategy. She didn't want to discuss it with Elinor; Iseut just wanted this pleasant journey to last for ever.

Elinor would have understood. She felt the same and had felt it in her previous life as Esteve too. To travel without a definite end in sight had then been the solution to her problems and it was the same now. Then she had been running from an unwanted marriage but, had she really understood it at the time, she would have seen that she was escaping bloodshed and horror as well.

And so it was now. Though the Lady's uncanny mood at the firing of Saint-Jacques had unnerved her, Elinor had in some ways shared it. It was as if the two women had died in the flames themselves and were now in a kind of limbo, waiting for their fates to be determined. Would they find paradise at the end of their journey or more flames – the eternal kind?

But for most of the time, the travellers tried not to think of this or anything else, but just concentrated on keeping to the path and taking care that their mounts did not pick up stones or thistles in their hooves. They saw only to their bodily needs – food, rest, refreshment and sleep – and did not talk of religion, or armies, or titles.

Very occasionally, when she spotted a distant castle up in the gentle hills, Iseut would sigh and Elinor would know what she was thinking.

Nicolas was a great source of strength to both of them. When they were out of earshot of other people, he would encourage Elinor to sing and the music she made to accompany their journey became a part of it. Sometimes Iseut would compose aloud – something she would never have done without parchment and ink in her own castle – and Elinor would fit the new words to old tunes. But no more laments; they would keep till safer times.

And so they came to Alba and rested for a while before continuing on to try their fortune at Chivasso. The broad-leaved trees were turning golden as they approached, in contrast to the pines and cypresses that kept their dark green spires pointed at the sky.

'There is a poem in that contrast,' said Iseut. 'Why some trees are evergreens and others lose their leaves. It is an image that could be applied to people.'

They were staying at an inn in Alba, having supped on duck with white truffles. The Lady had two rather hectic red circles on her white cheeks and Elinor thought she looked feverish.

'How so, my lady?' asked Elinor.

'Well, some people are unchanging. They continue on the same year after year and it is a shock to us when they die – even if it is at a great age – because they have never shown any sign of weakness or decline. People like Nicolas here, so stalwart and true.'

'So Nicolas is a cypress tree,' said Elinor, who did not like the melancholy that was creeping into Iseut's voice. 'What are we?'

'We are like little holm oaks,' said Iseut dreamily. 'This autumn has stripped everything from us and we are as bare as their leafless branches.'

'But that means will shall recover in the spring, surely?' said Elinor.

'Perhaps we will,' said Iseut. 'Though perhaps we shall just be wind-blasted and never see green again.'

'Then we must just hope that birds don't come and make their nests in us or woodsmen chop us down for timber,' said Elinor, casting anxious looks at Nicolas and talking nonsense just to keep Iseut from dwelling on dark thoughts. But her image was ill chosen.

'Chop us for timber,' echoed Iseut. 'Like the faggots I lit in my hall. Or the ones that burned the Believers. I wonder if Berenger is safe?'

Her thoughts really did seem to be wandering now and Elinor hastened to get her into bed in their chamber. Iseut was icy cold and Elinor chafed her hands and feet and piled all the clothes they had in their saddlebags on to the bed to warm her. She sent Nicolas to get fire for the logs in their grate, cursing her own thoughtlessness.

But as the night wore on, Iseut was hot again and cast all the coverings off and Elinor stayed up all night bathing her face with a cloth soaked in cold water.

Towards dawn, Iseut opened her eyes and asked for Elinor, though she called her Azalais in her fever.

'I'm here, my lady. It's Elinor.'

'Ah yes, the maid,' rambled Iseut. 'No, that was Garsenda. If I die, Elinor, you must go on to . . . to . . . where is it we are going?'

'Monferrato, lady and you will not die,' said Elinor fiercely, blinking back tears.

'But if I do, you must promise to go on without me. Swear it, Elinor.'

'I will swear if that is what you wish. But what should I do without you? I will not let you die.'

'I am burning like my castle,' said Iseut. 'What is left will be ashes.'

'No, no,' said Elinor, weeping over her friend. 'You will not. You will be a tree back in leaf, remember? One that comes back in the spring. I promise. We will wear green together.'

And eventually sleep came to both of them, though it was not a peaceful one, but full of nightmares.

CHAPTER SIXTEEN

A New Lord

The band of soldiers in Termes rapidly became a resistance force like the one at Cabaret. The Lord of Termes kept good healers and they were busy night and day tending the wounded who had been well enough to walk or ride into the castle. They were all desperate men, like Gui, who had seen terrible things.

Those who were uninjured, or who had recovered enough to wield a weapon, went out on raiding parties, harrying the French. Killing soldiers, stripping weapons to restock the armoury, even torturing prisoners for information – these became daily events. So war changes men, quickly and without question.

The news from captured Frenchmen was that the Abbot's force was reduced to about thirty knights and he had sent to the Pope for reinforcements. The French nobility were heading back north in droves, intent on getting their reward for forty days' service and looking after the grape harvest.

But the rabble of *ribauts* and hundreds of foot soldiers stayed on; they had no land to harvest or vines to tend and they were still living richly in the south. And there were plenty of empty castles to winter in.

So small groups of Frenchmen often ran into desperate

faidits or some of the rebels from Termes, Minerve and Cabaret. And then it did not go well for the northerners.

'They'll never take Cabaret,' said the Lord of Termes. 'It's three castles in one and Lord Peire-Roger knows what he's doing.'

'They'll not have Termes either, my lord, while there are knights left to defend it,' said Gui le Viguier, who had rapidly become one of the Lord's most trusted fighters. His wounds were healing, though his arm would never straighten again.

Bertran did not go out with the raiding parties. He still felt responsible for the people he had led out of Carcassonne and not many of them were fit enough to fight. Huguet and Peire became his special concern. The little boy had accepted his new name and they never found out what his parents had called him. He regarded Huguet as not just his saviour but a sort of older brother and Bertran as a substitute father.

The troubadour went to great pains to keep Peire innocent of the many cruelties still stalking the land. He was not allowed outside the castle walls and was only rarely permitted up on to the battlements. But he considered himself one of the fighting force nevertheless and was never seen without his wooden dagger.

One day a ragged man came to Termes and begged entrance. The porter let him in when he said he came from the Viguier bastide.

'It's the first word I've had of my family,' said Gui, as soon as he heard. 'I doubt it will be good, but send him to me.'

Once the man had been fed and washed, he came to Gui, who recognised his father's manservant under the emaciated form. The man fell on his knees but Gui lifted him up awk-wardly, clasping him with his injured arm.

'What news, Sicart?' Gui asked gently. 'What of my father?'

Iseut was ill for two weeks and as soon as she was recovered, Elinor took the fever from her and burned and froze as badly as her friend. Then the Lady, still weak, played servant to the woman who was supposed to be her maid. Without Nicolas, who appeared to have the constitution of an ox, they would never have got through this time.

Tirelessly, he procured herbs and remedies and brought healers to the inn. He ordered broth for the invalid and nour-ishing food for the convalescent. And he made sure that the fire in the women's room was kept well stoked. Even though sometimes the patient begged for it to be put out and the windows thrown open.

It was November before they were well enough to leave Alba and by then they were seriously worried about getting to Chivasso before winter really set in. Iseut was anxious to make good time on the road north but they could not press the pace too hard, as both women were still thin and weak.

'We must stop overnight at inns on our route,' insisted Nicolas. 'It is already too cold to spend nights in the open, especially since you've been so ill.'

Iseut chafed at the advice but took it. Since their fevers, both women had come to rely on Nicolas and he had become much more than a servant. They travelled as lady, maid and serving-man but when they were on the road they were just three companions and all thought of social degree was put to one side.

As they got nearer to the court of Monferrato, each of them had separate fears and worries about what they would find at the end of their journey. Iseut clung on to the reassurances that Taddeo the pilgrim had given her about the court there. Monferrato was famous even in the Midi for the welcome given to troubadours.

'The last Marchese and his troubadour were so close,' said Iseut, 'that they died side by side in battle.'

'Were they not on the same crusade as Lord Jaufre?' asked Nicolas.

'Yes but, unlike my lord, we know what happened to them,' said Iseut.

'They died in the Holy Land?' asked Elinor.

'No, the crusade was over. They were in Thessaloniki. It was only two years ago. A raiding party from Bulgaria killed the Marchese and sent his head to their Tsar.'

Elinor shuddered. Sometimes it was easy to believe that merciless cruelty had begun with the French invasion of the south but she was learning that the world had always been a harsher place than she had realised when she was *donzela* of Sévignan. Now she knew Iseut was suffering again, thinking that her own husband's fate could have been just as brutal.

'So the current Marchese has not held the title for very long?' asked Nicolas.

'I believe that his father gave up the title to him when he left for the crusade,' said Iseut. 'Taddeo told me that Guglielmo has been the effective ruler for the last five years.'

'So if he were not going to continue in his father's tradition as a patron of poetry and music, Taddeo would have known about that,' said Elinor.

'I'm sure he wouldn't have suggested going there if he had known any such thing,' said Nicolas.

'Well, we shall soon find out,' said Iseut. 'We'll be there tomorrow.'

Sicart's tale was brief. Thibaut le Viguier had taken the opposite line to the Lord of Sévignan.

'Once he heard what had happened at Béziers, your father said there was no way to keep the French out,' began the servant. 'So we packed up all we could manage to take with us and rode out into the hills, leaving the gates open and enough goods in the city to stop the army from pursuing us.'

'And my brothers?' asked Gui. 'Were they content to do as my father ordered?'

'No, sire. They wanted to stay and fight. But Lord Thibaut insisted they would do better to leave with their arms and horses. They went to Cabaret and are serving with Peire-Roger.'

'Good, I am glad to hear it. And where is my father now?' asked Gui.

The man shook his head. 'I am not sure, Sire. He sent me away when he heard of the forces at Minerve and Termes. He wanted me to find you or at least find news of you. No one knew what had happened at Sévignan.'

'That is a story for another day,' said Gui. 'So my father is a *faidit*, wandering in the south, keeping hidden from the French marauders. Well, I can at least kill as many of them as possible to make fewer to cause him trouble.' He turned to

Bertran, who had been listening to the man's account. 'You see? Lady Elinor would not have been any safer in my father's bastide than her own. She would now be wandering landless and ragged with him – and that if she were lucky. That's no life for a woman.'

'But life, all the same,' said Bertran. 'You must be glad that your father and brothers live.'

But he noticed that this was the second time Gui's thoughts had flown to Elinor. Perhaps it was the son who should have been proposed as a husband for her, not the father? He couldn't help wondering whether Elinor would have been so ready to flee from the handsome young knight as from the old widower.

The towers of the castle at Chivasso in Monferrato gleamed in the distance and the little party's hearts lifted as they saw them. It was more than two months since they had lived behind the protection of battlements at Saint-Jacques and, although they had encountered no worse danger on the road than an attack by fever, they were all eager to sleep again within such a shelter.

The gatekeeper had an easy life compared with his counterparts in the Midi; there were no hordes of armed militia threatening to besiege the castle, no mobs of refugees or looters, and only the occasional unexpected visitor.

So it was with interest that he inspected the three travellers from Saint-Jacques and called a small boy to take their names to the Marchese.

'Lady Iseut, the *Senhor* of Saint-Jacques, Lady Elinor of

Sévignan and Nicolas the *senescal*,' he drummed into the boy's head until he could repeat it back perfectly. He didn't suggest by so much as a glance that the ladies hardly lived up to their titles after two months on the road.

They were dusty, dishevelled and as thin as a pair of stray cats. But they sat their horses well, with heads held high.

Evidently the boy had passed on his message well for the Marchese's own *senescal* came to the gate to welcome the visitors, acknowledging Nicolas warmly, once he had courteously greeted the ladies.

'My master bids me to take you to a chamber where you may refresh yourselves after your long journey,' he said. 'And he will send the Marchesa's own maid to attend you.'

This was soothing to both women's nerves. They were shown to a richly hung chamber, while Nicolas took their horses to be stabled, and were brought hot water and soft towels. A serving-woman, better dressed than either of them, came to bathe them and dress their hair. She said nothing disrespectful but Elinor could tell from her eyes that she had not expected ladies to travel so ill-attended and so poorly dressed.

They took the two best gowns from the saddlebags that Nicolas brought up to the room, pale rose for Iseut and dark blue for Elinor.

Iseut sent the maid away once they had bathed and washed the dust from their hair and with a tiny pair of scissors snipped at the hems that Garsenda had sewed so long ago.

'I don't remember what was hidden and in what parts,' she said. 'We will have to hope the gems will match our gowns.'

With clumsy fingers, Elinor stitched the hems up again,

once Iseut had extracted a pair of diamond earrings and a pearl collar for her own ornament. For her own wear Elinor would accept nothing more than a fine silver chain for her neck and even then not the cross that went with it; that would have seemed disloyal both to her father and Bertran. But she had his brooch to wear on her dress and it gave her courage.

By the time the maid came back to brush their hair, the two women already looked much finer than when they had arrived and the serving-girl looked with satisfaction at her handiwork as they left to meet the Marchese. True that younger woman's hair was short for someone her age but it was a fine glossy brown and the older lady had such pretty blonde locks that they made a handsome pair.

Nicolas agonised for a while over whether to stay and guard the saddlebags or attend his mistress but in the end reasoned that even the meanest servant in the employ of so rich a marquisate would not need to pilfer, so he hastily washed his hands and face and hurried after the women.

On entering the Marchese's great hall, Nicolas had to swell out his chest and pretend to be the whole retinue of servants that Iseut deserved and should have had – would still have had if it hadn't been for the cursed French. At the head of the hall sat Marchese Guglielmo and his Marchesa, Berta, richly robed, on carved wooden chairs, as if King and Queen of their own Kingdom. And in a way they were. Monferrato was large enough to be a small kingdom and the noble family that ruled it went back generations – perhaps further than those of some monarchies.

But while the *senescal* noted with approval the richness of the hangings and the plate, Elinor was completely absorbed by the sight of the troupe of musicians and dancers. There were so many more than she had ever seen, even at the court of Maria of Montpellier.

The two best dressed, without instruments, must be troubadours, she reasoned, but there were others with fiddles, rebecs, flutes and tambours as well as a dizzying coloured swirl of *joglaresas* and acrobats. It made Elinor intensely homesick, not just for Sévignan or Saint-Jacques but for the travelling life she had led as Esteve.

The Marchese was courtesy itself, rising and coming forward to greet the women and leading them to seats beside him and his wife.

'Welcome to the court of Monferrato,' said Guglielmo. 'What brings my lady and her companion so far away from home?'

'I have no home, Marchese,' said Iseut, clearly and firmly so that all the court could hear. 'I left Saint-Jacques a prey to the French army – though they will have had scant joy of its strong towers and thick walls.'

Elinor found that she had been holding her breath; now she let it out very slowly. She had forgotten that Iseut was a poet. She was going to tell her story now and everyone in the court would be gripped by it.

While two women and their *senescal* had come to roost in Italy, Clara of Sévignan, her remaining daughter and their servant had found no such resting place. For weeks they had been wandering the hills of the Midi without any aim, except to escape the French. As time went by, they ventured further on the road by day and saw fewer signs of any soldiers.

Alys and her mother were still in such a state of shock that they hardly spoke. It had been bad enough seeing Aimeric shot down on the battlements but the sight of Lord Lanval climbing steadily on to the pyre had eclipsed even that. As far as Lady Clara was concerned she had but one child left and so certain was she that death or utter ruin would soon overtake them that she could not take thought even to protect that last human being who was dependent on her.

If their *senescal* hadn't made them stop for food and rest, it is doubtful that they would have survived the first few terrible days. They had come to Béziers and seen it nothing but a heap of ruins. They reined their horses and looked out at the devastation.

'I was married there,' said Clara quietly. 'In that cathedral that is now nothing but a wreck. Lanval and I stood at the altar in Saint-Nazaire and pledged ourselves to each other for life. That same altar where priests clung on to the crucifix and women and children hung on to the priests' robes screaming while French ruffians speared and burned them.'

She turned to her daughter and her servant.

'They did that in the name of my church to the Believers of my husband's religion. And to their own. I think the whole world has gone mad.'

They rode on to Narbonne, which had surrendered so easily to the northerners. But there were hardly any there now, only a handful to guard it against rebels.

The *senescal* persuaded Lady Clara to go to the court of the Viscount and throw themselves on his hospitality. Viscount Aimery was a cipher now, left his title as a reward for his surrender but no longer true lord of his own city. Still, he received them kindly enough.

'I should have believed Miramont when he came to see me last spring,' he said bitterly, when Clara had told him of the events at Sévignan.

'Our troubadour came here?' asked Alys. It was the first thing she had taken any interest in since the death of her brother and father.

Lady Clara hesitated then shrugged. What harm could Bertran's secret do any of them now? He was probably dead too.

'He was a Believer, like your father,' she told Alys. 'He came to Sévignan to warn us after the Pope's Legate was murdered.'

'And to me,' said the Viscount. 'He said that the French would not stop at killing heretics and he was proved right – look what they did at Béziers!'

'We passed it,' said Clara wearily. 'No church, no market-place left, nothing of that thriving and busy town – just ashes and ruins.'

'That is what Narbonne would have looked like if I hadn't surrendered,' said the Viscount. 'I know there are those who think me a coward for not resisting but at least my city still exists, unlike Trencavel's.' He lowered his voice, even though there were no Frenchmen in the room. 'And may one day again not be in foreign hands.'

'I sent our knights and foster-sons to join the rebels,' said Clara, 'but I have no great hopes. So many have been killed and the French army outnumbers them so vastly.'

'But most of the French have gone home,' said the Viscount. 'And though they may have reinforcements in the spring, our men have all the winter to regroup.'

'Then let us hope they do,' said Clara.

The court at Monferrato fell silent. Iseut had told them everything. They had heard of some of the disaster in the Midi: news of the massacre at Béziers had travelled far and fast. But that French soldiers had crossed back over the Rhône and sacked Digne and threatened Saint-Jacques was unexpected.

'So you fired your own castle?' asked Guglielmo. He was shocked and impressed in equal measure. He could not imagine being so desperate as to destroy any of his own castles.

'You are very brave,' said the Marchesa, her hand on her heart, picturing her own three little boys with the castle under siege. She was carrying her fourth child and her husband did not want her to be upset.

'Come, enough of such tragic tales for one day,' he said, taking Iseut by the hand. 'You and your companions are welcome guests at Monferrato. Stay as long as you wish. In fact, it would please me very much to have you and the Lady Elinor become part of my court. My wife is not so rich in noblewomen to be her friends that she would not welcome two more such lovely additions to the court. And my *senescal* will make yours welcome too.'

He stood and clapped his hands.

'We shall have music. And you can tell us the rest of your story over the coming days. For now we shall have feasting and dancing and push away all thoughts of warfare while we can.'

CHAPTER SEVENTEEN

Two Castles

Elinor and Iseut were assigned a chamber of their own in the castle, which the Marchesa took pleasure in furnishing with every comfort. At last the women were able to unpack what belongings they had saved from Saint-Jacques and put their pitifully few clothes and possessions into chests. All the jewels were unsewn now and, with the coins, were hidden under cloaks and dresses. Although Iseut was content to live as a dependent of the Marchese, at least for the winter, that money and those gems represented what was left of her independence.

But Guglielmo of Monferrato was a generous host and when his wife told him what poor clothing and adornment the two women had, he made them many presents of gowns and fine linen.

When they had been at court a week, he sent word that he would like a private audience with Iseut and there she told him about Jaufre and the Fourth Crusade.

The Marchese was a good listener. At the end he said, 'You know that my father left on the same crusade as your lord? They might well have met and known each other. The last Marchese was a good man and a good father. I fought alongside him in many battles with troublesome neighbours. And I would have gone with him to the Holy Land.'

'And why did you not?' asked Iseut.

'Because he forbade it. I am his only son, save my little half-brother Demetrio. And he is still only four. The Marchese insisted that I should stay and govern Monferrato, in case he didn't come back. And of course he didn't – like your husband.'

They were both silent for a while.

'I heard what happened to your father – it was terrible,' said Iseut gently.

'Yes,' said Guglielmo. 'It was, but I must not think of that now. I have to rule my lands as best I can and I must continue the tradition of my father's court. He was always generous to widows and orphans and I would wish to follow his example.'

'So I have heard,' said Iseut. 'And I have also heard that your father was a great patron of music and poetry. Did his own troubadour not fight and die at his side?'

'So they say,' said Guglielmo. He had his own views about troubadours; since his father's death many of them had written poems urging him to go and avenge the dead Marchese. But Guglielmo saw nothing to be gained by listening to their advice, except further bloodshed and a doubtful chance of victory. He preferred to stay in Monferrato and encourage the poets to write about something else.

'I am myself a *trobairitz* and so is my companion Elinor,' said Iseut. 'Though we are not yet greatly experienced poets and Elinor has started composing only since she came to me at Saint-Jacques. Yet we would both rather rely on your patronage than on your charity.'

This startled the Marchese out of his reverie about troubadours.

'Both *trobairitz*?' he exclaimed. 'Then doubly welcome at the court of Monferrato. We shall not expect to hear much from you yet but when you are ready to give my *joglars* something to perform, we shall be honoured to hear it.'

Iseut's heart lifted, till she saw how the Marchese was looking at her. It was a speculative assessment, not like a man attracted to a woman but more like a farmer assessing a cow he was thinking of purchasing. She saw with sudden clarity that he was mentally matchmaking. This great lord, for all his power, his army and his castles, was casting around in his mind to see if any of his knights might make a second husband for her!

She told Elinor her suspicions, as soon as she was back in their chamber.

'And he'll do the same for you, be sure of it,' she said.

'What shall we do?' asked Elinor. 'You surely don't think we should leave?'

The thought of returning to the road with no better destination in mind appalled both women. It was well into November now and the nights were cold. Their bedchamber with its own fireplace was welcoming and cosy and to go back on the road without a goal or plan would have been madness.

'No,' said Iseut firmly. 'We shall stay and eat the Marchese's meat and wear the Marchesa's clothes but we shall spend our days in composition and offer our songs and poems in return for their care. They'll never think of marrying us off before the spring and then we can decide what to do. Besides, it might be amusing to see whom Guglielmo has in mind.'

Elinor was not so sure; the only marriage proposal she had ever received had been far from amusing.

But at the next feast day, when they might have feared eligible suitors would be presented to them, the evening turned out very differently.

The *joglars* had sung and played and the dancers and acrobats and jugglers had entertained Guglielmo's guests, when his *senescal* came and spoke into his ear. The Marchese continued his father's tradition of never turning anyone away from his great hall during a meal and it seemed that a knight had come to the gate all the way from the Midi. Iseut and Elinor gathered that much but it seemed the man did not want to enter. He had asked instead for Guglielmo to come to him.

The Marchese was disconcerted; he considered it ill-mannered to leave his guests, who did indeed include possibly eligible suitors for the ladies of Saint-Jacques, but the knight had been most insistent and the *senescal* looked very grave.

With many elaborate courtesies and excuses, the Marchese left his board and the women glanced at one another, fearing something but doubting what it could be. He was not long gone, however, and brought the knight with him, making space for him at his table and pressing him to take wine and some sweetmeats at least.

Elinor recognised the red and gold of his surcoat; here was someone else from her homeland and she longed to question him.

Guglielmo stood and rapped the table, calling all to listen to him.

'This young man,' he said, 'has ridden hard over a long distance to bring bad news. Viscount Trencavel is dead.'

It was no different a fate from what Elinor had feared but it was so definite, so final. She had seen the young Viscount and his wife on several occasions; as her father's overlord he had even come to Sévignan more than once. She had heard about his capture at Carcassonne and about the way his titles had been usurped by the French victors. But dead! As long as he had been a prisoner in his own dungeon there might have been some hope – some talk of ransom or other bargaining for his release. But now all hope had died with him.

'The French "Viscount" de Montfort,' spat the Marchese, 'is giving it out that Trencavel died of dysentery. But I think we can discount that. The man was alone and unarmed, chained up in a dungeon. What would have been easier than to eliminate him with a dagger or rope? And what had he done, except own some fine castles and rich lands?'

'Does his son live?' asked the soft-hearted Marchesa, whose own little boys were no older than the small heir to Trencavel's title.

'He does, my lady,' said the knight. 'The Viscountess Agnes has accepted a pension of three thousand sols and is under the protection of the Count of Foix, with her son. But of course she is viscountess no more – that title is reserved for Alice de Montfort. And little Roger has lost his father's title to a Frenchman. Viscountess Agnes had to promise he would never try to get it back.'

'And the cur had Viscount Trencavel's body laid out in the cathedral for all to see,' said the Marchese. 'As if to honour him. He who was kept a prisoner in his own dungeon! There is no limit to the man's effrontery.'

Elinor felt that her heart might break. She had no idea if any of her family had survived the French onslaught on the south and she had been as horrified as everyone else when she had heard the news of the massacre at Béziers. But the word of this one death was somehow worse than anything she had heard so far because she could see a picture in her mind of the young Viscount, tossing his baby son up into the air and smiling as the boy crowed and the pretty Viscountess gazed indulgently at them both. Now the father was dead, almost certainly murdered, the son dispossessed and the wife a widow, dependent on the protection of another southern noble, just as vulnerable as her husband had been.

She could bear it no longer. Elinor whispered in Iseut's ear. All around them voices were raised in anger and shock as the news sank in. Trencavel had been a popular overlord and his fame had spread even into Piedmont. His death was viewed as an outrage too far.

Iseut spoke to Guglielmo and he clapped his hands again for silence.

'We shall honour Viscount Trencavel as a fallen comrade,' he said. 'As if he had died on the battlefield defending his lands and castle. Not having met his end in a dank and unhealthy prison, whether by disease or treachery. The Lady Iseut reminds me that we have at our court Lady Elinor of Sévignan, daughter of one of the Viscount's vassals. And she would like to sing for us a lament, written by Lady Iseut, but to a tune of her own composition.'

Elinor came down and spoke to the musicians. She stood straight and slender in a dark red gown and sang the *planh* that Iseut had written for her dead husband, to a tune she had been working on for months.

The *joglars* soon picked it up and produced a soft accompaniment on rebec and tambour. She poured into it all she felt about the destruction of the south and the loss of her own home and family. It was unusual for a *trobairitz* to sing in public but this was an unusual occasion and Elinor's plangent melody fitted the melancholy mood exactly.

When she stopped, there was long silence and then a roar of approval, as Guglielmo pledged a toast to 'Trencavel, Sévignan and the people of the south!'

'Well sung, Elinor,' said Iseut, when she sat back down, and the Lady's eyes were wet with sadness for the death of more than one man.

The news of the Viscount's death had reached Termes from Carcassonne as the garrison was settling in for the winter. Bertran was stunned. It seemed such a short time ago he had been with Viscount Trencavel in his castle, when the Legate came to arrest him. All the knights were similarly affected. The young Viscount had been liege lord to most of them, although many were older than him, and there was a warmth of feeling towards him that made his ignominious and unnecessary death seem all the worse.

They held a memorial Mass in the church at Termes and Bertran went, though he didn't take the Sacrament. He noticed about twenty others who refrained, telling him more clearly than he had known before who were what the Pope would call heretics. They never discussed religion in the garrison; whatever the reason this carnage had begun, it was clear now that it was all out war between the north and south.

The young Viscount hadn't been a Believer – or if he had he had kept it quiet – and he had never been accused of any crime. The Abbot of Cîteaux had broken with every honourable convention of law by not accepting the

Viscount's submission at Montpellier. It was Trencavel's uncle, the Count of Toulouse, that the vast army had been assembled to crush and by joining the French he had deflected the onslaught on to his nephew.

Feeling against the Count of Toulouse was running high; he was known to have sent his own representatives to Rome so that his lands wouldn't be confiscated. And if he succeeded, he would have lost nothing in this war that had caused so much death and destruction.

All the *faidits* wandering through the south, sheltering where they could in the empty castles abandoned by the northerners, blamed the Count of Toulouse for their situation, even more than they blamed the French.

Sévignan was one of the abandoned bastides. Bertran had gone with a small band, including Gui le Viguier, to check the lie of the land in his old lord's hill town. But though abandoned, it was not quite empty. Bertran knocked on the wicket gate and a grizzled head appeared.

'Friend or foe?' asked the keeper.

'Foe to the French,' said Bertran recklessly.

'Then friend to us,' said the man and opened the gate to the little party. When he saw Gui, nudging his horse through, he rushed up to cling on to his stirrup.

'Is it you, young master?' the old man asked. 'Lord le Viguier and your sister are here.'

It was true. No one knew what would happen in the spring, whether the French army would return to reclaim its prizes won so easily the summer before. But for now, in the unusually cold and wet winter in the Midi, the forsaken castles and hill towns could provide shelter and some meagre rations for the landless lords who had been ejected from their own keeps.

Lord Thibaut and Blandina were warming themselves by the one log fire in the deserted hall. They fell on Gui with joy when they saw him; they had thought him dead in the defence of this same bastide. Gui hadn't had the heart to send Sicart, the old *senescal*, back out into the wilderness to find his father. The messenger he had sent in his place had come back unable to find where Thibaut was. But the old man and his daughter had found their way to Sévignan after they had surrendered their own bastide.

Bertran left them to have their reunion in peace and wandered the keep looking for signs of the life that had once been his to share. All the tapestries and hangings had gone, looted by the French, and all the portable plate and furniture. The kitchen was cold and empty, though there were logs enough stacked in the hearth.

Bertran stood a moment to remember Hugo the cook, who had died so bravely.

Then he pulled his cloak tight about him and went up to the battlements. The walls were still intact, because of Lord Lanval's actions. Perhaps this castle would one day again be home to a member of the family? He longed for the war to be over and to bring Elinor here to her inheritance and restore her mother and sister to her. Perhaps even one day there might be a marriage for the *donzela*, maybe even to young le Viguier, and a good life rebuilt here, where the troubadour had spent so many happy hours before the war.

He shook himself; these were idle dreams. And it went against his religion to regret the loss of earthly possessions. It was all just matter. Even Big Hugo and Lord Trencavel had been made of the same gross stuff as himself and death had released their spirits from the dull heavy envelopes of their bodies. He should rejoice really, but Bertran was a man and a poet even though he was a Believer, and he could not bring himself to feel joy instead of sorrow as he stood in the cold empty castle of Sévignan.

As winter passed, Iseut and Elinor grew used to life in the Marchese's court. It was much bigger and grander than the homes they had been used to. It teemed with servants carrying logs to keep fires roaring in all the rooms and hanks of wool to stuff into any crack that might let the wind find its way through the thick stone walls. It was as warm as a mild spring day, as long as they stayed indoors.

And the more that life was confined to the castle, the more feasts and entertainments were put on to amuse the court. Food was plentiful if less varied than in summer and the women of Saint-Jacques began to recover some of the fullness of figure they had lost in their long flight to Monferrato. Without the possibility of walking or riding in the countryside they grew sleek and glossy as kitchen cats and fell into a kind of torpor.

Iseut had been right about suitors. Even in the cold months a stream of young and not so young Italian nobles visited Guglielmo, though Elinor couldn't tell if they had been summoned or if it was just the Marchese's custom to entertain widely in the winter.

She noticed one knight in particular, who seemed to be constantly, as if by accident, put in the way of Lady Iseut. He was called Alessandro da Selva, and was a vassal of the Marchese from one of the towns in the south-west of the Monferrato region. Alessandro was the older son of the Lord of Selva and would one day inherit a very substantial castle and fertile lands, the Marchesa told Iseut.

'Don't they make a handsome couple?' she said to Elinor one day when Iseut and Ser Alessandro had their heads bowed over a game of chess.

It was true: they looked very similar. The knight was about the same age and had the same fair hair and grey eyes as the Lady, though this made them look more like close brother and sister than a pair of courting lovers in Elinor's eyes. And she couldn't help noticing that Alessandro did not behave like a lover.

He had many conversations with Iseut, it was true. He was a cultured man, interested as much in poetry and music as in the knightly skills of hunting, jousting and warfare. But he didn't sigh or roll his eyes, never pressed his hand to his heart or recited poetry to Iseut. And Elinor couldn't help noticing that he often cast a look in her own direction.

Often when she thought she could watch his behaviour towards Iseut unobserved, Alessandro would look up, as if he felt her gaze on him and then she had to look away swiftly. It would not have been at all seemly for the young knight to think that she had any interest in him for herself.

It made Elinor smile. *I am turning into the kind of young woman my mother wanted me to be*, she thought, *if I can use words like 'seemly' even in my own head!*

And so the cold months wore on in Italy, in feasting and courtesy and warmth and with no fear of invasion or siege.

But in Montpellier, King Pedro had refused to accept Simon de Montfort's homage as his vassal.

'He may call himself Viscount of wherever he likes,' said Pedro. 'But Trencavel was my vassal and he was foully done to death. I won't be suzerain to that murderous French upstart.'

The Count of Toulouse, on the other hand, seemed prepared to do anything to win favour with the Pope and with the leader of the northern forces.

But a week or so later the bodies of two monks were found on the road outside Carcassonne. They were Cistercians, servants of Milo, the Papal Legate, and there were thirty-six stab wounds in their bodies. The fight back against the north had begun in earnest.

CHAPTER EIGHTEEN

Wearing the Green

The Abbot of Cîteaux was a disgruntled man. He had lost the leadership of the army and lost face in front of his men. True there was currently not much of an army to lead, but the Abbot felt about de Montfort as a man feels who has nurtured a wolf cub with scraps from his own table, only to be turned on and bitten in the leg.

Ever since Simon de Montfort had taken over Viscount Trencavel's titles, he seemed to have taken over as leader of the crusade and the Abbot had soon begun to regret elevating him to such a high position. In order to assert his own authority, the Abbot had declared many citizens of Toulouse to be heretics and demanded they and their property should be handed over to him personally.

But the Consuls of Toulouse resisted him. These men were not heretics, they claimed, and they wrote to the Pope, going over his Legate's head, asking him to intervene. And Innocent would not let his Legates enter Toulouse without a strong reason. It made the Abbot gnash his teeth with frustration. Toulouse was the prize he had kept his eye on all along and it seemed to be slipping out of his grasp.

And the wretched Count was the slipperiest of all his opponents, for all he was supposed to be on the French side now. The Pope was too trusting and the Abbot had written to him saying, 'If the Count of Toulouse, that enemy of peace and justice, should come before your Holiness, take care not to be deceived by his lying tongue.'

Three important towns – Avignon, Nîmes and Saint-Gilles – were ready to renounce their allegiance to the Count. But Raimon of Toulouse was wily as a fox and had destroyed some of his own frontier castles, just to keep a swathe of neutral territory between his lands and those of de Montfort, making sure that hostilities didn't break out between his followers and the French. He had gone back to King Philippe-Auguste himself and sent representatives to Rome. He was determined to beat the French at their own game.

Well, we shall see, thought the Abbot. He had heard it said in the south that 'A reconciled enemy never makes a good friend.' Between de Montfort and the Count of Toulouse, he felt thoroughly oppressed but he was not beaten yet. If the Count did not keep all the promises he had made during his humiliation at Saint-Gilles, he would have him hounded out of all his territories. And once Toulouse was his, the Abbot wouldn't care about de Montfort. Let him posture in his castle at Carcassonne; that was nothing but a child's toy fort compared with the rose-pink city of Toulouse.

Elinor and Iseut passed their first Christmas out of their own country, keeping vigil on Christmas Eve with all the court in the cathedral of Chivasso and celebrating Mass at dawn. Gifts were given and received, Iseut insisting on using some of their supply of money to make handsome presents to the Marchese and his wife, though the jewels and lengths of velvet and satin they got in return far surpassed what they could afford to give.

In January came the news that the Count of Toulouse's latest excommunication had been lifted.

'So there should be peace in the Midi,' said the Marchese. 'If the Pope has forgiven the Count of Toulouse then the very cause of the crusade has been removed.'

The two women began to dream that they might go back in the summer.

'But to what?' asked Iseut. 'My castle lies in ruins, my lands burned or pillaged. I would have no more there than here.'

'Perhaps Sévignan still stands?' said Elinor. 'You could come and live with me. That would be fair exchange for the months I spent at your court.'

But Elinor was doubtful of her own welcome, since she had run away. She did not know that she was now the *Senhor*.

'There will be time to decide,' said Iseut. 'Besides the Count of Toulouse has been excommunicated and restored to favour many times before. There is no guarantee this will be the last. We should do nothing hastily.'

Elinor agreed but she wondered if something more was preventing Iseut from planning to leave. The young Lord of Selva had spent all of the winter at Monferrato and he did seem to be Guglielmo's preferred candidate even if not Iseut's.

***

The leader of the resistance was Peire-Roger, Lord of Cabaret. He was no longer young and it made him reckless. He had the strongest castle in the region, three fortresses in one on a rocky ridge, surrounded on three sides by sheer cliffs. Simon de Montfort had tried to take it in the autumn and had to retire defeated.

Peire-Roger, who had fought bravely in the suburbs at Carcassonne before escaping with his knights, had spent the cold months launching raids on the French. By the spring the northerners had lost forty castles to the raiders, as well as the ones left empty by the nobles who had returned to their harvests in France. And Simon de Montfort had no more than five hundred men left to defend his eight remaining strongholds.

It really did seem as if the south was winning back much of what it had lost the summer before. The Lord of Termes and his raiding parties had played their part in taking back bastides, Sévignan included, though they had not needed to fight for that one. They had lost few men and were in constant contact with the garrison at Cabaret.

The men at Cabaret and Termes had the advantage of knowing the terrain, while the remaining French were defending unknown territory and were easily ambushed when they ventured away from the castles, even when the raiding party was outnumbered. And word had spread that the Abbot of Cîteaux and Simon de Montfort were no longer on good terms. 'It is a bad season when wolves eat each other,' said the people of the south.

Then in March everything changed again. And it was a woman who changed it.

Alice de Montfort brought reinforcements south to her husband, meeting him at Pézenas with a huge army. And more crusaders followed throughout the spring. After a hard winter, which had caused the rivers to overflow and made movement difficult, it had turned very warm and more and more northern knights came south to fight for their forty days and get what they could in return.

Simon's cruelty was given a huge boost by having so many new recruits; now he could take vengeance for the French losses of the winter. He put down rebellions brutally, hanging and burning with great zeal. But it was his actions at the fortified town of Bram that brought real fear into the rebel garrisons.

Bertran was with the Lord of Termes and Gui le Viguier when the news came. The messenger from Cabaret could hardly tell them what he had seen without retching; they had to feed him sips of spiced wine and let him speak at his own pace.

'We were at dinner with Lord Peire-Roger,' he said, 'when they came. A sentry had spotted them coming through the valley.'

'Who?' asked the Lord of Termes gently, because the man was shaking so much.

'About a hundred of them,' he said. 'From Bram. They came slowly, so slowly. It wasn't natural. We went up to the battlements to watch them approach. There was one man in the lead and they were all roped together. As they got nearer we saw that their faces were just masks of blood . . .'

He couldn't go on for several minutes.

'What had the bastards done?' demanded Gui, clenching his fists.

'Blinded them,' said the messenger. 'All save the leader, who had been left one eye to guide them to what the French call 'the rebels'. And, and, they'd all had their lips and noses cut off too.'

'Sweet Jesu!' said Lord Raimon, while the other two put their hands to their mouths as they felt their gorges rise.

'Who did this foul thing?' asked Bertran.

'De Montfort,' said the messenger bitterly. 'The worst of them all. He is so powerful with his new forces that he sees himself as a giant hammer and all the Midi his anvil.'

'And the poor wretches from Bram?' asked Raimon.

'Dying like flies,' said the messenger. 'Their wounds had festered and they can't take proper nourishment. The healers at Cabaret do what they can for them but I doubt any of them will survive into summer.'

'What kind of life would it be for them if they did?' said Gui. He had a young man's horror of disability, far greater than his fear of death. Even his own crooked arm was a badge of shame to him, though he had gained it valiantly.

Bertran was distracted. Now that French reinforcements had come he could not imagine that the garrisons in Termes and Minerve could hold out for long – perhaps even Cabaret would fall if there were big enough siege engines to hurl stones at it. He could not face the thought of Huguet and Peire being subjected to the cruelties of the wolf de Montfort, not after losing Perrin at Béziers.

'My lord,' he said. 'Could you spare me a small guard to take Huguet and the boy into safety? I'd like to see them as far east as possible. If they could get to Saint-Jacques, the ladies there would look after them.'

The Lord of Termes looked doubtful. 'They would be in danger from the French all along the way.'

'They are in danger if they stay here,' said Bertran. 'Would you have happen to them what happened to the men of Bram?'

The Lord winced. He had grown fond of the boy and the child.

'Let me go,' said Gui. 'I'll take them and come back. Bertran is a good man but he is a poet not a knight. I can see them safe to Saint-Jacques and come back before summer.'

And see Elinor, thought Bertran. An old pain invaded his mind, to be quickly suppressed.

The Lord was debating whether it was better to lose Bertran, his wise counsellor, or Gui one of his best knights. But he saw how desperate the situation was.

'Very well,' he said at last. 'Take four men, le Viguier, and turn back as soon as you have got them somewhere safe, Saint-Jacques or wherever. Rest one night only and return. Perhaps you will still find us alive if God wills it.'

If God is here, thought Bertran. He buried his disappointment about not seeing Elinor because he knew Gui would be the better guard for the two boys. Now all he had to do was to persuade them to go.

Alessandro da Selva was in a quandary. He had been invited to the castle of Monferrato specifically to court Lady Iseut of Saint-Jacques. And he did like her; she was like a sister or a kind woman friend to him. But it was her dark-eyed friend who really attracted him. And he dared not show her any attention lest he offend both Iseut and his liege lord.

In the end, he went to lay his problem before the Marchese.

Guglielmo was vastly amused.

'She has no dowry, you know,' he said. 'Only the dresses

she stands up in and those were given to her by her friend or my wife.'

'But that is not Elinor's fault,' said Alessandro. 'Did she not have to leave her home to escape the army?'

Neither woman had told the Marchese about Elinor's time as a *joglar* or the real reason she had left her home. They had talked about the persecution of the French, and Iseut's own escape had been so dramatic that it had been easy to gloss over the original reason for Elinor's being at Saint-Jacques.

'What about Iseut?' asked Guglielmo. 'Will she be disappointed if you seem to have transferred your affections?'

'I don't think so,' said Alessandro. 'I think she feels about me much as I do about her. We are friends and no more.'

'Would you like my wife to find out?' asked the Marchese.

Alessandro was happy to leave such a delicate task to a woman. And so it was Berta who came to Iseut for a private audience and it was quickly established that the one lady was indifferent and the other likely not to be averse to Alessandro's suit.

When Elinor heard about this conversation, she blushed to the roots of her hair.

'But I shall never be able to speak to him again!' she exclaimed. 'He really said that to the Marchese?'

'I don't think you have ever spoken more than two words to him or he to you,' said Iseut, smiling. 'And I think it's time you did. How else are you to know if you really like him?'

'And you really don't mind? You don't want to marry him a bit?'

'I really don't mind and I don't want to marry him even slightly,' said Iseut. 'If you want to encourage Alessandro, you have my blessing. And the Marchese's, according to the Marchesa.'

Elinor's mind was in a whirl. How could that heart which had for so long carried the image of Bertran the troubadour make room for a new love? She felt disloyal and wretched. But then in a moment she was excited at the prospect of seeing Alessandro again, looking into his grey eyes knowing that he had told the Marchese that he wanted to court her.

And if he did, would she accept him? What other future could there be? She had known for a long time that Bertran would never marry her or anyone else. If she did not accept someone, she was likely to spend the rest of her life at the court of Monferrato, dwindling into a dependent spinster – someone to teach the children and sit at the bottom of the table. And if she were to marry – well, Alessandro was certainly an intriguing proposition.

⊰⊱

The Bishop of Toulouse was Simon de Montfort's ally. And, what was more surprising, he had once been a troubadour. But, nearly fifteen years ago, Folquet had abandoned his wife and children and taken holy orders. When the Legates forced out the Bishop they considered to be too friendly to Count Raimon, Folquet, now a fanatical churchman, had been an obvious choice.

Being sympathetic to de Montfort's ambitions to take the city, he organised the good churchmen – by which he meant those who thought as he did – into a society called the White Brotherhood. They dressed up in white robes with crosses on the front and held meetings and processions to make themselves feel important.

Officially they had been formed to combat moneylending and charging interest, which made it easy for them to persecute the Jews. But there were Christian moneylenders too, who enjoyed the protection of the city's older rich families who had been forced out into the suburbs by the new up-and-coming men, who were all fanatics like the Bishop.

In their part of the city also lived the bleachers, cobblers, tanners and weavers, where the majority of the Believers came from. As soon as the aristocrats saw the White Brothers taking up arms against not only moneylenders but heretics, they formed their own Black Brotherhood. The two bands roamed the city armed with swords and banners, some on horseback, and there were frequent outbreaks of fighting in the narrow streets.

When the Abbot reached Toulouse, at the end of March, the city was in a state of civil war. And he was no nearer to getting rid of Count Raimon. But the troops that Alice de Montfort had brought her husband had restored the French army and all the castles that had been taken last summer and recaptured by the south over the winter were all gradually coming back into French hands. The tide was turning again and it was time to crush the resistance; Toulouse would just have to wait.

In Monferrato, spring came early. Alessandro spent more and more time with Elinor and she was getting over her embarrassment at knowing he liked her. Iseut watched them both with amused pleasure. Alessandro taught Elinor to play chess and she found to her delight that she was really good at it. At first she thought he was just letting her win, in order to gain favour with her, but then she saw a worried frown as he could not get his king out of the trap she had set.

He sat back, raising his hands and laughing.

'You have defeated me utterly, my lady,' he said. 'You should have been a general at the head of an army.'

'Maybe I should,' said Elinor lightly. Then she remembered Béziers and shuddered. Alessandro was instantly repentant.

'I'm so sorry,' he said. 'I forgot you have had experience of what an army can do to its victims.'

'Not really,' admitted Elinor. 'I left both Sévignan and Saint-Jacques before the French got to either bastide. But I know what they are capable of and they were close on our heels when Lady Iseut fired her castle.'

They sat in sombre mood until a servant came to tell Elinor that Guglielmo wanted to talk to her. She curtseyed to Alessandro and went to the Marchese's private room, her heart beating fast. What could he want with her? Surely it was too soon for Alessandro to have made a declaration and wouldn't he have made it first to her rather than the burly, bearded Marchese?

The very thought made her lips curve so that it was with a smile on her face that she entered the room.

And saw before anyone else Huguet the *joglar*.

She knew it was not 'seemly' but she rushed to clasp him in her arms as if he had been her dear brother.

'Huguet!' she exclaimed. 'I am so pleased to see you. But what has happened to you? You are so altered, so thin. Tell me everything. Where is Perrin and what news of Bertran?'

It was only then that she registered the other people in the room: the Marchese, a child she didn't recognise and – could it be? – her old dancing-partner, Gui le Viguier.

Alessandro was seriously put out. He had been so happy that afternoon, playing chess with Elinor, happy even when she beat him. He had been going to turn a pretty phrase about how she had captured his king as she had captured his heart. But somehow they had got on to the subject of war instead and the mood had gone wrong for courtship. Then Elinor had been summoned to the Marchese.

And now a strange knight, much younger than him and closer to Elinor's own age, was sitting beside her in the place Alessandro usually claimed for his own. True, neither of them was saying much but Elinor would not look in Alessandro's direction either and she was terribly pale, toying with her food. To Alessandro's jealous eye, this looked like lovesickness and he observed his rival with deepening dislike.

The stranger knight was good-looking, or at least Alessandro imagined he would be pleasing to a woman. He was broad-shouldered and slim-hipped and his brownish-blond hair was newly trimmed. True, he had an awkward right arm, but that just showed he was a valiant fighter as well as elegant courtier – all that a knight should be, in fact.

But if Alessandro could have seen into Gui's mind, he would have found a far from complacent courtier, let alone suitor. Gui was playing over again the scene when Elinor had come into the room, smiling and lovely in a green gown. How lovingly she had embraced poor troubled Huguet and how her first words had been of Bertran! He was jealous, quite as jealous as Alessandro because he now saw how beautiful and womanly Elinor had become and because he believed her affections to be given elsewhere.

It didn't matter that he was incorrect about the state of her heart; he had understood rightly that she was not for him and he felt overwhelmingly sad about it.

And then he had been forced to tell her that both her father and brother were dead and how it had happened; she would not let him spare her any details. And of the death of Perrin at Béziers, which had affected her almost as badly. Gui kept from her only the story of the mutilated victims from Bram. The little party had left Termes immediately, as soon as Bertran had been able to persuade the boys that it was no longer safe for them to stay and that he was sending them to Elinor.

Only the magic of her name had been enough to make Huguet leave Bertran's side and where Huguet went, there the child Peire would follow. But when they had arrived at Saint-Jacques and found the ruins and ashes that were all that was left of Iseut's castle, it had been hard for them all not to fall into despair.

But as they came down from the mountains, a shepherd told them what had happened. About the Lady's giving away all her belongings and riding to Monferrato with 'the other lady, the dark one' and hope had risen again. The land around Saint-Jacques was all burned, the vines uprooted and the crops destroyed by the petulant Frenchmen who had hoped to get rich spoils from the castle. The shepherd's flock had had very little to feed on over the winter but the grass was beginning to grow back in the lower fields.

So Gui and his little band had taken the road to Monferrato, as Elinor and Iseut had the autumn before. And now he would stay only one night before returning to Termes; his new lord and the others would be wondering what had happened to him. Gui wondered that too. He feared that he would be leaving the better part of himself behind in Italy.

CHAPTER NINETEEN

Love Tokens

Everything changed for Elinor with Huguet's arrival. Up until then, she had been able to feel that – apart from some anxious hours before they left Saint-Jacques and the shock of seeing Iseut fire her own castle – the war in the south had not really touched her.

But seeing Huguet so diminished from the merry boy she had known when they were *joglars* together and hearing Gui's news had stripped all comfort away. Her father was dead, had died horribly, and Aimeric had died too, defending their home. She felt a wretched traitor for deserting them just because she hadn't wanted her parents' choice of husband.

'And now I will never be able to tell him how sorry I am,' she sobbed to Iseut the night that the party from Termes had arrived and the two women were alone in their chamber.

Iseut held her friend and let her cry as much as she needed to.

At last, exhausted, Elinor sat up and brushed the hair from her face.

'My mother and sister are out there somewhere,' she said. 'I must do what I can to find them. At least I could say sorry to Maire. And maybe they too could settle here in Monferrato?'

'The Marchese is generosity itself,' said Iseut, glad that her friend's thoughts had at last turned to practical matters. 'I'm sure he would not mind two more mouths to feed. Look how he offered to take in the two boys – and they are not even fellow nobles.'

'But how can I find them?'

'Why don't you ask the young knight from Sévignan?'

And so, next morning, before he left to return to Termes as promised, Elinor asked to see Gui le Viguier.

At first he was thrilled but he soon realised that what she wanted from him was no declaration of love.

'I don't know where they went, my lady,' he said. 'But I shall ask for news everywhere we stop on the way back and I promise I will deliver your message if I possibly can.'

He paused then added, 'Do you have any messages for anyone else?'

What can I say to Bertran? thought Elinor. When she considered how her feelings for him had been changed not by anything he had done or failed to do but by the mere existence of Alessandro da Selva, she could sense the embarrassment showing on her face.

'Please tell Bertran de Miramont that I thank him for entrusting Huguet to my care, and the little boy. Tell him I shall look after them. And tell him that I am at the Marchese's court here in Monferrato and am well.'

'That is all, lady?' asked Gui.

'That is all,' said Elinor. 'And thank you, also, Gui, for all the news you have brought me. Though it was unwelcome, it was better for me to know.'

She was pale, with dark bruises under her eyes. Gui thought she had probably been awake all night. He found her painfully beautiful.

'May I take no token from you, lady?' he asked.

Elinor thought at first he meant for Bertran. Then she saw the way he was looking at her.

'I might not survive the summer,' said Gui. 'The French have reinforcements and have recaptured all the castles we took from them in the winter. They . . . they do not treat prisoners kindly. It would mean a lot to me to have something from you to carry next to my heart.'

Elinor was dismayed. She was inexperienced in these matters; if she gave him something would that mean he was her accepted lover? But then she felt reckless. Gui was going back into danger and he probably would die soon. She would never see him again. So what harm would there be in giving him a token?

But not Bertran's brooch. That was still precious to her in memory of her old love. She took from her waistband a silk handkerchief edged with lace that the Marchese had given her at Christmas, and proffered it to the knight.

To her alarm, he kissed it and would have kissed her too, she was sure of it, but then Guglielmo came in and Gui was ushered away to horse, for the journey.

Later she watched from the battlements as he rode out with his small guard party. And from a high window Alessandro watched her.

'What shall we do, Maire?' asked Alys. 'It is well into spring now and I'm sure the Viscount wants us out of Narbonne.'

Lady Clara was undecided. Her daughter had never seen her like this. She had spent the whole winter drowsing like a hedgehog and was too lethargic to deploy her usual spikes.

'We must get away,' insisted Alys. 'Everyone says the soldiers are coming back. The woman we must call Viscountess de Montfort brought thousands of men to her husband at Montpellier – you must have seen how many French there are now in the streets of Narbonne.'

'What does it matter, whether we go or stay?' said her mother. 'We'll be just as dead here as anywhere else.'

Alys could not bear this fatalistic streak that had invaded her mother. Clara and Elinor had always been the strong, decisive ones, while the younger sister had been docile and ready to go along with whatever was suggested. Now it seemed once again their roles were to be reversed and she must make the plans.

'Well, I think it would be safer if we made our way east, Maire,' she said.

'And why do you think that?' asked Lady Clara.

'Because that is what Bertran advised Perrin and Huguet to do,' said Alys. 'And that is where the *joglars* took Elinor.'

It surely didn't matter what she said now, not now that Aimeric and her father were dead and Sévignan taken.

'Elinor?' said her mother. It was as if Alys had slapped her smartly across the face and woken her from a deep dream. 'What do you know about Elinor?'

'She dressed as a boy,' said Alys, her words tumbling out. 'I cut her hair and Huguet gave her some boys' clothes. She took Mackerel.'

'She took the pony,' said Clara. 'I knew that. But I didn't know you had helped her.'

If this had been the old days, back at the castle, how the mother would have raged against the disobedient child! But now the two of them just gazed at each other in silence. The news about her older daughter had at last roused Clara to some energy. Her husband, son and home were lost, but she saw that there was still something she could regain from her old life.

'Where did they go?' she demanded, gripping Alys's arm. 'Tell me again. Tell me everything.'

Alys did not know much but she embroidered her tale enough to convince her mother that they must set off immediately. The Viscount of Narbonne was indeed quite willing to let them go; to be sheltering even the wife and daughter of an admitted heretic was far too dangerous to want to prolong the risk.

He wrote them a safe conduct, which he knew was probably useless, but hoped that two women and a manservant would not be tempting enough prey for the French. And then, as soon as they were gone, he forgot about them.

This time they avoided Béziers; they had no wish to look again on its ruins. They travelled slowly towards Montpellier, stopping in every town and village to ask if anyone knew where Lucatz and his troupe had gone. But no one could tell them anything.

So they continued east, taking cover whenever they saw groups of French soldiers or smelled burning pyres.

Huguet and Peire settled in Monferrato and seemed never to want to leave Elinor's side. The *joglar* gave up his care of the boy to the women of the court with a sigh that was part sadness and part relief. The child needed mothering and was soon blossoming under all the petting and spoiling from Elinor, Iseut, the Marchesa and the other ladies at court. He had made a special pet of Iseut's little dog, Minou, and the two were inseparable.

Huguet himself sat quietly in the corner of whatever room Elinor was in, playing soft tunes on his flute or fiddle. Sometimes he joined in with the Marchese's *joglars* and sang poems written by the court's resident troubadour. But mostly he composed *planhs* of his own, their haunting, melancholy sounds floating round the thick stone walls of the court like morning mist.

His presence put a new constraint on Elinor's meetings with Alessandro. The Italian knight's expression told her that something was wrong, that something had changed between them since the little band had arrived from Termes but she didn't know what it was. Alessandro was not jealous of a boy *joglar*, but he was intensely jealous of Elinor's life before he had met her. And he suspected the handsome knight with the crooked arm had played too important a part in it.

One day in late April, he came to see her, wearing full armour.

'Oh is there a tourney?' asked Elinor innocently.

'No, my lady,' said Alessandro stiffly. 'My armour is not just for sport and games. We are going to war.'

Huguet gave a small moan and his expression was much like Elinor's own.

'Do not frighten the boy,' she said. 'What do you mean? Who attacks Monferrato?'

'No one,' said Alessandro. 'But the Marchese means to show the rebels at Cuneo who is their master and I am to ride with him.'

'Cuneo?' said Elinor stupidly. She remembered the wedge-shaped town where she and Iseut had stopped to rest last summer and eaten rabbit stew. It seemed a lifetime ago. She had no idea what Alessandro meant by 'the rebels'. The only ones she knew of were the brave men of Termes, Minerve and Cabaret. And towards those she felt kindly; Bertran was one of them and he had sent her the boys to heal.

'It will be a real battle,' said Alessandro, sounding like a boy himself. 'Will you not give me a token, as you did to the knight from Termes?'

So that is the trouble, thought Elinor. *He thinks I favour poor Gui.*

But it was too late to undo such a misunderstanding when he stood before her just waiting to put on his helmet and ride out to fight. And just like Gui, he might not survive what was to come.

Still, she gave him a green silk girdle from round her waist and he wound it tightly round his sword arm, never taking his eyes from her face.

'Goodbye, Lady Elinor,' he said.

'Goodbye, Ser Alessandro. Fight well and please come home.'

She hadn't added 'to me' but he hoped that was what she meant.

The Marchesa was a bit better informed than the women from Saint-Jacques.

'You know my husband supports Otto's claim to be Emperor?' she said when the army had left. 'Well, he is going to meet him at Cuneo with the Marchese of Saluzzo and they will crush the rebels.'

'What rebels?' asked Iseut, who was as ignorant of Italian and German politics as Elinor was.

'Why, those who have set up a commune there,' said the Marchesa. 'Don't you know they refuse to recognise any feudal lord? They pay no dues to Monferrato or Saluzzo and such revolutionary ideas must be subdued.'

Elinor wasn't so sure. When she was growing up in Sévignan, she had accepted that her father had vassals and was himself vassal to Viscount Trencavel and ultimately King Pedro of Aragon. But now Trencavel was dead and his titles given to a Frenchman as casually as if they had been old pairs of shoes. And King Pedro had become a real person to her since she had met his abandoned wife and tiny son in Montpellier.

Perhaps the 'revolutionaries' of Cuneo were just being realistic and accepting that the old systems must change. But the Marchesa was clearly certain that her husband should take arms against this unconventional town.

And so was Alessandro, thought Elinor. Perhaps he will die in what he thinks is a just cause, wearing my token, and he will never know how I felt about him.

Simon de Montfort was riding high again. His wife's arrival with reinforcements in the spring had acted like a tonic on his spirits. And winning back so many castles had restored him to optimism. These heretics might take a long time to crush but, if the Pope approved fresh forces every spring, then he could do it. He no longer bothered to confer with the Abbot of Cîteaux, who had started out as leader of the crusade.

But he thought it was time to turn his attention to the three rebel castles of Minerve, Termes and Cabaret, and he began with Minerve. It was defended by steep gorges on three sides and de Montfort brought his biggest siege engines to bear on the walls. He had a new one, called *La Malvoisine*, 'the bad neighbour'.

When the defenders saw the huge trebuchet being trundled into place, their hearts sank. It was aimed at their main water supply and there were three others positioned to rain boulders on the village. The bombardment went on for six weeks.

'There's only one thing to do,' said the Viscount of Minerve at last. 'We must launch a sortie, catch them by surprise and destroy that bad neighbour of theirs.'

There were only two hundred men in the garrison and it was a small party that set out by night, creeping round the north of the village on the far side of the ravine. They had brought bales of straw and wodges of animal fat with them which they packed round the giant machine and quickly set fire to.

The bad neighbour had just begun to catch when an unfortunate soldier came out of his tent to relieve himself. He was quickly silenced with a lance but his initial cry of horror on seeing the flames licking round the trebuchet brought the rest of the French besiegers down on the party and they fled back to the walls.

Their one chance of surviving the siege had gone up in smoke, unlike the mighty *Malvoisine*. Their water supply had been cut off and the citadel shattered; the Viscount saw nothing for it but to negotiate a surrender. He had heard of the horrors at Bram earlier in the year; messengers had come from Termes where the last of the mutilated men were dying, so he was not feeling brave or hopeful when he entered de Montfort's tent.

It was a tricky problem for the French leader too. If he let the entire garrison go, it would hardly be an example to the other rebel bastides at Cabaret and Termes. But conventions of war demanded that a free surrender should be accepted and the inhabitants of the besieged city spared.

And then de Montfort had a piece of luck: the Abbot arrived. With relief, he handed the problem over to him. But the Papal Legate, who had not been at all squeamish at Béziers, where the city had resisted the army, balked at killing men who had raised a white flag of surrender.

Still, he had a trump card to play.

'We will spare all the heretics who agree to convert,' he said.

There was some muttering among the crusaders about this because they thought the heretics would just pretend to give up their barbarous beliefs. But the Frenchmen still knew nothing about the Perfects, men and women, of the south. The Legates went through the ruined streets of the citadel knocking on doors and calling on heretics to repent and save themselves from the fire.

The clergy led the army, singing the '*Te Deum*' and carrying a huge gold cross. But the Perfects of Minerve took no more notice of it than they had of *La Malvoisine*; their time had come.

'One hundred and forty of them, men and women,' said the Viscount's messenger, who had taken the news to Termes. 'Only three went over to the Roman Church. The rest were burned. Some of them leapt joyfully into the flames and none resisted.'

'We'll be next,' said the Lord of Termes grimly. 'Now that they have destroyed one rebel stronghold, the French will not stop there.'

And Bertran was glad that he had sent Huguet and the boy away. But Gui had not yet returned and he wondered if the knight had found Elinor.

At Montpellier, Clara and Alys had a rare piece of luck: they found Lucatz. The Lady Maria, still clinging on to her title and her little son, had made them welcome and when they asked about the troupe that had left Sévignan more than two years earlier, she remembered the boy who had sung the lay of Tristan and Iseut.

'Their troubadour is here again now,' she said. 'But with different *joglars*. I'll command him to have them play in your honour tonight.'

Alys was overcome with joy but her mother was nervous. It was the first time she had met a dependant of her old court since she had ridden away from its occupied walls and the winter had sapped her of her spirit.

But she need not have worried. Lucatz was delighted to see his old *domna* and her daughter, though soon sad again when they told him what had happened in their bastide.

He ordered his new youngest *joglar* to sing a *planh* for Sévignan, its lord and the heir to its title and lands.

After dinner, he was invited to come and sit with the ladies and Maria enquired after the *joglar* who had sung for her at little Jacques' baptism celebrations.

'Young Esteve?' said Lucatz. 'There was always a bit of a mystery about him. We came across him shortly after we left Sévignan, saying he had lost his troubadour. But I ran into Ademar last summer and he'd never heard of him.'

'Where did you last see him?' asked Lady Clara, unable to believe there might at last be news of Elinor. 'He, he took a pony from our stables,' she added, to explain her interest.

'I knew that dapple grey looked familiar!' said Lucatz. 'I left the boy at Saint-Jacques. The Lady Iseut there was very taken with him and asked him to stay and learn the poems she and her friend were writing. He seemed a good lad – I can't believe he was a common horse-thief.'

'What about Perrin and Huguet?' asked Alys. 'I see you have all new *joglars*.'

'Ah, they left me when I went into Italy,' said Lucatz. 'They headed back west and I don't know what happened to them.'

'Why did you not stay in Italy yourself?' asked Clara. 'You have heard what has been happening. We at Sévignan were not the only ones to lose everything.'

Lucatz bowed. 'I know, my lady. There is material in the south for a whole boxful of laments. But I had to see for myself. And now that I have, I think I shall return east. It is becoming harder and harder for a troubadour to remain in his native land – especially,' he lowered his voice, 'when some people think all of us are heretics.'

While the troubadour was talking to the nobles, one of his *joglaresas* was eavesdropping. She was a dark, strong-faced woman who was familiar to both Alys and Clara from the days in their old home, though they had not seen her for over two years. She gave a secret signal to Alys, who soon made an excuse to leave the table and met her in the corridor outside.

'You are looking for news of your sister, are you not?' said Pelegrina.

'Of course!' said Alys. 'You knew of her disguise! Tell me how she was when you last saw her.'

'She turned back into a woman,' said Pelegrina. 'The Lady Iseut's friend saw through her disguise and she stayed on with them in Saint-Jacques.'

'So we should ask for her as Elinor again when we travel east?'

Pelegrina shifted uncomfortably. 'Lucatz doesn't know, but we heard the French had set fire to Saint-Jacques.'

Alys clutched her throat. 'Not Elinor too,' she whispered.

'Don't despair, lady,' said the *joglaresa*. 'I remember when we were at the Lady Iseut's court that she was advised to travel east if troubles came. If you find Saint-Jacques in ruins, my advice is to seek the Marchese of Monferrato.'

CHAPTER TWENTY

The Lodestone

'I can't believe it!' exclaimed the Lord of Cabaret when the message reached him.

Simon de Montfort, after his victory at Minerve, had left his mighty siege engines outside Carcassonne. They were packed into ox-carts, ready to roll on to his next target. It was too good a chance for the rebels to pass up. The giant catapults stood, with a small detachment of guards, like a child's abandoned toys, not put away at night by the nurse-maid.

In the darkest part of the night, the raiding party from Cabaret fell upon the siege train that was slowly trundling the trebuchets towards Termes. Peire-Roger himself led the attack before the machines were out of sight of the walls of Carcassonne. And the rebels were spotted; soldiers ran out of the garrison and chased them away.

But the Cabaret rebels were like hyenas, which run away when the lion approaches but return to the carcass as soon as the more powerful beast sleeps. At dawn, they attacked the train again and set fire to the machines. And they almost got away with it. But the crusaders came to the defence of the siege train again and soon they had pressed Peire-Roger and his men back to the river.

Casualties were heavy and the water ran red.

'How did you escape?' asked Peire-Roger's men when he made his way back to Cabaret with only a handful of wounded rebels. Their lord was soaking wet and in a very bad mood, stinging from dozens of small wounds, but his face split into a big smile at the question.

'I rode through the city and out the other side, shouting "Montfort, Montfort!"' he said. 'And they thought I was a Frenchman!'

Peire-Roger had not succeeded in capturing de Montfort's siege engines but he had held them up and when the crusade's leader arrived with most of his army at his next target, Termes, they were not there. He reached the heavily-fortified city in mid-August.

The massive castle stood on a sheer rock above the village and had a reputation for being impregnable. It was certainly a daunting sight to the Frenchmen.

The Lord of Termes had made good use of the time bought for him by the Cabaret rebels' raids. The castle was well stocked and had taken in many mercenaries to give extra manpower to the rebels. Now they looked down from the walls at the crusaders, as overwhelmed by the size of the army as the Frenchmen were by their castle.

'So, it has come at last,' said the Lord to his band of close advisors. 'I'm glad you were back in time to join us for it, Gui.' He clapped the young knight on the shoulder.

'So am I,' said le Viguier grimly. He had no intention of being taken prisoner.

Bertran saw him touch for the hundredth time the lady's handkerchief he wore in his jerkin. The troubadour was sure it was Elinor's but, although the knight had given them a full account of the long journey to Saint-Jacques and beyond to

Monferrato, where he had safely left the boys, of the lady of Sévignan he had said only that he saw her and told her of the fate of her home and family.

Bertran had almost as much of a death wish as the young knight. He was now fully-armed and prepared to defend Termes, the castle that had given him shelter, and its lord, who shared his religion. He had given up the pretence of being Jules; it didn't matter now who knew him as the troubadour-spy. He hadn't done anything wrong.

From the very beginning, two and a half years ago, he had tried to put things right, riding hard after Pierre of Castelnau's assassin, and then warning all the lords of the south about the coming storm. But now, besieged in Lord Raimon of Termes' castle, he was just another fighting man and not a very experienced one at that.

He hoped to die honourably and closed his mind to the atrocities the French had done to the men of Bram and in many other places. But he had to think what he would do if Termes were forced to surrender and de Montfort offered the same terms to the Perfects and Believers that had been given to them at Minerve. There were only a few Perfects within the keep at Termes and none of the ordinary Believers at Minerve had chosen the bonfires. But Bertran felt that if he were prepared to die on the battlements for the right to prac- tise his own religion, he should logically be ready to perish in the flames rather than give it up in order to gain mercy.

In Chivasso, the Marchese and his army were still away and Elinor found the time lay heavily on her hands. She tried to compose but had no encouragement from Iseut, who also seemed weary of poetry. The weather was oppressively hot and the whole court seemed to be holding its breath, as if waiting for something momentous to happen.

Peire was thriving. The days when his eyes clouded over and he seemed to be remembering his earlier life grew fewer and fewer. He had attached himself to Iseut and for that Elinor was glad. Her friend needed someone to love, she decided – she who had lost husband, child, friends and home – and the boy needed someone to love him.

He was about the age that the baby Iseut had lost would have been if he had survived and he was a comfort to her. She never thought about him as a farmer's son, a peasant – only as a lost child who needed mothering.

And if Peire was like a son to Iseut, Huguet was a brother to Elinor. Not one like Aimeric, so much older and stronger, but someone who had been a friend and companion and suffered such terrible griefs that the two of them did not need to talk; it was enough to sit quietly together and remember.

Sometimes they played music or Huguet taught her his new *planh*s and Elinor taught him the one she had written for Iseut's words. It seemed as if all her thoughts were turned towards sadness and loss now. She felt like an old woman who had been deprived of all her family but she was still only sixteen.

The Marchesa was friendly to her but busy fussing over her newborn daughter, Beatrix, her first after three boys.

'You will see, Elinor,' she said comfortably. 'When you are married. It is good to have boys first – it will make your husband happy. But a girl is a present for the wife, a child you can always treasure.'

But Elinor did not think she would ever have a husband now; she was getting a bit old to marry and she had no dowry. And she did not know if Alessandro of Selva would return from the war or whether, if he did, he would still like her.

Nor did she think her mother had ever regarded her as a treasure! Alys maybe, but not difficult, disobedient, awkward Elinor. She wished now that she had been a better daughter.

Then, one day in high summer, the Marchesa sent to say that the ladies of Saint-Jacques had a visitor. Neither of them could imagine who it could possibly be.

'Someone with news of my mother, perhaps?' said Elinor.

But it was a man who waited for them in the Marchesa's receiving room and a familiar figure. Iseut cried out and moved towards him.

'Lord Berenger!' she exclaimed. 'How wonderful to see you! We thought you had perished at Digne.'

Her eyes sparkled with an energy Elinor hadn't seen in her for months.

Berenger came forward and kissed both their hands. He looked long and hard at Elinor.

'I am so glad to find you both safe,' he said. 'When I saw what was left of Saint-Jacques, I thought the worst. It has taken me all this time to find you.'

He was touched by the warmth of Iseut's welcome. His eyes kept shifting between the two women and, suddenly, Elinor saw with great clarity what had happened. A bubble of laughter floated up inside her and spilled out; there was nothing she could do to stop it. She held her hands to her mouth but the laugh and the words came out together.

'You spoke to Garsenda, didn't you?'

Berenger looked embarrassed.

'What is it, Elinor?' asked the Marchesa, who dearly loved a joke.

'It is a silly thing,' said Elinor, striving to straighten her face and anxious to preserve Berenger's dignity. She too had been impressed by how happy Iseut was to see him. 'It is just that a meddlesome maid of Lady Iseut's thought that I . . . that she . . . that I might be a young man in disguise!'

Now the whole court laughed and Elinor realised how very much she had changed since she could pass herself off as a boy.

Berenger was unsure whether to join in. But here was Iseut, whom he had loved for so many years, smiling lovingly back at him and looking even more beautiful than he remembered. And there was her 'secret lover', so obviously female.

'What would Ser Alessandro have to say if you were?' said the Marchesa, wiping tears of laughter from her eyes.

And that made Elinor feel good too, to know that the heir of Selva was acknowledged to be her suitor still.

So it was a merrier party at dinner than had gathered at Monferrato for some time.

Berenger told them his story. It was true that the French had besieged his castle at Digne and had caused some damage. But his garrison had fought back bravely. Although he had been forced to flee, he had gained time enough to gather money and valuables and set off through mountain paths the crusaders could not follow. He had doubled back alone to Saint-Jacques and seen the ruins smoking from a distance.

'And then I thought that you had fared worse than me, lady,' he said to Iseut.

'I did it myself,' said Iseut quietly. 'I couldn't bear to see it in French hands.'

Reinforcements were slow in joining de Montfort's encampment at Termes. Large though his army was, it wasn't big enough to surround the walls and some of the soldiers were beginning to drift back to their harvests, their forty days' service completed.

And when small groups travelled to join the French force they were often set upon by Cabaret raiders and sent on to Termes horribly mutilated and unfit to fight.

Bertran sometimes saw these disfigured Frenchmen from the walls and despaired. It was bad enough to be standing on the edge of the abyss, wondering merely what type of death he and the garrison would shortly meet. But to see that their fellow rebels had been so corrupted by French cruelty that they resorted to the same atrocities made him sadder than anything that had happened in the last two years.

The fate of the men of Bram, which had made him send Huguet and the boy away, had produced a terrible effect on the garrison at Cabaret and in other places; they no longer regarded the French as human like themselves. It could be felt even in the castle at Termes, where the men jeered at the soldiers beneath their walls and launched raiding parties to capture their banners. Bertran was sure that if any Frenchman were to be caught by the garrison, he would be tortured just as badly as the men of Bram.

And Bertran was worried about the Lord of Termes too. He seemed distracted, often forgetting what he was saying in the middle of a sentence. Several times he asked for Peire, forgetting that the boy was no longer at Termes.

The siege stretched out interminably through the summer and, at the very end of August, fresh troops came to join the Frenchmen. At last the trebuchets began to have an effect on the walls of the castle. But the defenders had some siege engines too and they knew what Simon de Montfort looked like.

Twice he was nearly killed: the first time a bolt from a ballista pierced the leader's tent while Mass was being celebrated. The soldier standing behind de Montfort was killed. Then a boulder from a mangonel on the castle walls crushed one of the sappers as de Montfort was talking to him. He had even had his arm round the poor wretch's shoulder before he was struck.

'Third time lucky! Third time lucky!' chanted the defenders and even the French saw these narrow escapes as a bad omen. De Montfort was so worried that he stopped eating.

But inside the castle at Termes morale was no higher. The water supply was running out. And his mercenaries were pressing the Lord to surrender; they knew they would receive no clemency from the French unless the castle was yielded up.

And in the end, by October, the lack of water was so acute that Raimon did suggest terms on which he would surrender. He would give up the castle for the winter but keep his lands and even take the castle back in the spring.

'They'll never agree to that,' said Gui.

But de Montfort was so desperate that they did and a day was arranged to let the French enter the keep.

The night before, torrential rain began to fall and all the

wells and cisterns inside Termes were filled back up to the brim. The defenders ran out in the rain laughing and letting the water trickle into their throats. When the French Marshal arrived, plodging through the mud, Raimon de Termes refused to hand the castle over.

'Go back!' de Montfort ordered the unfortunate soaking man. 'Take any terms you can get, as long as I have this castle for the winter!'

Two of the senior defenders of Termes felt they shouldn't renege on the terms that had been agreed, just because the rains had come; one of them was Bertran. The others refused and the siege went on.

'You see?' said the Lord of Termes. 'God sent the rain – he is on our side.'

Bertran feared more and more for Raimon's reason.

Large sections of de Montfort's army had disappeared back north. But the blessed rain which had filled the castle tanks was to prove the defenders' downfall. The cooks used it to make dough for bread but the rainwater had mingled with the stagnant mess left in the bottom of the tanks by the dry summer and was full of disease.

Soon dysentery was spreading through the castle and the rebels became desperate to leave. Banking on their superior knowledge of the area, they organised their secret departure from the castle and had nearly all escaped when a French guard raised the alarm.

Bertran was with Lord Raimon, doing his best to see him safe out of the castle and on the way to Cabaret. But Raimon was now delirious and insisted on going back into the castle for something.

'What, my lord?' asked Gui le Viguier, who was also part

of the bodyguard. 'We have no time to go back. We must escape.'

'The boy, the boy,' said Raimon. 'I need his little sword.'

He pulled himself out of their grasp and ran back towards the keep. Immediately he was captured by the French.

'Run!' said Gui. 'Save yourselves! There is nothing more we can do for Lord Raimon.'

When the Marchese of Monferrato came back from his wars, Alessandro was not with him. Elinor's heart sank when she saw no sign of him among the returning knights.

But at supper that evening, the Marchesa reassured her. 'Sandro is well,' she said. 'But his father has died and he had to go back to his castle – he is the Lord of Selva now.'

Guglielmo took a great liking to Lord Berenger and promptly gave him a castle he had taken from the rebels who had been beaten at Cuneo.

As the women settled in for their second winter under the protection of Monferrato, Elinor sensed a change in Iseut. She, Berenger and Peire seemed to have created a new family. Elinor asked her about it one day in November on a rare occasion when she found Iseut on her own.

'I was homesick, Elinor,' said Iseut. 'And I didn't know it. Berenger reminds me of Saint-Jacques. Even you had only a short history with me there but he knew me before I was married, knew my husband Jaufre, even came to my wedding. Ever since he came here, I feel in touch again with my past.'

'It seems to me you are thinking of the future,' said Elinor. She wanted so much to be happy for her friend but all she could feel was a terrible loneliness. Iseut would marry Berenger, she could see that, and would take Peire and go and live with him in his new Piedmontese castle, and Elinor would be alone at Chivasso.

Well, if it was to be, she would still have Huguet and their music.

'It is true,' said Iseut. 'Berenger has asked again to marry me and I have said yes. But I also said I would not leave Monferrato without you and the young *joglar*.'

Elinor was speechless.

'Come with us in the spring,' said Iseut, taking her hands. 'We can try to make a new home, combining all that we remember best of Saint-Jacques, Sévignan, Digne – yes and Monferrato too. It will be a castle filled with music and poetry and perhaps one day, more children for Peire to play with.'

It was not long after this conversation that they heard of the fall of Termes and imprisonment of Lord Raimon. But there was still no news of Bertran or Gui le Viguier.

Instead news came that threw the Marchese into confusion.

'The Pope has excommunicated Otto!' exclaimed the Marchesa. 'And now he supports Fredrik as German Emperor. Poor Guglielmo doesn't know what to do. He is wondering whether to change sides himself.'

And in the midst of this upheaval, Lady Clara and Alys arrived at the court.

Elinor could not believe her eyes; she flung her arms round her sister and then abased herself at her mother's feet.

'I'm so sorry, Maire,' she sobbed. 'I should never have disobeyed you. And now Paire and Aimeric are both dead and we have all lost our home.'

'But not because of you or anything you did,' said Clara, lifting her daughter up and embracing her with more warmth than she ever had in the past. 'Still, I am glad that you have heard that news already.'

'And you all have a home with us as long as you need one,' said the Marchesa warmly. 'I told you Elinor, didn't I? A daughter is a treasure to her mother and now yours has two.'

'Two more for our new castle,' whispered Iseut, before being introduced to the Lady of Sévignan.

'The Lady of Sévignan is not me but my daughter,' said Clara, holding tight to Elinor's hand. 'I should like to announce here before the court that my Lord Lanval made her his heir after our son Aimeric. And though her inheritance is now in the hands of the French, the bastide and lands of Sévignan belong by right to Elinor. I hope one day she may retrieve them.'

'Until then, as my wife says,' said the Marchese, 'you are both welcome at my court, wherever I keep it, and in any of my castles.'

He looked round with satisfaction at his dependants. 'Everyone comes to Monferrato,' he said.

'Everyone comes to Monferrato,' echoed Elinor. 'It is true. First Iseut and I, then Huguet. Did you know Huguet the *joglar* was here, Maire? Then Lord Berenger. Even Gui has been here. It was he who told us what had happened at Sévignan. Monferrato is like a lodestone, drawing everyone to it.'

Everyone but Alessandro, she thought. *Monferrato has released its hold on him.*

CHAPTER TWENTY-ONE

Lady of Selva

King Pedro of Aragon could not hold out any longer against accepting de Montfort's homage. Not only was the Frenchman carrying the titles that had belonged to Viscount Trencavel, he was now the master of Minerve and Termes. During the long siege of Termes, where fortune had wavered from one side to the other so often, the eyes of the south had been on the fortress and its fate.

And then had come the sudden victory. The old Lord of Termes was now incarcerated in the dungeon at Carcassonne and his forces scattered. Only Cabaret remained of the three once impregnable rebel fortresses.

In late January, King Pedro was on his way to Montpellier, when he was waylaid at Narbonne by a serious deputation. The Count of Toulouse was there, along with the Abbot of Cîteaux and Simon de Montfort. The Abbot begged the King to accept de Montfort's homage.

Pedro didn't like it; it would mean he had accepted the French overrunning his territories in the south. But reluctantly he agreed and let de Montfort kneel to him. Then he decided to go even further than this and spurred to Montpellier and his wife in haste.

The Lady Maria was astonished by her *senescal* bursting in

to tell her that her husband was in the bailey with a hundred knights. In moments he was in her room.

'Madam,' he said, bowing low.

But Maria was used to his grand courtesies.

'What do you want?' she asked.

'My son,' he said.

Maria felt winter enter her blood.

'What for?' she demanded, instinctively shielding little Jacques with her body. But the boy, who was not yet three years old, was fascinated by the big man in armour, with the gold circlet round his head. And now this grand figure was bending down and holding out his arms to him; he was irresistible.

'Come here, Jaime,' said his father, using the boy's Spanish name. Maria watched like one drugged as her son willingly put himself in his father's embrace. His chubby hands reached for the crown and Pedro, laughing, let him take it.

'Do you suppose I mean him any harm?' he asked, turning to Maria. 'He is my son and heir. I merely want to give him, briefly, into the care of his future father-in-law, Simon de Montfort.'

This was not news to reassure a mother.

'De Montfort?' cried Maria. 'The French wolf?' She reached for the child but the King swung him up into his arms.

'I am going to pledge him in marriage to de Montfort's infant daughter,' said Pedro. 'I have accepted his homage and it will strengthen my alliance with France.'

'And do you not care what happens to our child?' asked Maria, now sobbing freely. She had seen in an instant there was nothing she could do against the King and a hundred knights.

She could grab the child and make Pedro tear him from her arms but that would only frighten Jacques and make him scream. She did not want that to be her last sight of him.

'Nothing will happen to him,' said Pedro. 'De Montfort is a family man. His wife Alice is with him and they have a brood of children.' He tickled Jacques under the chin. 'How would you like to meet a nice little French girl to play with?' he asked.

'Play,' said the boy, still fascinated by the gold crown in his hand.

'You see,' said Pedro. 'He will be fine. Now, get your women to pack his clothes and toys and prepare your farewells. You will see him again soon. And Alice de Montfort will be like a mother to him.'

He could hardly have thought of a worse thing to say.

❦

Spring came to Monferrato and when it did, Lady Iseut of Saint-Jacques married Lord Berenger of Digne in the great cathedral of Chivasso. The Marchese gave her away and Elinor, Alys, Clara and Berta were all her attendants. She was twenty-six, very old for a bride, but of course she had been married before.

As soon as the feasting was over, they moved to the castle given to Berenger by the Marchese. They renamed it Castelnuovo – the new castle – and with the money they had both managed to rescue from their own bastides, together with further handsome presents from Guglielmo, they were able to furnish it in style.

They took with them Elinor and Huguet, Clara and Alys. And of course, the child, Peire, who was now nearly eight. The Marchesa was devastated to see them go, especially Elinor, of whom she had become very fond.

'You must come and see us often,' said Iseut. 'And bring baby Beatrix. I think that Castelnuovo will be a good place for children.'

Elinor was happy for the first time for many months. The war in the south seemed very far away, even though she knew there were battles and skirmishes right on their doorstep. That warfare was about feudal loyalties not about persecuting people who believed something different from the Pope in Rome. It didn't make it less bloody but it seemed less personal to Elinor. And she had her mother and sister back; they were a family at Castelnuovo.

Berenger claimed to be no more than a farmer now, taking a minute interest in the lands that had come with the castle as part of Guglielmo's gift. He and Iseut often talked of going back to the mountains in Occitania when the war was over but no one knew when that would be. The Lord and Lady's two senescals had settled down to a good understanding and Nicolas had shared with François a plan that one day they would go back to the ruins of Saint-Jacques and dig up the plate and valuables buried there.

But for the time being, they were all content to live at Castelnuovo, and that contentment only increased when, in the summer, it was clear that Iseut was expecting a child.

By then the news had reached Piedmont that Pedro, the King of Aragon, had formed an alliance with Simon de Montfort.

'That poor child!' exclaimed Elinor, when she heard that the little boy had been handed over to Simon de Montfort by his father. 'And his poor mother! He was all she had left.'

'Well, and the Seigneury of Montpellier,' said Berenger.

'And I wonder how long she will have that,' said Iseut.

The next piece of news was that the Count of Toulouse had fled from the council at Montpellier and been excommunicated again. Finally they heard that Cabaret had surrendered. The heart had gone out of the rebels after the French victory at Termes. The Lord of Cabaret did not want to spend his last years languishing in a dungeon like the Lord of Termes and had negotiated a deal with Simon de Montfort.

But in all this time there was no word of Bertran or of Gui le Viguier. Gradually, Elinor began to accept that she would never know what had happened to either of them.

Then one night a richly caparisoned horse rode into the bailey at Castelnuovo and Nicolas announced the Lord of Selva. Elinor had been playing the flute while Huguet sang and played the fiddle and Alys was teaching Peire to dance the *estampida*.

The boy was tripping over his feet and Elinor had to put down her instrument in order to laugh.

'I know just how you feel, Peire,' Elinor was saying. 'I could never master the steps.'

And then she looked up and saw Nicolas and behind him, Alessandro.

He looked older and a little more careworn but the smile that lit his face was entirely for Elinor, even though he had first to pay his respects to the castle's lord and lady.

At dinner, he was seated next to Elinor.

'You are a difficult lady to find,' he whispered, showing her that he still wore the green girdle under his jerkin.

'Not by choice,' said Elinor. 'And I'm very glad you have found me.'

Bertran passed a miserable winter after the capture of Termes. He felt wretched that he hadn't been able to save Lord Raimon but Gui had convinced him there was nothing they could have done. They went to Cabaret and spent the cold winter months there. Physically, they lived in reasonable comfort; Cabaret was a well-provisioned castle. But it was hard to believe that the French would ever leave the south now.

The pattern had been set of fresh recruits joining the army every spring from the north and there was no reason to believe that this wouldn't carry on for years, until not just the heretics but all the landowners of the south had been dispossessed.

When Bertran heard that King Pedro had accepted de Montfort's homage, he knew it was all over for the resistance. It was about then that he decided to go to Italy but it was many months before he set out. He slipped out of Cabaret just before the surrender of the city, bidding Gui farewell. The young knight was sorry to part with him.

'What will you do?' he asked.

'Become a troubadour again,' said Bertran. 'In whatever castles and palaces still value poetry and music. And you?'

Le Viguier hesitated. 'I've half a mind to come with you,' he said. Then he grinned. 'Only my voice would scare your patrons away! No, I'll stay till Cabaret yields to the French, then go with Peire-Roger or with any *faidit* that needs a fighting arm. I'm a knight-mercenary now.'

'Never that,' said Bertran. 'You wouldn't join forces with de Montfort or the Bloody Abbot.'

Gui spat contemptuously. 'Perhaps I'll see you in Monferrato one day?' he said. 'You will go there, won't you?'

'One day,' said Bertran. 'I'd like to see Huguet once more.'

'Huguet,' said Gui. 'Yes, of course. Take the *joglar* my greetings. And the child. And any other friend you find there.'

As Bertran rode away, Gui watched him go, fingering the handkerchief in his jerkin, which was now tattered and stained.

The troubadour journeyed slowly eastwards, avoiding every sign of French activity. From Cabaret, he skirted Minerve, now in French hands, and went on to Narbonne. There the Viscount told him about Clara and Alys and how they had left his court the previous spring. Bertran did not stay long; the court was too full of Frenchmen.

When he reached Béziers, he drew up his horse and sat for a long time contemplating the ruins and thinking of Perrin. He wondered where Nahum the Jew was now, and whether he still kept the key to his house of ashes. The charred skeleton of the cathedral of Saint-Nazaire stood stark against the sky. From here Bertran chose the low road, on which he had travelled as a prisoner with the Papal Legate two years before. But after Montpellier, he turned further south along the canal and into the marshes, wanting to keep a good distance between him and Saint-Gilles where he had been rescued from prison by the *joglars* and *joglaresas* and where he had witnessed the Count's humiliation.

It was a lean few weeks, since the low-lying land was home only to wading birds and reed-cutters, and it took a long time to get through the delta and into Provensa. By the time Bertran reached Marseille it was nearly winter.

The cold weather seeped into his bones but after a few nights' rest, he carried on along the coast road. Then a racking cough engulfed him and he decided he must overwinter in some sympathetic noble's court.

By the time Iseut's baby daughter arrived in the depths of winter, Elinor was Lady of Selva. She had married Alessandro in Chivasso, with the Marchese of Monferrato standing in place of her father. Alys was her only bridal attendant and there were tears mixed with the joy of all three women from Sévignan as they missed the people who should have been there.

But for Alessandro the happiness was unalloyed. He gave his bride a beautiful grey mare as his wedding gift; Elinor had long outgrown Mackerel, who was now more of a mount for Peire. She stroked the horse's soft white nose and thanked her new lord.

'What can I give you, Sandro, to match such bounty?' she asked. 'You have known from the beginning that I have no dowry, if Sévignan is lost.'

'I want no dowry,' said Alessandro. 'Just you to be my lady for ever.'

He had persuaded Elinor to bring her mother and sister with her to the court where he was now lord. But he had to let her go again for Iseut's confinement. Their castles were only one day's ride apart.

And Elinor would not have missed it.

'You have what the Marchesa of Monferrato would call a treasure,' said Elinor to her exhausted friend, cradling the warm soft newborn in her arms.

Iseut smiled weakly. 'I hope Berenger won't be too disappointed,' she said.

'He will be delighted that you and the baby both survived the birth,' said Elinor. 'What shall you call her?'

'She looks so peaceful,' said Iseut. 'I'd like to call her Serena. But perhaps her second name could be Leonora?'

That was Elinor's new name in Selva; the servants had all converted it to a form easier on Piedmontese tongues.

So when Berenger was allowed to meet his daughter, he was introduced to her as Serena Leonora. And he thought she was as beautiful as her mother.

A few days later, Elinor was back in her own castle. As she arrived on the grey mare who had been her bridal gift, she rode into the bailey scarcely able to believe her luck. Of all the futures open to her when she had left Sévignan four years earlier, she would never have guessed that she would be married to an Italian lord, let alone one she could love. Alessandro had heard the horse's hooves in the courtyard and came running out to meet her like an eager boy; Elinor saw more than one castle servant turn aside to hide their indulgent smiles. The young Lord was popular and his people had taken Donna Leonora to their hearts.

'How is Lady Iseut?' asked Alessandro, after he had kissed her. 'And the baby?'

'Iseut and Berenger have a healthy daughter,' said Elinor. And it counted entirely in Alessandro's favour that he didn't look disappointed – even by proxy.

'You wouldn't mind a little girl?' she asked him, smiling.

'Not at all,' said Alessandro.

'Good,' said Elinor. 'Because I cannot guarantee that I am carrying a son for you.'

It was perhaps not how he should have been told, out on the cobblestones, with his wife smiling down on him from the fine mare he had given her, but Alessandro was far too happy to mind.

Bertran got to Piedmont in the spring. He was much thinner and had barely survived his marsh fever of the winter. But the warm sunshine helped heal him faster than any poultice or tisane. He rode the same horse he had bought after his rescue from Saint-Gilles. She had seen him well through raids and battles and his long journey through the Camargue.

And now they were approaching a fine-looking castle, where Bertran hoped to receive a good welcome. Italy had been kind to him so far and he was glad to have left the troubles of the Midi behind him. He knew there had been fierce fighting between rebels and Frenchmen through the winter but it all seemed far away and dreamlike now.

There was no longer any pretence that the Count of Toulouse was on the French side though his great city of Toulouse remained technically in his hands. But Bertran, who had once been willing to fight for Raimon as his overlord, no longer cared what happened to the traitor count. Still, he was glad that the rose-pink city had not yet fallen.

He pulled his mind back to his present situation. As he approached the castle, he asked a passer-by what bastide it was.

'Selva, Sire,' was the answer. 'In the Seigneury of Lord Alessandro.'

The names meant nothing to Bertran but he announced himself at the gate as a troubadour from the Midi and was courteously admitted. Once he had stabled his horse, he asked if there were other troubadours and *joglars* at court and was taken to where the musicians were housed.

There he received a warm welcome; although there were dancers and musicians, there was no resident poet currently.

'The Lady herself writes poetry,' said one of the *joglars*.

'Who is your *domna*?' asked Bertran. 'And what sort of lady is she?'

'Lady Leonora da Selva,' said the *joglar*. 'Married to the young Lord only a few months. As for her sort, the very best – young, beautiful and very favourable to our calling.'

'So I shall not find it hard to compose a song for her?' said Bertran, smiling.

'I think not,' said the *joglar*.

Bertran decided to compose a new poem. There was something about the atmosphere at Selva that lifted his heart. Perhaps because he was so near Monferrato, he thought of a poem by Raimbaut de Vaqueiras, who had been the old Marchese's favourite troubadour:

'*All good usage rules in your court: generosity and courting, elegant clothing and handsome armour, trumpets and games and rebecs and songs, and at dinner-time it has never pleased you to have a keeper at the door.*'

Now he set himself to think of a new *canso*. He hadn't yet set eyes on the Lady of Selva but that never presented a problem for a troubadour. As he started to compose, Bertran thought of all the women he had written love songs for, the *domna*s of so many castles and bastides. They had never been written from the heart but were more exercises of his skills.

And then Bertran began to think of Elinor. He wondered where she could be now and whether he would find her at Monferrato. Gradually thoughts of her began to influence his choice of words and he found himself writing for a dark lady.

After two days, the *canso* was ready and Bertran had given it to a *joglar* to put to music. There were several standard tunes that could be used for new love songs.

Until then, he had not attended dinner in the great hall, though the Lord had sent him a message of welcome and a servant with specially-chosen delicacies.

When he entered the hall, his eyes were dazzled for a while by all the candles and torches but it was a cheerful place. It reminded Bertran of Sévignan, before the war came. He looked at the nobles gathered at the main table and identified the Lady whose praises he had written for the *joglar* to sing. He was relieved to see that she was not only very beautiful but also dark.

Bertran rubbed his hand over his eyes and wondered if the marsh fever were returning. He kept thinking he saw people he knew. Perhaps it was just his memories of Sévignan but he thought briefly that the Lady Clara was there, and Huguet.

Elinor had recognised him straight away. Her heart tilted to see how much grey there was now in his dark hair. But something stopped her from sending for him. She waited until after the platters were cleared away and the musicians had played. Then a *joglar* stepped forward and indicated the troubadour. He took up his rebec and sang the new *canso*.

Elinor listened to the praises of the dark *domna*; it was just as beautiful as the love song she had wished for when she was thirteen. But it was like a distant view of a high mountain – something fine and admirable but remote.

The court was very pleased with it; they applauded both Bertran and the *joglar*. And then Huguet came down and embraced him and took him over to Lady Clara and Alys. Bertran was bewildered.

'It is wonderful to see you, my ladies,' said Bertran. 'But why are you all here? How do you know the Lord of Selva?'

'He is my husband, Bertran,' said the Lady of Selva, coming down to take his hand.

Bertran did not know her at first and then he saw the brooch. Elinor always wore it on her dress, in memory of her first love and her old life.

When the troubadour saw it, he knew at last who Lady Leonora must be.

'It was for you,' he said quietly. 'It was your own song, no one else's.'

Elinor thanked him with a full heart.

'And now let me present you to my lord,' she said.

Third Time Lucky

Toulouse, June 1218

The women sweated and strained to lift the huge blocks of masonry into the bucket of the trebuchet. They were standing on a platform in the Bourg outside the city. Toulouse had been under siege by the crusaders since Count Raimon had returned the previous September. But it had not gone well for the French leaders, who had spent a miserable winter in the gloomy Roman fort of the Château Narbonnais outside the city walls, while Raimon and his supporters were warm and well fed within the city.

In May, de Montfort's wife Alice had brought reinforcements again and his brother Gui was leading part of the army. But the Count had also received reinforcements and Toulouse continued to resist. In desperation to take this prize, Simon de Montfort was building a 'cat', an enormous wooden shelter on wheels that would enable an assault party to move right up to the walls in safety.

And then the Toulouse defenders scored a direct hit; a lucky shot from a trebuchet within the walls crushed the 'cat' and killed many Frenchmen inside it. The next day while it was being repaired by the carpenters, de Montfort was hearing Mass in his tent, praying for a speedy end to the interminable siege. His prayers were about to be answered but not in the way he hoped.

By then, the women were heaving their blocks into the trebuchet and two parties from Toulouse launched a joint sortie on the carpenters' compound. De Montfort ran to the battle where he found his brother bleeding from a bad wound, his horse dead beneath him.

'To the gate, to the gate! To me! De Montfort!' yelled Simon, urging his men to block the gate out of which more defenders were pouring.

And then the women on the trebuchet found their mark.

De Montfort, who had seemed blessed with the luck of the devil till now, took a direct hit to the head with a chunk of stone and was killed immediately.

There was a pause in the battle as the French, appalled, realised what had happened. And then the cry went up from the rose-pink city 'Lo lop es mort!' – 'The wolf is dead!' Church bells were rung and the streets resounded with drums, cymbals and trumpets. The wolf was dead indeed, lying under a blue cape, his head and face smashed by the women of Toulouse, and the crusaders defeated – for the time being.

Elinor and Iseut both greeted the news with relief, for their people and for the families they had now. Iseut had a second child, a son, named Jacopo, in memory of Saint-Jacques and in honour of the Pilgrim Way to Compostela. And Elinor had borne Alessandro three sons – Corrado, Ranieri and

Alvise – before getting her own 'treasure', a daughter named Pelegrina.

But Bertran was not there to hear the news. He had stayed two years at Selva, long enough to hold Ranieri in his arms and write a song for his baptism but had died soon after from a fever. Huguet, answering the troubadour's dearest wish, found him a Perfect to administer the *consolamentum* before he died.

He was buried in the cemetery of the church at Selva, even though he had never taken the Eucharist there. Elinor had a tombstone erected with words from an earlier troubadour:

Like the candle
which consumes itself
to provide light for others,
I sing, suffering,
Not for my own pleasure.

She was in the habit of visiting his grave whenever there was important news to impart. So on the day she heard the news of Simon de Montfort's death, in late August, she went to sit near his tombstone, with Pelegrina on her lap.

The child reached up to grab the red brooch her mother always wore and managed to dislodge it. It fell on the stone and Elinor heard it split.

'Oh no,' she said, jumping up to retrieve it. 'There, there, don't cry, little one. I'm not cross. Let Mama get her brooch.'

The dull metal of the setting had cracked away, revealing bright gold hidden underneath. Elinor had worn this brooch for twelve years and never known its secret.

She showed it to Alessandro who sent for a jeweller from

Turin. It took a while for him to reach Selva and by then Elinor could see that not just the mount but the stone itself had a false exterior.

The jeweller, once he had carefully removed the brooch's outer layers of pewter and red glass, sighed contentedly.

'One of the best rubies I've ever handled,' he said. 'And the size of a pigeon's egg.'

'Ruby?' said Elinor stupidly. She had always assumed that Bertran's token had sentimental value only.

'Oh yes, my lady,' said the jeweller. 'And a ruby of that size would be owned by only the richest crowned heads of Europe. I am not surprised you wear it always. It is a great treasure, worth a small city, I would guess.'

It soothed something in Elinor to know that Bertran's gift had such a great value and she wore it still, in its newly revealed glory. But she did not value it more now that she knew what it was worth in the world's eyes. And she never sold it. She kept it as an heirloom for her other treasure.

HISTORICAL NOTE

Troubadours and Cathars

There was a period of a few decades in the thirteenth century in Southern France when noble women were regarded as almost equal to men under the law. They could inherit property from fathers or husbands and received a bride price, rather than having to pay a dowry on marriage.

This coincided with the middle period of the troubadours, aristocratic songwriter-poets, who composed (mainly) platonic love poetry and songs, dedicated to the wives of their liege lords. (They are not to be confused with *joglars*, or minstrels, usually of a lower social rank, who were performers of songs and other types of entertainment. Their female equivalents were *joglaresas*.)

And at this time some aristocratic women, highly articulate and educated, wrote their own love songs and debate poems. These women were *trobairitz*, or female troubadours. However, they did not idealise men in the way that the troubadours idealised women and they wrote some pretty straightforward verse about the pains and pleasures of love.

Some of this took place in the south of France, in the area today known as Languedoc, where many of the noble families were Cathars, that is to say they were dualists, who believed in the separation of good and evil forces and did not believe in the Incarnation of God as Jesus Christ. They did not call themselves 'Cathars' but Credentes (Believers) or True Christians. The most advanced of them (those who became monks and nuns or preachers) were known as Perfects or *bons hommes* and *bonnes femmes* – 'good men and women.' Even ordinary Believers aspired to become Perfects at their deaths.

The Albigensian Crusade

The inciting incident for the whole Albigensian Crusade, as the war against the Cathars was called, was the murder of the Legate, Pierre of Castelnau, but it is my invention that the crime was witnessed by a troubadour. (And that the same troubadour was witness to many other terrible things recorded in the course of this book.)

From 1209 to 1229 the Cathars were ruthlessly persecuted by the Pope, who promised their lands to any Northern Frenchman who would fight forty days in the crusade against them. This was a lot easier than travelling to the Middle East to gain land and fortune. Many thousands of Cathars and non-Cathars alike were slaughtered in the rush to cash in and take their lands and wealth. They showed little resistance, being pacifists. Later, some were offered the opportunity to renounce their beliefs and become good Catholics but in the beginning there was no mercy.

What happened at Béziers I have recounted truly. The Abbot wrote to the Pope, '*Today, Your Holiness, twenty thousand citizens were put to the sword, regardless of rank.*' It was a thriving and prosperous fortified city run efficiently by Viscount Trencavel, who lived in the bigger city of Carcassonne to the west.

Raimon-Roger Trencavel was a remarkable young man. He had inherited his title when he was only nine and had managed to hold on to it at a time when it was difficult for minors to grow to manhood, let alone retain their lands.

He had been hoping for a peaceful future, with his wife Agnes and their little son. Bertran was bringing news that would lead to the break-up of that dream. Trencavel was only twenty-four when he died in the dungeon at Carcassonne.

The Count of Toulouse

Raimon VI, Count of Toulouse, was an extraordinary character. He was married six times. His first wife, Ermessinde, died childless after four years of marriage. The second was Beatrice Trencavel, who bore Raimon a daughter but later became a Perfect. It was not difficult to get the Pope to grant him a divorce from her since she was a declared heretic.

Wife number three, Bourgogne of Cyprus, lasted a year before Raimon divorced her. Then there was Joan of England, sister of Richard the Lionheart. She gave the Count his only heir, another Raimon, who would be the seventh count of that name. Joan left the Count and took refuge in a convent, but a respectable one of the Church, at Fontevrault. She had been carrying another child. They both died, from the results of Joan's having to be sliced open to release the baby.

And once he had his son and heir, who grew and thrived, Raimon had been able to please himself about a fifth wife, another Beatrice, but this marriage also ended in divorce, in 1202. His sixth and last wife was a good dynastic choice. She was Eleanor (Leonora) of Aragon, King Pedro II's sister.

Raimon VI was therefore uncle to Raimon-Roger Trencavel twice over, being his mother's brother and the ex-husband of Trencavel's Beatrice – though that marriage was not referred to during the crusade, because of her being a heretic.

The Feudal System

It is perfectly possible for a lord to have vassals and yet himself be a vassal to another lord of higher rank or to a king.
Hence Bertran is vassal of Lanval, who is vassal of Trencavel,
who is vassal of Toulouse, who is vassal of King Pedro! The
only figure to whom Aragon is vassal is the Pope.

King Pedro is suzerain (= overlord) to Toulouse and all
those below him.

The Languedoc and the Langue d'Oc.

The region of southern France that we know as the
Languedoc got its name from the language spoken there. This
was the 'Langue d'Oc', the language of Oc where 'Oc' meant
'yes'. In northern France they spoke the 'Langue d'Oïl' the language of Oïl, where 'Oïl' meant 'yes' (= modern day French
'oui').

This language has been called Provençal in the past but
this is misleading, because it was not limited to Provence; the
preferred term used now is 'Occitan' and I have provided a
glossary of Occitan words used in *Troubadour*.

After the Crusade

During the crusade troubadours became distrusted – some
were forbidden to compose – and many fled from Occitania
into Northern Italy or Spain.

Most of the characters in Troubadour are fictional but I
have made even the historical ones do some fictional things.
I could find out virtually nothing about the Papal Legate
who was Bishop of Couserans, for example, so felt no com-
punction in having him interrogate Bertran de Miramont. Or
in making Simon de Montfort the leader who suggested

betraying Raimon-Roger Trencavel. Someone did it and why not Montfort the wolf? It is perfectly in character.

Only Jean-Charles-Léonard Sismondi, in the mid-nineteenth century, has the detail that some citizens of Carcassonne escaped through a series of caverns to Cabardes, but it was suggested first in 1645 and was too good an idea to resist.

There is no historical record of the 'Nightingale of Carcassonne' or that a couple of *joglars* were, for good and ill, at Béziers. I have shamelessly stolen the words of William of Tudela for Huguet's *planh* at Termes.

Fate of Historical Characters
Simon de Montfort was made to yield up the child of Maria and King Pedro in 1214 and the proposed marriage with his daughter never took place. The boy was already an orphan because his father had been killed at Muret in 1213 and his mother, Maria, had died some months before. But little Jacques/Jaime was raised by the Templars and eventually became King of Aragon, a strong and well-made man, known as James the Conqueror.

The Abbot of Cîteaux never got his hands on Toulouse. He became Archbishop of Narbonne and was dead before the end of the crusade.

Pope Innocent died in 1216 and was replaced by Honorius III.

Guglielmo, Marchese of Monferrato, died in 1226 when about to set off to defend his father's conquests in Greece. His Marchesa, Berta, had already died in 1224.

Raimon of Toulouse lived another four years after Simon de Montfort's death. He was excommunicated at the time of his death and his body was not allowed to be buried in hallowed ground. He and his son, Raimon VII, managed to recapture much of their territories before the crusade ended in 1229. But when Raimon VII died, twenty years later, the County of Toulouse passed to the French King of the time, Louis IX (later Saint Louis). That marked the end of Occitania as a separate entity from France.

Pierre of Castelnau never did become a saint. The man whose murder set off the whole crusade remains merely 'Blessed Pierre'.

List of Characters

Aimeric de Sévignan, a knight

Alessandro da Selva

Alys de Sévignan

*__**Arnaut-Aimery,**__ Abbot of Cîteaux and Papal Legate

Azalais de Tarascon, a *trobairitz*

Berenger, Lord of Digne

Bernardina, a *joglaresa*

*__**Berta,**__ Marchesa of Monferrato

Bertran de Miramont, a troubadour

Blandina le Viguier

Borel, ferryman between Arles and Saint-Gilles

Clara de Sévignan

Elinor de Sévignan

*__**Ermengaud,**__ Bishop of Béziers 1205–8

*__**Folquet de Marseille,**__ Bishop of Toulouse, formerly a troubadour

Garsenda, servant of the Lady Iseut

*__**Guglielmo VI,**__ Marchese of Monferrato

Gui le Viguier, a knight, foster son of Lord Lanval

Hugo, the cook

Huguet, a *joglar*

Iseut de Saint-Jacques, widow of Jaufre, a *trobairitz*

*__**Innocent III,**__ Pope (1198–1216)

Lanval de Sévignan

Lucatz, a troubadour

Maria, a *joglaresa*

*__**Maria de Montpellier,**__ the Lady of that city

*__**Milo, Papal Legate,**__ a Cistercian monk

Miqela, an old servant in Sévignan, formerly a wet nurse

Nahum, a Jewish spice trader of Béziers
*Bishop of Couserans, a Papal legate
*Otto IV of Brunswick, Holy Roman Emperor
*Pedro II, King of Aragon
Peire, a child orphaned at Béziers
Pelegrina, a Catalan *joglaresa*
Perrin, a *joglar*
Philippe-Auguste, King of France 1180–1223
*Pierre of Castelnau, Papal Legate, murdered in 1208
*Peire-Roger, Lord of Cabaret
*Raimon VI, Count of Toulouse
*Raimon-Roger Trencavel, Viscount of Béziers, Albi, Rezés
and Carcassonne
*Raimon, Lord of Termes
*Renaut de Montpeyroux, Bishop of Béziers, 1208–11
*Simon de Montfort, one of the most ferocious leaders of the crusade
Thibaut le Viguier, a nobleman
Victor, a jailer at Saint-Gilles

* = a historical character

GLOSSARY OF OCCITAN WORDS

Amic	Friend
Amistat	Friendship
Canso	Love song
Canso de gesta	Song about heroic deeds
Cortesia	Courtly behaviour
Domna	Lady
Donzela	Young girl
Dolcment	Gently
Dolor	Sadness, grief
Estampida	Vigorous dance
Familha	Family
Fin'amor	Courtly love
Joglar	Minstrel
Joglaresa	Female minstrel
Joi	Joy
Joven	Young boy
Noiretz	Foster-son
Oc	Yes
Planh	Lament
Ribaut	A ruffian (literally 'ploughman')
Senescal	Senior male servant in a castle
Senhor	Lord of a bastide, castle or city
Senhoria	The position and authority of a feudal lord
Tenso	Debate poem
Trobairitz	Female troubadour

GLOSSARY OF MEDIEVAL WORDS

Bailey	Courtyard of castle
Ballista	Siege engine, like a giant crossbow
Bastide	Fortified town
Consolamentum	Ceremony of being received into the Cathar faith
Believer	What would now be called a Cathar
Chansons de Geste	French songs about heroic deeds
Demesne	A lord's lands, castle and property
Faidit	A lord who has lost his demesne
Fealty	Allegiance owed by subjects to their lord
Fief	A vassal's source of income, land and labour
Hippocras	Spiced wine
Keep	The main tower of a castle
Mangonel	Wooden siege engine
Perfect	A man or woman who had received the consolamentum and lived according to the strictest rules of the Cathar belief
Rebec	A small stringed instrument played with a bow
Saltarello	A lively dance involving jumping or leaping
Seigneury	The position and authority of a feudal lord
Solar	A private or upper chamber in a medieval house
Suzerain	Sovereign or feudal lord over other kings or lords; overlord

Trebuchet	Wooden siege engine, like a massive catapult
Trencher	Platter, sometimes wooden, sometimes made of bread
Vassal	A free man who held land (fief) from a lord to whom he paid homage and swore fealty. A vassal could be a lord in his own right.

ACKNOWLEDGMENTS

Dr Susanna Niiranen, of the Department of History in the University of Jyväskylä, Finland, kindly read and commented on this novel. She specialises in the women troubadours of Southern France in the 12th and 13th centuries. Norman Allum was most helpful in the Languedoc.

And Alessandro Barbero, Claudia Grosso and Riccardo Pergolis all provided invaluable information on the court of Monferrato. In spite of their assurances that the court would have moved around, I have taken the view of the *Enciclopedia de La Repubblica* (Utet, 2003) that it would have been at Chivasso, because I needed it to be somewhere!

I am very grateful to Nicolas Gouzy and Véronique Marcaillou of the Centre for Cathar Studies in Carcassonne for their assistance and support.

I have read many books and articles about troubadours, *trobairitz*, Cathars and the Albigensian Crusade while researching this book. Among the most useful have been Yves Rouquette's *The Cathars* (Loubatières, 1998), Jonathan Sumption's *The Albigensian Crusade* (Faber, 1978), Stephen O'Shea's *The Perfect Heresy* (Profile Books, 2001) and Laurence Marvin's *The Occitan War* (Cambridge University Press, 2008). On troubadour life and poetry, Linda M. Paterson, *The World of the Troubadours* (Cambridge University Press, 1993), and F. R. P. Akehurst and Judith M. Davis (eds), *A Handbook of the Troubadours* (Berkeley, University of California Press, 1995), have been invaluable.

I'm grateful to the Bodleian and Taylorian libraries in Oxford and, as always, the utterly wonderful London Library.